# Bag Boys

## Christopher Conway

Bag Boys is a work of fiction, although much of the story is true. Places, events, and people in many instances are real. All others are from the imagination of the author.

Bag Boys is inspired by the remarkable life of Phil Sigismondi.

## Acknowledgments

Bryan Pugner, for encouragement, suggestions, editing, and mostly, for friendship

Thea, thanks for the ideas and editing

Jean Marx of Time Flys for editing and publishing

A special thank you to Phil and Lorraine. Without them, this book would have been impossible.

*To Lori, Zac, Audrey and Brandon*
*for always being there for me*

# TABLE OF CONTENTS

Foreword

Chapter 1      NUMBERS

Chapter 2      LEARN A NEW TRICK

Chapter 3      THE OLD MAN

Chapter 4      FINDING ME

Chapter 5      THE BOYS

Chapter 6      WATCHING

Chapter 7      FIGHTER

Chapter 8      TIMES ARE CHANGING

Chapter 9      SIXTEEN

Chapter 10      INFAMY

Chapter 11      TRAINING

Chapter 12      FORT BENNING

Chapter 13      THE WAR

Chapter 14      THE NEW LIEUTENANT

Chapter 15      WHAT YOU SEE

Chapter 16      SURRENDER

Chapter 17      HOME

Chapter 18      MARY

Chapter 19      I MUST BE CRAZY

Chapter 20      CHANGES

Chapter 21      SAVE A WRETCH LIKE ME

Epilogue

# FOREWORD

When I first met Phil Sigismondi, I was immediately drawn to his humor. He was incredibly charming and every part of him dripped with charisma. He had a mischievous boy-like smirk with a delightful twinkle in his eyes. He was clearly handsome and carried such a deep inner strength in everything he did. Ironically enough, he was the doorkeeper at the local church youth group. Working the doors, he made sure that curious teenagers did not sneak away to find nearby trouble. Phil was eighty years old at the time.

Not too long afterward, I became the local minister at Phil's church and he felt the need to share his story with me, concerned that his past transgressions could somehow disqualify his involvement with our teens. It was here that I first heard the story of *Bag Boys*. After assuring him that he would be able to continue to monitor the doors, the next words I uttered were, "You need someone to record these stories and make them into a book."

As the years passed, I found it harder to imagine that the Phil I knew was the same guy who used to be referred to as Funeral. The Phil I knew was kind and soft-spoken. He was held in tremendous respect by young men and endeared by young women when he regularly asked them, "Have I told you lately that I love you?" I have grown to simply love this man.

As I was reading Chris Conway's book, *The Glove Slinger*, I often thought of Phil's story. Little by little, I would share some of Phil's adventures with Chris hoping he would get the itch to tackle his story. And now, I am so humbled and grateful to have played a small part in this wonderful project.

Although some of the accounts and characters of this project are fictional, Chris has done an amazing job capturing the essence of life on the Baltimore Block and a young street kid who became one of the greatest men I have ever known. Bag Boys is a wonderful tribute to a great man. Phil Sigismondi is my hero.

*Bryan Pugner*

# Chapter 1

# NUMBERS

*A bag boy is a kid the Mob uses to run numbers. That's how I got started.*

You know the feeling you get when you think everything is perfect? Nothing can go wrong? So far, this day is perfect. I don't have school; we were let out for the summer the day before, Friday afternoon. Come Monday, my old man will drag me down to the work site. But not today. The sun's shining, but not too hot. It appears no one needs anything from me; I have at least a few hours to myself. I can daydream in a field in a park, staring up at the sky if I want. I can kick a can down to the waterfront. Just as I am about to make my move to destinations unknown, I hear a shout from across High Street.

"Come here, kid!"

I know he is yelling at me because he's looking right at me. What I don't know is that my life is about to change. I have seen him before. Who hasn't? He's hard to miss. Besides being enormous—the biggest, fattest man I've ever seen, he is always on the same street corner, seeing everything like a circling vulture. But this is the first time he calls me.

I freeze, stuck to the ground.

"Kid! Get over here!"

My feet start to move. I don't tell them to, they just do. Next thing I know, I'm standing under him— under because I only come up to his belly button.

"You know me, right?" he asks.

"Yes, sir," I manage through chattering teeth.

He starts laughing a huge belly shaking laugh. "You scared of me?"

I don't want to lie, but I don't want to tell the truth, either. "Sorta, I guess," I finally spit out.

"Well, this is your lucky day, kid. Today is the first day of an education you'll spend the rest of your life thanking me for," he says.

I don't know what to say, but manage, "I go to school already. I'm only eight."

Again, he laughs his huge belly shaking laugh.

"This education will be something you can actually use. Not a waste of time like you is gettin' from the sisters down at St. Leo's."

St. Leo's is the name of the school I go to. St. Leo the Great Roman Catholic Church, and school is the center of our universe. Everyone in the neighborhood goes there, to the school I mean. My father doesn't believe in the Church and my mother won't go alone, so we never go on Sunday morning.

His name is Joey Galbo, a street boss of sorts. His nickname is Beans. Galbo, sounds like Garbo, Garbo like Garbanzo. Garbanzo beans. Beans. A nickname is as easy as that. He probably got it when he was my age.

"What's your name?" he asks. "Mine's Beans, nice to meet you."

"Paulie," I say. After a pause, I add my last name, "Signori."

"Paul, like the apostle. Apostle Paul," he says. "You ever heard of him at that school you go to?"

"I guess so," I answer. Of course, I had, but I didn't say as much out loud.

"Well, you should have. He's a great man, a saint even."

I can see that he's thinking as many seconds pass—me staring up at him, and him staring at nothing.

"How about I call you Pistol?" he says, obviously very proud of himself. "Sounds like apostle, but people will think you're tough. Pistol Paul. No, Paulie the Pistol." Big Beans stops talking, and seems to be thinking some more. I wait.

"No, that's not gonna work. We already got a Pistol in the crew," he says while shaking his big head.

I'm kind of glad. I don't really want to be called Paulie the Pistol.

"I see you leaving Pastorelli Funeral Home, you work there?" he asks.

See? I told you, he sees everything. "I clean the tables after Mr. Pastorelli embalms people," I answer.

"At eight years old?" he asks. "He's got you cleaning dead people's tables?"

"Yes, sir," I answer.

"Hmmm, that sounds a little odd to me, but okay, I guess," he responds. But I can tell he's still thinking. Then, like a bolt of lightning, it hits him. "Funeral!" he yells. "I'm gonna call you Funeral!"

I spend the next few seconds thinking about the nickname Funeral and what my mother will think. Will she call me that? I don't think so. She hates nicknames. She calls all of us kids by our full names—my older brother is always Nicholas and my younger brother is Frank, and my younger sisters are Norma and Gloria. Nicky is two and a half years older than me; he takes care of Frankie, Glory and Norma, the baby. She doesn't have a nickname, just Norma. Nothing sounds right. Can't be Norm, that's a boy's name. We tried Orma and Orm, but both of those nicknames kinda suck, so we just call her Norma.

Whenever my mom works late—that's if she has a job— Nicky takes care of the younger kids. I take care of myself. When my dad isn't working, he's drinking and not home. We don't like it much when he's home.

For the next ten years of my life, actually for the rest of my life except for when I'm in the Army, I'm called Funeral. The guys in the Army call me Siggy.

❖❖❖

The first day I work for Beans he sends me on some errands. That's what he calls it, errands. Simple stuff, really. Anyone can do it, but he tells me he wants kids—little kids like me. Take a bag to a guy at a night club, or a store, or wherever he sends me. He tells me not to look into the bag, so I don't. The guy at the night club, or wherever I go, gives me two bags to bring back to Beans. One bag has a bunch of papers with numbers on them. No one seems to care too much about this bag because no one says I can't open it, but the other bag is tied shut. I'm not supposed to look inside this bag, just like the closed bag Beans gave me. I make trips to five different places that first day, all on the same couple of streets less than a mile or so away from the neighborhood. People call it The Block.

I'm a bag boy. I carry the daily numbers in one bag, and bring back cash in the other, the one I'm not supposed to look in. The game is numbers and everyone plays. Beans is a Mobster. I don't know that at the time, nor do I know that what I'm doing is illegal. Afterwards, he gives me a dollar, which is a lot of money, and tells me to bring two friends tomorrow.

Phil Carollo and Tony Mazzotti—my two best friends—and I start to work for Beans the next day, and every day after that for as long as I can remember. We're the three musketeers, we're always together. Beans tells us that teenagers are too stupid to do the job, but really, he's tired of the cops harassing the older kids. Nobody ever notices little kids except their parents.

Our education has started. He teaches us all about gambling and the numbers. Who we can trust and who we shouldn't. Who always pays, who will give us trouble. He teaches us what to do if we get stopped by the cops.

"Act stupid and hide the bags," he says.

Acting dumb is easy since we don't even know what we're doing! But hiding the bags will be hard, so we decide if acting dumb doesn't work, we'll just run. He also tells us what to do if someone tries to steal from us. It's kinda like what we do with the cops, but one thing is for sure—never give the bags up no matter what. Beans teaches us how to be street smart, too. People throw that saying around like it means nothing, but it does mean something to us, and we get it, we learn how to be street smart. We learn how to spot trouble, and how to avoid it even faster. Another thing, we never rob, steal, or cheat. Not from anyone. We soak in every word he says.

I live on Albemarle Street, in a row house, in Baltimore. We call it Little Italy.

The year is 1932.

Running numbers that summer is the most exciting thing I have ever done. It's too bad that I can only do it after my father is done with me. But that's okay with Beans. He doesn't really need me, Tony, and Phil until the afternoon. And he lets me keep working for Mr. Pastorelli cleaning the tables.

My father is a laborer, a mason working with bricks and cement. When he's able to find work, hired at a building site, he drags me along, but only in the summer when school's out. I'm his son; I'm supposed to help my father. He makes me mix cement and carry buckets so he doesn't have to. The more work he finishes in a day, the more he gets paid, and I save him a bunch of time. But he never pays me. Beans pays me. Mr. Pastorelli pays me. I get a dollar a day from running the numbers and a quarter for every embalming table I clean. Whatever I earn, I give to my mom.

I don't really understand what happens to the money my father earns. I learn, much to my dismay a couple of years later, that he spends his money drinking. And when he does come home, he takes out his anger and frustration on my mother and us kids.

Running numbers makes me feel important. It's like a game to us—which one of us can run the numbers the fastest and get back with the money first. The faster we work, the happier Beans is. On any given day, we can have a dozen or more stops. Bars, night clubs, dance halls, coffee shops, markets, and restaurants, it doesn't matter where—they all play the numbers. And the Mob makes the rules. They set the numbers. They collect the money. They pay the winners. They always keep their cut.

The numbers is like an illegal lottery, but not to be confused with gambling, which the Mob also controls. Eventually, we carry the bags for real gambling, too, like betting on boxing matches or betting on the horses.

Numbers are set by horse racing, at least ours are. If my number is "532," I'm betting that the fifth horse in the third race at the number two track will win. But I'm not betting on a horse in a race at a track. It's all random, and the Mob sets the particulars. For this game, say the number two track is Saratoga in New York. No one knows this, of course, going in. And if you are lucky enough to guess the right horse, race, and racetrack, your number hits and you win. Everyone that plays—and just about everyone plays— tries to figure out the system, or has their own system for picking numbers. What they're really doing is guessing and praying. Guessing the numbers and praying they hit. It is everyone's big chance to make some extra cash. And everyone needs extra cash.

It's also cheap, you can buy-in for as little as a dime, and you can buy as many numbers as you want. More than one person can have the same number, in which case, you split the proceeds. The payoffs can be huge. Hundreds, or thousands, of people can be playing, and thousands of dollars can be riding on a game. That dime buy-in can net you hundreds of dollars. This is going on all over the city; there can be hundreds of games going on simultaneously. The flow of money is astronomical. And we carry it all.

We're the bag boys.

The country is in the middle of what is known as the Great Depression. We don't know what it's called, but we know that many of our fathers don't have steady work and none of our families has much money. Most of our moms are out looking for work, too. Many nights, we only eat bread and potatoes, or stew with vegetables but not much meat. We have chicken a lot. Thankfully, we usually don't go hungry. The money I bring home is sometimes the only money we have.

Sometimes, it isn't enough.

# Chapter 2

# LEARN A NEW TRICK

I'm very good at running the numbers for Beans, so good that I never lose a penny or the numbers. We heard about a kid who lost the money bag. No one ever saw the kid again. We heard that Beans' friends broke both of his legs and he was in the hospital for almost a month. When we asked Beans about it, he just laughed his huge belly shaking laugh, but he never denied that it happened the way we heard it.

I'm ten, and after running the numbers for two years, I know everyone on The Block, and everyone knows me. I'm not sure how or why, but I have a feeling that won't go away. I know something is about to change.

"Funeral."

"Yeah, Beans?"

"Come on, take a walk with me."

"Where to?"

"You got somewhere better to be?"

"No."

"Okay, then walk with me."

Along the way, Fish and Bats join us. Eddie Fischetti and Vinnie Battaglia are associates of Beans. Both are not quite made men, but they're still high-up and important guys. A made man is what the Mafia calls someone who's high-up in the organization, but also because of blood—they're related to someone else even higher up in the Mob. Beans and Fish and Bats may not be made guys—bosses yes, made guys no—but they still can't be touched. Meaning, no one ever messes with them.

They're always together, like me, Phil and Tony are always together. I'd bet that the three of them started out just like me and my friends. Fish and Bats have their own bag boys that work The Block, too.

Oh, and The Block, that's what the red-light district is called. It's loaded with night clubs, dance halls, strip joints, and bars. Dozens of them, maybe even a hundred. It's packed with people all hours of the day and night. At night, it's so bright you'd think it was the day.

Sometimes people look like their name. Eddie "Fish" Fischetti looks like a fish, believe it or not. Just don't say it to his face—his thin face with puckered lips and big eyes, just like a fish. Vincent Battaglia does not resemble a baseball bat, nor does he swing one, but the nickname Bats fit him nonetheless. I know something important is about to happen if all three of these guys are taking me for a walk. My heart starts pounding. I think about taking off at a full sprint, maybe I can outrun whatever trouble I'm in. But I can't for the life of me figure out what I could have done.

"You remember what I told you that first day, two summers ago?" Beans asks me after a long silence.

"Um, that I was gonna be a bag boy?"

"Nope. Guess again."

"Honestly, I don't remember, Beans."

"I told you, you were about to get an education of a lifetime. Remember now?"

"Yeah, Beans, I do. Now that you reminded me."

"Well, Funeral, my little friend, you ready for your next lesson?" Beans asks. Not waiting for an answer, he adds, "See that guy across the street? I want you to go over there and fight him."

We are standing on Baltimore Avenue, in the middle of The Block. The guy across the street is just someone minding his own business. And he's twice my age and twice my size.

"What are you waiting for?" Beans asks.

"I can't fight that guy," I answer.

"Why not?"

I think about my answer for a time. "Because he's bigger than me."

"So, what. Go fight him."

I have three men staring down at me. Big, full grown men. They're not smiling, nor will they take no for an answer. I walk across the street, tap the guy on the shoulder and punch him in the face.

"Why the heck did you do that!" he yells. "You're gonna pay for that you little…" He grabs the front of my shirt with both hands and shakes me three violent shakes before rearing back and blasting me in the face. I don't remember anything after that.

I regain consciousness at one of the night clubs on The Block, the Two O'Clock Club; I run the numbers for the club. Beans is laughing and telling a story, but stops mid-sentence when he sees that I'm alive and awake.

"Here he is!" he shouts. "My new street fighter! And in this corner, The Funeral!"

He's weavin' and bobbin' like a boxer, pretending to throw a punch. It's all a big joke to him. All of his friends are laughing and clapping. I'm nothing more than entertainment for him and his friends, or so it seems. My eye is already swollen shut and my head is pounding.

"Tomorrow we'll teach you the basics. We'll make a fighter out of you," Beans finally says after all the theatrics are over.

You see, they want two things: first, to find out if I will follow their orders, and second, to see how tough I am. I didn't know it at the time, but Beans and his friends also made Phil Carollo and Tony Mazzotti fight guys that day, too. Beans nicknamed them Thrill and Naughty.

❀❀❀

"In a street fight, Funeral, anything goes. No such thing as cheating. You take the guy out as fast as you can, however you can. Sure, it's great to know how to box and all, but I say, hit 'em first, hit 'em hard," Beans Galbo tells us.

Me, Thrill and Naughty listen as Beans talks, and at the same time, he's showing us some of his favorite moves. He likes the 'grab behind the head and pull down into your thrusting knee' move. Or the basic 'knee 'em in the groin' first, and then while they are bent over, 'blast 'em in the face.' Or just 'kick him in the groin.' Sometimes, he says, you just need to throw the first punch. But once you throw first, don't ever stop until he's down.

That was the mistake I made in my first fight, he says. I punched the guy and then just stood there and waited for him to hit me. Beans says that if I had punched him in the face, then kicked him in the groin right away, and then started pounding on his face, I would have won my first fight.

"But I wanna learn how to box," I plea.

"Yeah, me too," Thrill chimes in.

Naughty is shaking his head up and down. He agrees, too.

"We got a kid, about to turn pro, Killer Marino. He owes us a favor, he'll teach you guys a thing or two," Beans announces after a minute or two of his customary thinking time has elapsed.

The three of us exchange excited glances. Larry "Killer" Marino is a local hero, a real boxer! A couple of times a week for three weeks after that first fight, we're getting boxing and fighting lessons from Killer. And there really is a difference between boxing and fighting, according to Killer Marino.

❋❋❋

"A good boxer doesn't get hit," Killer tells us. "A good boxer knows when to play defense and when to counter-punch. You guys know what a counter-punch is, right?"

We shake our heads side-to-side. We don't.

"A counter-punch is when you punch back after your opponent throws a couple of punches," Killer explains. "So, this is how it happens. Funeral, come here, I'll show you guys. Funeral throws a couple of jabs, that I dodge, and a right uppercut that misses. See how he's left himself open? This is my counter-punch. Bam, right to the jaw. You guys practice, let me watch."

After a while, we start to catch on.

"Footwork, footwork, footwork, you guys are gonna practice footwork until you can't see straight," Killer tells us repeatedly. "And then balance. After that, I'll show you how to block punches. Then the jab, right and left cross, uppercuts, body shots."

"What about the knockout punch?" I ask.

"Just about any punch can be a knockout punch. Depends on where you hit the guy," Killer says. "Hit a guy in the nose is always good. You got blood and his eyes water, he can't see," he adds. "You ever heard someone say 'hit 'em on the button?'"

"That's your chin, right?" I answer.

"That's right Funeral, hit 'em on the button, put 'em to sleep," Killer Marino says. "You guys are gonna need tough knuckles, too," he adds.

"How do ya get tough knuckles?" Naughty asks.

"Here, I'll show ya." Killer Marino drops to the floor and starts doing push-ups on his knuckles. "I want you guys to do a hundred push-ups a day on your knuckles. And don't cheat, do 'em on the hard floor like I just did."

After we did a few, and they hurt like heck, we got up. Killer holds out his hands for us to see. His knuckles are huge and gnarled. "Trust me, you'll thank me later after you split some guy's melon open with the knuckles you're gonna have. And you won't break 'em either."

The last thing he teaches is the head-butt.

"It's a good move on the street, and some guys use it in the ring. Guaranteed to make 'em bleed," Killer says. "Your head is real hard. Go on, feel your head. You wouldn't want to be hit by it, right?"

We now have the knee-'em-in-the-face, knee-'em-in-the-groin and the head-butt, plus we have the footwork, defense and punching of a boxer. The head-butt becomes Thrill's go-to move in a fight.

I guess the head-butt was the second to last thing he taught us because the last thing was a piece of advice. Killer Marino told us it was always better to fight in a group when we were in the clubs or in a street fight. He told us to fight with our backs to each other, like the Romans. He called us Roman gladiators; we are the decedents of the greatest warriors the world has ever known, he said. If we always have each other's back, we can never lose. We live by that rule.

Besides learning how to fight, we still run the numbers every day, even on Sunday. And I clean Mr. Pastorelli's embalming table. And since it's summertime and I have no school, my father makes me carry buckets when he has work.

❊❊❊

"Hey Funeral, see that kid over there? Go kick his head in," Beans tells me the next afternoon before the numbers need running. "I've got a big game upstairs at the Sandwich King, so make it fast."

We're sitting in front of Maruzziello's Grocery on High Street playing cards. Beans is warming up for the big game later that night. Sometimes, the poker game can last for days, and me and my friends make a bundle of money by running food and drinks up to the Mob guys who are playing. As for the kid across the street, I know him. He's just a neighborhood kid, younger than me.

"Awww, come on Beans, he's just a kid."

No one says a word. A whole minute passes. I get up and walk across the street. Two quick punches and a vicious knee to the face and the poor kid's out cold, bleeding on the sidewalk. Once it's done, I walk away, down the street, passing block after block for miles. How far I end up walking, I don't know.

At ten years old, I no longer have a childhood. I never really had one to begin with. I'm not sad about having no childhood because I don't really know anything different. For as long as I can remember, my family didn't have money, or stuff, and my father wasn't nice to me. I've always had to work, but I don't mind working, it's just what I do. I don't have toys to play with.

And now I must fight people—little kids even—because I'm being told to. I guess it's just what I should do. So, I walk and walk until stumble upon a discovery.

I stumble upon Colonial Stables.

Horses are beautiful, magnificent creatures. I see them every day on the streets pulling carts full of fruits and vegetables, the Arrabers calling out and hawking their goods, but I never take the time to notice the horses. I'm always too busy and they are in the way. Watching them run free, I see them for the first time. I walk to the horses' stable and watch a man brush a horse's coat. Another horse is being saddled.

"You wanna give it a try, young fellow?" the old man saddling the horse says with a grin.

I know he is talking to me, but I turn around to check if someone is behind me. "I've never done it before," I say.

"Now's as good a time as any to learn. Come on, I'll show you how. It's easy. And she's a doll, wouldn't hurt a fly. If you treat her like a lady, that is."

He points out what everything is: the bit in her mouth and the reins, followed by the noseband, cheekpiece, browband, headstall, and throatlatch.

"And this here is her saddle. You put your foot in the stirrup and grab hold of the pommel. And then you throw yourself up onto the saddle," he says. "There you go now, just like a pro."

I'm sitting on a horse, sitting up high over the world. I realize for the first time how tall horses are. I'm nervous, shaking in my boots. Even my hands are shaking.

"Take her for a little spin around the yard. It's okay, she knows what she's doing. Just give her a little nudge."

I give her a gentle tap with my boot and she starts walking. I tap her again and she starts trotting. The old man I left behind is hootin' and hollerin'. A few more people come out of barns and stables to see what's going on. I have never felt so free in all my live. Before I know it, she's running, and I'm holding on for dear life, holding the reigns tighter than I thought I could. I cannot explain the feelings of exhilaration I'm experiencing. A few minutes later, she slows down and trots back towards the old man.

"That was quite a ride, young fellow," he says. "I'd like you to meet Suzy, Brown Eyed Suzy. She's past her prime now, probably fifteen, doesn't get out that often. My name's Jack O'Donovan. You can call me Jack."

We shake hands.

"I'm Funer... I mean Paulie. Paulie Signori," I say.

The smile on my face must be telling because old Jack starts laughing. His cracked and wrinkled face is glowing, almost as much as I suspect mine is. He pulls off his cap and runs his fingers through his sparse, reddish hair.

"I'll make you a deal, Paulie Signori. If you promise to treat her like a lady, and brush her good, and keep her clean, you can come out here and ride her whenever you want," Jack tells me. "Here, let me show you how to do that." He starts taking apart all the equipment she has on her face and neck and head, then he takes off the saddle. "Here, you take the brush. That's right, brush her with the grain, long strokes. Isn't she beautiful?" He says, more to himself than me. "Oh, and she loves apples." Suzy chomps the apple right out of his hand!

Brown Eyed Suzy has enormous brown eyes. And if you look closely, you can see that she has eyelashes. Her coat is dark brown; she has a white patch on her forehead. I spend the next hour listening to Jack O'Donovan talk about horses. In the process, he tells me everything he knows, which is a lot. I listen more intently to Jack talk about horses than I did to Beans when he taught me about being street smart or Killer Marino when he taught me how to fight.

It's already getting dark before I head back to The Block. I know Beans is going to be mad at me. This will be the first time I'm late running the numbers.

❖ ❖ ❖

I am right—he cuffs me in the back of the head as soon as I show my face.

"You can't just walk away like that, Funeral," he says. "I like you. You're smart, handle yourself good, show respect, don't talk too much. I like quiet. You've never questioned me, until today, or said no." After a long pause, he adds, "I like you. And because I like you, I'm gonna forgive you, even though you're making me late for my poker game."

"I don't mind fighting, Beans, honest I don't, but can I pick the guy?"

"We'll see."

That's all he says. Not sorry I made you beat up some little kid, or don't worry Funeral, you won't have to do that again. Nothing. And as if to prove a point, he makes me beat up another little kid the next day.

The next fight I have, though, a week later, is with a man. I almost have him, too. But in the end, he knocks me to the ground. I'm beat up pretty good, so Beans stops the fight and chases the guy away.

After over two months' worth of fights, I'm getting pretty good. Most kids my age in the neighborhood are afraid of me, even some of the older kids, too. I'm not very big, about average size I would say, but word's starting to spread, and no one messes with me; or with Thrill and Naughty either, for that matter. We're all getting good at fighting.

Kids we don't even know say hello to us.

Occasionally, I get to see a softer side to Beans Galbo, like today for instance. I watch as he's talking to—comforting really—a middle-aged lady I've seen in the neighborhood, a few streets down from where I live. She is crying and carrying on, but Beans has his big arms around her, patting her back. Eventually, she leaves him, still crying.

"Funeral, after you collect today's money bag, I need you to do something for me."

"Sure Beans, whatever you say."

"You see that lady who was in here?"

"Yeah, the one who was crying and all."

"That's the one. She lost her husband today. He got squashed at the job site," Beans says in an unusually quiet tone for him. "He was one of my regulars. Loved the ponies. I need you bring Mrs. Bartolini today's winnings. Wouldn't you know it, she had today's number."

I know that she did not have today's number. She didn't even play the numbers. Whenever a gambler who was always straightforward and honest dies, the Mob donates the daily winnings to the widow. No doubt a horseshoe made from dyed green carnations will appear at Pastorelli Funeral Home for the wake, sent by the Mob to honor the dead man.

It sucks that the summer is almost over. The only good thing about the summer being over is I don't have to carry buckets for my father. I will say that lugging those heavy buckets all summer sure has given me some muscles! I'm about to start the fifth grade.

❊ ❊ ❊

I watch her that first day walking to school. She must be new to the neighborhood because I've never seen her before. She walks funny, all hunched over, sorta. I'm not sure if she has something wrong with her or she walks like that on purpose, and she's small, real small for her age. I find out later that day that her name is Helen. All the kids in our grade and older ones, too, pick on her, call her names, some even push her down. I watch her cry.

I don't have any friends besides Thrill and Naughty, and of course, Beans, Bats, Fish, and the other kids that run numbers for them, but they're mostly acquaintances not friends. I have no time for a social life outside of the numbers, and the night clubs we run numbers for. When school is over—and I didn't learn a damn thing at school anyway by the way—I can hardly read—I race to Mr. Pastorelli's Funeral Home to see if he needs me, or to old Joe's junkyard, but that's a story for another time.

By late afternoon, I finally end up at Beans' corner to start working the numbers. But before I take off, I can't help but notice poor Helen getting tormented by a gang of kids. I don't understand why. Why pick on a defenseless little girl? It makes my blood boil, but I'm too busy, I have places I need to be. It doesn't dawn on me that I'm beating up little kids too, when Beans tells me to.

It starts all over again the next day. Some kid pushes her down and she skins her knee. I can't take it anymore. I walk across the street and punch the kid right in the nose, like Killer taught. He's a seventh grader, and big, but I don't care. The gang stops torturing Helen the second their friend hits the ground. I turn and face them, six guys in all.

"Who's next?" They all look at each other. No one says a word, no one moves. "Whoever touches her or bothers her again deals with me," I say.

I like the way helping her makes me feel. It turns out that I like looking out for people that need looking out for.

As far as I know, Helen graduates from high school at St. Leo's and no one ever bothers her again. I even heard that one year she is voted class president. As for me, I pick up a shadow. For as long as I go to school that year, when I pass her house, she bolts out the door and follows ten steps behind me. If I stop, so does Helen.

Finally, a few days later, I ask, "Why are you following me?"

"Because you're my hero," she says.

"Could you just walk with me? Following me is creepy."

I now have three friends.

# Chapter 3

# THE OLD MAN

Sometimes things are not always as they seem. I'm not saying that my father isn't mean, because he is, but sometimes something else might be going on. When I was four, or maybe it was when I was three, he fell off a work truck and broke his collarbone. I don't remember it happening and won't find out about the accident until after his death. What I do know is that the word love is never said in our house. Not by my father, anyway. He might have said the word, and meant it, when I was real young, but I don't remember. What I remember is he drinks and gets mean. And he beats my mother. Most times, he beats us kids, too, but my older brother Nicky more than the rest of us because he always tries to get between him and my mom.

Now that I'm older, both me and Nicky get between them and we both get beatings. We try to protect our mother as best as we can. She's defenseless against him. He leaves my two sisters alone, and my younger brother most of the time, but we all live in fear. We don't have a pleasant home life. We don't have flowers in a vase on the kitchen table. If we had a vase, it would most likely end up broken.

He never says anything to me about his shoulder, or his back, or his arm always hurting. I guess he has me hauling buckets around during the summer because he can't. I wonder what he does when I'm at school.

I don't have to wonder much longer. It is late 1935, before my twelfth birthday—I was born April 3, 1924—and he finally lands a job with steady work. The job is with the Works Progress Administration. The WPA is part of President Roosevelt's New Deal. Half of all of Baltimore's out-of-work or part-time laborers get jobs, my old man being one of them. Anything that needs cement, and luckily everything needs cement, means my dad has steady work. His job is helping to build a swimming pool.

I am with my father building the swimming pool at a recreation center because my father pulled me out of school not even halfway through the fifth grade and I never go back. I don't have a choice, and no one can stop him. I go to work at the job site with my father hauling buckets—again. The buckets I lug now are water buckets, I'm a water boy. The men need water for the cement mixers, I'm their mule. When they're thirsty, they holler for me.

"Bucket, here!" they yell, and I must run the right drinking water bucket.

White man and black man work the job, side by side. No one ever argues, or fights, or says bad things about each other; everyone just works. I never see any prejudice against black people, but there's two water buckets. One has a "W" for white painted on it, the other a "C" for colored. The men can work together, side-by-side sharing sweat and strain, but they can't drink from the same bucket.

❋ ❋ ❋

He always takes the money I earn on the job, but he doesn't know about the money I make elsewhere, like working for Beans or Mr. Pastorelli, because I hide it from him. I give the money to my mother when he isn't around. I always find ways to make money. I don't steal it, but I do have some creative ways of getting it. Working for Mr. Pastorelli at the funeral home is money I earn, but it's never much. Running numbers as a bag boy is steady, and it pays well, but even that's never enough. My mom has a hard time finding work. Plus, she has three little kids to take care of.

"What's the matter, Mom?" I ask, even though I already know.

"I've got nothing, Paul, nothing to give you kids," she answers.

"Don't worry, Mom, I'll go to the bank," I tell her.

An hour or so later, I'm back with ten, fifteen dollars. She doesn't ask how I get the money, she's just grateful to have it. She can buy groceries, or pay off her credit bill with Mr. Maruzziello at the grocery.

Like most neighborhoods we have a junk yard. Old Joe Lucci owns it. I call him Mr. Joe. By most standards, he's rich; he has a nice house with no upstairs neighbors. He owns a car. The Mob guys all have cars, but not a lot of ordinary people in the neighborhood do.

I cut a hole in the junk yard fence, way in the back, out of sight. I pull my wagon around back and wait for the coast to be clear. I sneak into the yard and search for the right stuff. Iron always pays the most. I don't know how Mr. Joe gets the iron in the first place, or what he does with it after he gets it, but there's always scrap iron in the junk yard. I haul as much as I can carry and load the wagon.

"Hi, Mr. Joe," I call out.

"What have you got for me today, Paulie?"

"Scrap iron I got from the work site," I answer.

"Let me take a look."

He examines the iron, occasionally making what sounds like satisfactory noises. "This is high quality iron, Paulie. I can give you twenty cents a pound."

"Come on, Mr. Joe, fifty cents a pound."

He thinks for a few seconds and comes back with thirty or forty cents, but eventually we make a deal at fifty cents a pound. I think he just likes to haggle with me. I can have anywhere from ten to twenty pounds in the wagon.

"You drive a hard bargain, Paulie Signori." He always says the same thing.

"Thank you, Mr. Joe, I'll see you when I have another load." I always say the same thing in reply.

I know I can't do this trick too often or Mr. Joe will get wise. How can he not realize that I'm taking scrap iron out of the back of his junk yard and selling his own iron back to him in the front?

This isn't the only trick I play. He pays good money for cardboard and newspaper, which he also pays for by the pound. Can I be the only kid smart enough to think of this? First, I wet the cardboard I collect from the grocery stores and restaurants. I know all the store owners, restaurant owners, bar owners— you name it—in the neighborhood or on The Block because I run their numbers. I have the run of the place, so to speak. All I have to do is ask, and they give me whatever I want. I collect all their cardboard and soak it with water to make it heavier. I wrap the wet cardboard around a brick making it even heavier. To cover up the trick, I wrap dry cardboard around the bundle and tie it up with string. Easy as pie and no one is the wiser.

Mr. Joe doesn't pay nearly as much for cardboard as he does for iron, but I can do this as often as I want, a couple of times a month, at least. I don't see selling weighted cardboard or selling someone his own iron as cheating or stealing. I don't really think about it one way or the other. I'm getting money for my mother is how I look at it.

Sooner or later, everyone gets greedy. One day while scrounging in the junk yard I see what I think can be my greatest score yet. The vase is one of the most beautiful things I have ever seen:  big, ornate, and expensive-looking. I grab it.

"Mr. Joe is gonna pay a lot for this!" I exclaim out loud. I can't believe my luck.

When I pull my wagon up to the front of the junk yard, Mr. Joe is in his office. I don't even bother with any iron.

"Paulie, it has been a while since I have seen you," he says.

"Yes, sir, Mr. Joe, I've been real busy lately," I say. "But I have something today."

I show him the vase. He takes it out of my hands and looks at the beautiful piece of porcelain closely. He takes off his glasses and pulls it close to his face. I'm beginning to get nervous.

"This is a beautiful piece, reminds me of a vase I have out back," he says. "Where did you get such a lovely vase?"

"It was my grandmother's," I answer, starting to sweat.

"Why do you want to sell it, Paulie?"

"What do I want it for?" I answer.

"I see your point. I'll give you twenty dollars."

"I need twenty-five," I say out of habit more than anything else.

"Always driving the hard bargain, Paulie," he says.

Five minutes later I'm walking out the door with twenty-five dollars! It's my biggest score. I walk home and give my mother the money—all twenty-five bucks. She's so overcome with joy that she starts crying. I guess it doesn't occur to her to ask me how I get the money. She calls me an angel; I leave to meet Thrill and Naughty. It's that time in the afternoon—numbers need to be run, and I'm a bag boy.

❊ ❊ ❊

My mother hears the knock on the door a couple of hours later. She has already been to the market and back and is making dinner for the kids.

"Mrs. Signori, It's Joe Lucci from the junk yard," he yells through the door. Before my mother can say hello, after she opens the door to our crappy little row house, he erupts. "That lousy, good-for-nothing, two-timing son of yours stole my vase!" he yells as he holds it out for my mother to see. "Then he sold it back to me! For twenty-five dollars!"

"Oh," my mother says. "So that's where he got the money."

❀ ❀ ❀

I must march down to the junk yard as soon as I get home to face the wrath of Mr. Joe, junk yard owner. He repeats the same string of curses he had for my mother, only worse. He finally calms down after about five minutes of yelling at me.

"Paulie, I let your mother keep the money. She already spent some of it on food, and I know how much your family needs it."

He, like everyone else, knows my father is a good-for-nothing drunk and doesn't provide for his family. But an unwritten law is no one ever interferes with another man's family.

"Thank you, Mr. Joe," I manage, with my hat in hand.

"Under one condition—I will only be paying you half for the iron you bring me. The other half will go towards paying off the debt." He then adds, "And you'll have to stop wetting the cardboard and wrapping it around bricks."

At least one of my tricks survives the day.

Good thing I've got another scheme up my sleeve. Our house backs up to a morgue, which is close to Mr. Pastorelli's funeral home where I work. When a dead body shows up to the morgue, they take the clothes off the dead person. Sometimes the family wants the clothes, sometimes not, but either way the clothes end up in a box outside the morgue. I take the clothes and bring them home. Hey, if I don't take them, someone else will. My mom washes and presses them, and I shine the shoes; then I sell the stuff in front of our house on the street.

❈ ❈ ❈

*I'm floating above my bed. My eyes are open; I can see everything in my room. I can see Nicky sleeping. I hear a strange noise. I'm sitting up looking across my bedroom. I feel something poke me in the face. I see darts coming at me, hitting my face. It hurts. I cry out. A figure from across the room, hidden in the shadows, is coming toward me, throwing the darts. I see its face and I cry out again. It's the face of the devil. His bony fingers are scratching me, tearing at my flesh. He's pulling on me. He's trying to pull me into the basement!*

I wake up screaming. Nicky sits up with a start. "What is it, Paulie?" he asks.

"The nightmare, Nicky," I say. I don't need to explain it as he already knows.

When I was five, we moved into a new house after our landlord raised the rent on our old house, but it's not the house we live in now. We moved here two years ago when I was seven. I didn't like our last house. It was haunted, I know it was. It all started when my father busted up the gravestone that was in the basement and made me and Nicky carry the broken pieces out to throw away. That's right, we had a grave in the basement.

I didn't like the basement before my dad got rid of the gravestone. I especially didn't like it after. It was dark—only one little light bulb hanging in the middle of the room provided light. The ceiling was so low my father couldn't stand, and the floor was dirt. It was always cold down there.

My mother told our new neighbor about the gravestone and what my father had done. I heard the woman gasp. She said we would be forever haunted by the ghost of the dead person. She also said that the devil would come after our souls. I was never more scared in my life. I was only five. Every so often, I still have the nightmare about the devil trying to steal my soul.

❀ ❀ ❀

Just because my father and I work the same job site doesn't mean that we get along. Sure, I see him all the time, but he never talks to me. He mostly just ignores me. We don't spend breaks together or eat lunch together. When he does talk to me, it's never more than a couple of words, and he never uses my name. He calls me kid or sometimes just you.

"You, come here," he demands.

"Yeah, Dad, what do you need?"

"Run the chalk line." I have to drop everything and help him. "Now get the trowel," he orders.

"Which one?" I ask.

"Plastering trowel, idiot."

"How am I supposed to know which one you need?"

He mutters something in Italian—probably calling me stupid or useless or something worse. This is the extent of our conversation throughout the day. Mind you, I have my own work to do, but he's forever calling me to bring him something or hold something. Bring the long float, then the bubble level, then a plastering trowel, it never ends. Oh, and of course, I must carry his buckets. Maybe having me do stuff for him is the only way he knows how to connect with me. Maybe this is his way of showing affection.

Then we go our separate ways when the whistle sounds at three in the afternoon with not so much as a thank you for your help or even a goodbye. He most likely goes to a bar to drink his money away, me to meet up with the guys. I still have to work; it seems my day never ends.

Prohibition ended over a year before so he doesn't have to sneak around looking for places to drink, although The Block never stopped thriving and the bars never stopped serving. Prohibition didn't mean people stopped drinking, and Baltimore never endorsed the law. The state of Maryland, and the city of Baltimore, were the wettest state and city in the country. I think the Mafia probably had something to do with that.

I don't know how he is able to pull it off—the drinking I mean—and still be able to get to work on time, and be able to work the next day, but he does. He isn't the only one, either. It seems like most of the men leave the job site and head straight to the bars. I see men I know by sight all night long. I'm there also, but not drinking a pay check away. I'm working. At eleven, going on twelve, I'm running numbers, collecting bags, delivering money, running errands. I stay away from home as much as possible. But eventually, I always end up back there.

❊ ❊ ❊

I hear the crashing and the yelling before I reach the door. The yelling is always in Italian. I understand the language—

even speak a little—so I know what is happening. It happens all the time. When I burst through the door, his fist is raised. My brother Nicky is already on the floor, his mouth bleeding. My sister Glory is crying in the corner, hiding behind the overturned kitchen table. I don't see Frankie or Norma. They're good at hiding. He doesn't even bother to look up. Instead, he finishes his swing, connecting with my mother's face, sending her flying across the room into the wall. Then he looks at me.

He curses in Italian. "Pezzo di merda marcio!" he yells. "Ho intenzione di battere!"

I know exactly what he said. He curses and says he's going to beat me. I've been fighting in the neighborhood or on The Block for the better part of a year, 3 or 4 times a month, every month. I win most of them, and I can take a beating and keep on coming. Even against guys older, bigger, and stronger. But my father scares me. He isn't a very big man, but he's also stronger than anyone I have ever seen. When he needs to, he can fling bags, fifty pounds or more, of cement ten to fifteen feet like it's nothing. You can see the muscles in his arms bulging.

Many times, it's me and Nicky together that finally gets him to stop. I jump on his back and Nicky grabs an arm, and together we try to wrestle him to the ground. He gets winded pretty easily—he smokes packs of cigarettes all day—and he's drunk, so after several minutes of the struggle, he usually gives up, but the damage is already done. But not this night. He's in a rage like I haven't seen in a long time. Just seeing my fourteen-year-old brother on the ground crying tells me everything I need to know.

"He's gonna kill her, Paulie!" he shouts. Nicky is more scared than I have ever seen him.

My mother is lying limp on the ground. I think she is already dead. He turns on me. I try to run, but there is nowhere to go. He catches me by my hair. I have the sides cut close, but I let my hair grow long on the top, longer than most guys. I wish it was shorter. After tonight, it may not matter. He'll either pull it all out or I'll be dead.

First, he throws me to the ground. Then he grabs my coat and pulls me back up. Then he throws me to ground again. My back feels like it's broken. I can't move. He pulls me up a second time and open-hand slaps me hard across the face. My nose starts to bleed. Out of the corner of my eye, I see Nicky pull himself off the ground and leap onto his back, his arms wrapped around his neck. Nicky is the bravest kid I know. He's going to kill me—and my mother—for sure if not for Nicky. Like all the many times before, he eventually tires himself out and passes out, drunk, with other peoples' blood on his hands.

Not too long after, Nicky breaks his wrist. He's a great step-ball player. Step-ball is like stick-ball, but it's played on steps, or rather, home plate is on the steps that lead to the front porch. All the houses have steps and a front porch. You try to hit the ball, with a stick like stick-ball, across the street. A homer is if you hit it on the porch across the street. Nicky falls off the steps while running and breaks his wrist. He ends up having surgery, but something gets messed up because afterwards he can't use his fingers on his right hand—they're all stiff. After the accident, he can't work. Before the accident, he worked with the old man, like me, but now he can't. I think it makes my father hate him even more.

❈ ❈ ❈

He was born Paolo Signori in the Lombardia region of northern Italy in the town of Bergamo. He said he was born in the year 1900. The name Signori means "Lord," like "Knight," in English. He says that his family came from important people once upon a time. His older brother, Marco, sent for him when

47

he was seventeen and Paolo, my father, traveled to America alone. He settled in Baltimore, in Little Italy, and that's where he met my mother, Lucy. At that time, after the Great War, America had many people coming to her shores, looking for a better life. My father was luckier than most, he had his brother living and working in America. He also had an Italian community already established in Little Italy. He didn't have to learn English right away because everyone spoke Italian. He did learn the language over time, but he never lost the accent. None of us kids have an accent. My mother makes us only speak English.

She was born in America, from a large family that was very poor. Her father was glad she found someone to marry her. He had one less mouth to feed. She was only eighteen when they married, and they had their first child a year later. I came two and half years after that. They never spoke of the child they lost. They had three more after me over the next six years. I think they may have been in love then.

Now my mother is a beaten woman, in more ways than one. Physically and emotionally, she's beaten. And she is only thirty-two years old. She tries to find work to support her children—her husband keeps the money he earns for himself—but she hardly leaves the house. The often-bruised face probably plays a role. By this time in her life, she almost never shows emotion. I guess it becomes harder and harder for her to show love. My father gave up on love a long time ago.

My father started out as an apprentice to a mason that his brother knew. There was a booming construction spree at the time so he had plenty of work. As he got older and better at his trade, more construction companies sought him out. Then he fell off a work truck and broke his collarbone. They gave him morphine in the hospital. Then the Great Depression hit a couple of years later. He, like my mother, had become a beaten man. He started drinking because he couldn't get morphine. I

48

did not know this at the time. He started to hate his life and his family.

I hate the man, but I can't help but love him.

# Chapter 4

# FINDING ME

I find a father figure of sorts in Beans Galbo. Honestly, he is never mean to me. He only cuffed me in the head that one time when I was late getting back, after riding Suzy, and he never yells at me, never says a curse word at me, and he protects me. Although, he can be very bossy, always barking orders, always telling me what to do. We have a strange relationship, no doubt, but deep down I know he likes me. Maybe even loves me? I don't know—he never says it, of course. We see each other almost every day, have since I was eight. I work for him, and he uses me, and I make him money, but if I really need anything, he's the person I go to.

I try not to ask favors of him very often or have him take care of a problem, and I never tell him about my home life, although I suspect he knows. There are many nights that he tells me not to bother going home; I can sleep in one of the Madam's empty rooms.

The Madam is Mrs. Russell. She is the head of the house. The empty room in the house that she is head of is in a house of ill-repute, a brothel, called the Mother's Milk, or the MM Club. It also turns out that Mrs.—although she isn't married— Russell lives one floor above me on the third floor, the top floor of the row house we live in. She has it all to herself. I see her practically every day of my life. I have for as long as I remember. Come mid-afternoon, she's always perched on her third floor window sill, looking out over the neighborhood. Little Italy has lots of neighborhoods. I never see her until mid-afternoon because she works all night taking care of the girls at the night club. She may have been a showgirl or a dancer at some point in her life, but not anymore. I still think she's pretty enough to be one, but nowadays, all the girls really are girls, some as young as seventeen, but most are probably closer to twenty.

She sits in her window in a robe, smoking a cigarette and drinking coffee. Me and the guys, Thrill and Naughty, and some of the older kids, spend a lot time across the street, playing cards and hanging out. Sometimes, I swear, her robe pops open just enough so we can see in. I think she does it on purpose just to tease us. For some reason, she has a soft spot for me, maybe because she hears my father yelling all the time. She always calls me by my name and says corny, embarrassing stuff like how cute I am.

One day she calls me up to her house. I try not to be nervous —I'm almost twelve and can handle anything—or so I think.

"You're the worst card player I've ever seen," she says, standing in the frame of her open door, robe barely covering her. "Come on in, I'll teach you a thing or two."

I'm too nervous to speak so I followed her in.

"Grab a seat, I'll be right back," she says. "Oh, and get a beer out of the ice box."

A beer does sound good. Maybe it'll help calm me down.

"You have all this space just for yourself," I say out loud, but mostly to myself, because of course, she knows she has the whole house to herself.

"That's right, Paul, all to myself. You're welcome to come up anytime you want," she yells from her bedroom.

At first, I think it's a come-on to me, her inviting me up to her house anytime, but after spending a few minutes with her, I realize that she only feels sorry for me and really wants to help me. She comes back out of her room dressed in her nightly outfit of expensive-looking clothes, befitting a Madam of the house. She sits down on the sofa with a deck of cards in her hand and starts dealing blackjack: four hands and a dealer. Blackjack is the hot game everyone's playing. It's new on The Block, so most people are not any good at it. The gambling houses are making a killing with it.

"I'm going to show you how to win at blackjack. Come over here, sit by me."

Four cards, face up are arrayed in front of her and one is face down for the dealer. She flips another card face up on each of the four cards and one face up for the dealer—an eight. The first player has a five and a four, for a total of nine.

"The nine takes a hit." She drops a queen on top. "Player one is good. Always assume the dealer has a ten or a face card underneath, Paul. And nineteen beats eighteen."

The next pile totals thirteen. "You hit the thirteen if the dealer's face-up card is seven or higher. The dealer has to stand on seventeen. Do you understand?"

"Not really," I say. I have just started playing, and almost always lose.

"The dealer has to hit at sixteen, and the odds are good he'll bust. Let's keep playing, you'll catch on." She then drops a seven. "Oh, that's very good. Player two now has twenty. Thirteen plus seven, but an eight would have been better, as that'd be twenty-one. Anything higher and it's a bust."

She makes her way around the game and flips the dealer's hidden card—and sure enough—it's a king or ten. The dealer has eighteen. Two of the player hands won and two lost. We play game after game for a couple of hours. Towards the end I'm really catching on, almost always knowing when to hit or stay. I even learn when to split my cards and play two hands. I'm almost late meeting Beans I'm having so much fun.

The next afternoon she doesn't need to call me up. I knock on Mrs. Russell's door at exactly three-fifteen in the afternoon. That's how long it takes me to run home from the job site, fifteen minutes.

"You don't go to school anymore, do you Paul?" she asks as she's shuffling the deck.

"No, ma'am, my father pulled me out of school to work."

"That should be illegal," she says. "How much did you learn when you went? How well do you read and write?"

I'm not stupid, I know that much, but I also know that I'm not book smart, so to speak. I'm street smart, remember? I stumble around looking for an answer when I finally say, "No, I don't read or write too good. I guess I didn't learn much."

"Well, Paul, I don't read or write well," Mrs. Russell corrects. She puts the cards on the table, not dealt, and goes to a book shelf. She returns to the sofa with two books, F. Scott Fitzgerald's *Tender is the Night* and William Faulkner's *As I lay Dying*. "You'll probably like Fitzgerald better," she says, handing me the book.

I'm surprised at how heavy and thick it is. She doesn't expect me to read it, does she? I thumb through a few pages, close the book, and put it on the coffee table where we had played cards the day before.

"We'll play cards for an hour and read for an hour," she announces. Maybe she sees how scared I look because she adds, "Don't worry, Paul, I'll help you with the words you don't know."

Over time, we probably read a dozen books together. Mark Twain is by far my favorite author. After a while, I don't even have to ask her what some of the big words mean. I've learned the meaning of hundreds of new words, but I can't use them in front of the guys. I can never let on—with the guys I mean— that I have become smart. I know they will never understand.

Oh, she also teaches me how to count cards while playing blackjack, which is quite a trick. Most people stop playing against me because I never lose. That goes for regular five card poker or seven card stud, which she also teaches me. I keep these skills for the rest of my life.

I think I'm sort of a surrogate child to Mrs. Russell, who never had any children of her own. Whenever we're together—in her apartment, on the street, anywhere—she always introduces me as her son Paul to anyone we meet. I'm not sure what she gets out of our relationship. Like I said, maybe I'm a surrogate son, but I know what I get—the mother I don't have. Someone who teaches me things, important things you can't learn on the streets, like how to treat a lady. She also teaches me how essential it is to look after less fortunate people, to help and protect people who can't help themselves, like I did for Helen at the start of fifth grade.

❀ ❀ ❀

On the night of my twelfth birthday, five of the girls from the MM Club hold me down and take advantage of me. They think it's the best present a kid my age can get. Mary Kelly, Grace Campbell, Betty Parker, Sandy Matthews and Sarah Gilbert take turns rubbing on me, touching me and kissing on me. I try to fight back, honest. Sarah is the prettiest and only seventeen, the closest to my age. I don't fight back too hard when it's her turn.

The night starts with Thrill and Naughty throwing a party for me on The Block, at the Two O'Clock Club. Beans and his friends are there, too. They're always at the club, it's their favorite spot. I have more than a couple of beers, more than at any one time before. There is no drinking age to speak of, and we drink plenty of beer. I guess I get drunk, I don't remember. I do remember waking up with five girls on me. This is at the house, Madam Mrs. Russell's, where I sleep when I don't go home. I wonder if she's in on it? Girls taking advantage of me doesn't stop after that night, either. It's never five at once again, but I'm waked up a lot after that night by one, or sometimes, two at a time. They call it playing. They say I'm like their little brother and they're teaching me things.

"Well, Paul, do you like it?" Mrs. Russell asks.

"I don't know. I try to stop them. Sometimes they leave me alone."

"I have an idea. If you stop fighting them and act like you like it, I bet they'll leave you alone for good."

The next time I sleep at the MM Club, Sandy Matthews and Mary Kelly come into my room. Mary starts to take my belt off and unbutton my pants. I settle on the bed and put my hands behind my head. I smile and close my eyes. Both girls make a funny "humph" sound and leave the room.

It's the last time it happens.

I am fortunate to have Mrs. Russell. Despite my sometimes-rambunctious behavior, she never ceases teaching me. "Paul, would you rather be ebullient or churlish?" she asks out of the blue.

"I'm mostly churlish, but I would rather be ebullient, I guess, Mrs. Russell," I answer.

"That's good, Paul. I don't think I would like the churlish you," she says. "And if you ever became too obdurate, I will stop inviting you up to visit with me."

"I'll try to always be agreeable, Mrs. Russell."

This type of banter can go on for hours while we play cards. She's always teaching.

❄ ❄ ❄

"I'm certainly glad to see you again, Paul Signori."

I had a couple of rough weeks—my father beating us all nearly to death, Beans pushing me into more and more fights, and the girls holding me down on my birthday. I need to escape, and walking the many miles to the stables is the best escape I can come up with. I haven't forgotten the excitement, the exuberance I feel when I'm riding Suzy.

"Mr. Jack, I want to learn how to ride," I say. "Really ride—ride as good as you."

"Oh, my boy, those are the most wonderful words I could possibly hear," he says. "I would be pleased to convey whatever knowledge I may have on the subject onto you."

I'm happy that I know what the word conveys means. I also like the way he talks. This being only the second time I meet him, and the first time I was so overcome with the excitement of riding a horse for the first time, I missed how small he is. He's barely as tall as me, and I've just turned twelve.

"I would also be pleased," I say. "If you taught me how, I mean."

He laughs. "I like you, Paulie. You get right to the point. I suppose you would like to see Suzy again. She's been waiting for you to come back, you know. Even told me as much just the other day."

Now I laugh. "Horses can't talk, Mr. Jack."

"Ahh, but this beauty can," he says. "When she was a filly all those years ago, she was quite a runner. Won a few races, I'll have you know." He looks away, and then adds, solemnly, "Now she's just an old mare."

"Did you ride her?"

"Oh yes, quite a few times back when I was a jockey."

I know what a jockey is, of course, and I'm not surprised to hear that he had been one since he's so small. Together we saddle Suzy, and I climb aboard her. Jack walks us around the fenced-in yard, talking non-stop about how to handle a horse. He finally lets her go, opening the fence's gate, and off we go. She runs free, as I am merely a passenger. The wind blows my hat off and I shake my head, sending my long hair streaming freely in the wind. I can stay up here forever.

Like always, though, my thoughts of Beans, and numbers, and fights, and money, and my mother, and my father, and everything else starts to cloud my mind. I know I need to end the ride—end my joy—and return to the troubled life I lead.

But I have finally found something special—something that requires nothing of me except my presence, and a horse running free. With Jack's teaching, I can really ride! I saddle her. I brush her, clean her, and feed her as many apples as I can carry. I know I have found something that loves me and I love back.

I'm lucky. I have found a respite from the violence that permeates my life. I can experience something that's more wonderful than I most likely deserve, certainly better than anything else that my life can provide. My weekly trips to the stable riding Suzy and the responsibility of taking care of her provide the only escape from the reality of my life. I believe that she does wait for me, for whenever I arrive, Suzy greets me with uncontrollable excitement. She brays and whinnies and bounces on her front hooves. She takes off running on an excited lap around the fenced yard, finally stopping directly in front of me. She nudges my chest with her long, beautiful muzzle. We then spend the next hour or so riding on the wind.

❊ ❊ ❊

In my world of violence, I'm desperately trying to find, and maintain, some semblance of normalcy and morality. I know right from wrong and the Mob has taught me the creed that they live by: Never steal from the family, never disrespect the family, and always stand with the family. It's also acceptable to take advantage of suckers. Or anyone not associated with the family for that matter, regardless of whether the family is right or not, always side with the family.

But I'm not in the Mob family yet.

I certainly don't learn ethics at home—not with a father who spends all the money he earns on himself and drinking and beats his family on a whim. I guess that's why I take advantage of Mr. Joe from the junkyard. There's also no moral code on the job site. Look out for number one is the most common phrase I think I hear. That, or stay out of another man's business. The times are tough, the work's hard, let men be men, blah, blah, blah. I hear it all. But not with the Mob, and I want to be part of it—the same with Thrill and Naughty. The two of them have been my family for as long as I can remember.

As far as I can tell, God doesn't play much of a role in the day-to-day living we do. It's not that I don't believe in God. It's just like with most aspects of my life—I don't have the time to think about such things.

# Chapter 5

# THE BOYS

April 3, 1938, my birthday:

It's a beautiful spring afternoon, clear and bright and sunny. After putting in my eight hours at the lumber yard—I now work at a lumber yard—I want nothing more than to celebrate with Thrill and Naughty. Maybe we'll end up dancing and drinking on The Block. Maybe we'll run into some girls who are not strippers.

Me, Tony Mazzotti, and Phil Carollo were all born within two months of each other, but I'm forever reminded that I'm the youngest, which means I'm the last to turn fourteen. We've grown up together, and fast, on the same block only a few doors apart in the part of Baltimore City called Little Italy. Our community is just about one hundred percent Italian by my fourteenth birthday. Little Italy is over twenty-five blocks of flat-front row houses, usually two or three stories high with a basement. Row houses are common throughout the city. I guess that any row of continual houses, an unbroken line, where common walls are shared is a row house. We've got neighbors on both sides, and share a wall with each of them.

Every neighborhood within Little Italy has an abundance of shops and restaurants. You don't have to go very far to get what you need. You don't even have to leave the neighborhood if you didn't want to. And everyone pretty much knows everyone else; it's hard to be anonymous. Sometimes, I get the feeling I'm living inside of a box, surrounded on all sides by walls. It's almost impossible to find any peace and quiet while living here. There are always people around everywhere, crowding into me. My house is no different—it's always crowded and noisy—it's especially loud when my father is home and yelling. I wonder what our neighbors think. I can hear them yelling and fighting sometimes, but I never bother checking to find out why or what's happening. They probably are content to mind their own business also.

My mom and Mrs. Satori from next door sit on the front porch and smoke cigarettes and gossip sometimes. Sometimes our other neighbor, Mrs. Carboni, joins them. None of them seem very happy as they're always complaining. I'm polite when I see my neighbors and say hello, but mostly I ignore them. On any given warm summer night, you can see a sea of people, all sitting on their small front porches, watching the goings-on all around them. This is probably the most peaceful time of all—everyone outside talking and no one yelling and fighting with each other. Kids running up and down the street, boys playing stick-ball or step-ball, teenage girls gathered in groups watching the boys.

I'm nothing more than a casual observer of all this activity, as I am too busy to participate and hang around. Most everyone knows what Thrill, Naughty, and me do, but no one ever questions us, and most—if not all—of the men in the neighborhood, my father included, have seen me working in the clubs or fighting on the street. Most just say, "How are you doing, Paulie?" and we leave it at that.

I see Thrill and Naughty just about every day since we live so close to each other and work together for Beans and the Mob. The two of them have been my family my entire life. Italian families don't have a coming-of-age celebration, but for us, fourteen is a turning point. We already considered ourselves men—we've been taking care of ourselves for years —regardless of what the rest of the world might think. But we have been too old to run the numbers for a while. We have become teenagers; we're too stupid to run the numbers. We think that maybe our time working for Beans has come to an end.

"Why don't you guys come down to the Two O'Clock Club tonight?" Beans says that afternoon. "We can celebrate Funeral's birthday."

I didn't even know he knew it was my birthday. Naughty Mazzotti has a hard time hiding his excitement. We all do, but he speaks first, "That would be great, Beans! What time? Nine?"

"Yeah, Naughty, nine would be perfect. We got something special planned for you guys," he says as he turns to walk away. "And wear something nice, you bums."

We watch him walk away. Our relationship with Beans has changed over the years. It's morphed more into a boss-employee relationship as opposed to us being kids helping him out. He expects a lot from us, but he also treats us like the men we think we are, as opposed to boys. We appreciate that since we feel like men. It has been six years since we started working for him, but like I said, Beans has already stopped using us to run numbers. The last couple of months we've been hanging around the clubs at night running errands or doing odd jobs. Tonight, is either going to be a grand farewell or we'll be starting the next chapter of our lives in organized crime.

We pray it's the latter.

"What do ya think it's gonna be, Funeral?" Thrill asks.

"Beats me," I say. "But I hope he keeps us," I add a few seconds later, but mostly to myself.

I don't want to stop working for him. Deep down I know it's not right—illegal even—but I want to be part of something. I want to feel like I'm important, like I'm needed. I don't know what to expect tonight.

Most of the kids who were bag boys, running the numbers, never do anything for the Mob once they stop being bag boys. Why would we be different?

We part ways, agreeing to meet, dressed in our best suits, in front of my house. For my birthday, my Uncle Marco said I can use his extra car. Marco has a car title company; he always seems to have a car for me to use when I need one. I don't have a driver's license, how could I? I'm only fourteen, but Marco taught me how to drive when I was twelve. My uncle lives a couple of streets away and has been a constant in my life for as long as I can remember. He's nothing like his brother, my father. Marco is a decent man—good to his family—but unfortunately, he never interferes with his younger brother and his family. Although he does help me out of a jam every now and again, and he lets me drive his extra car.

My friends and I plan on going to our party in style.

Things have quieted down at home lately, too. The old man still drinks every night, but he comes home and passes out more times than not, and the beatings have started to taper off. Me and Nicky can handle him now without too much trouble if we're together. But he still beats Mom when we're not around and the younger kids, too, sometimes.

I stopped working the WPA job a few months back and only do side jobs with the old man now. We build porches and steps and walls, mostly. I started working the job at the lumber yard, sanding window frames, as soon as I quit the WPA. The lumber yard is just down the street, across from Mr. Joe's junkyard. Oh, and I don't take Mr. Joe's iron from him and sell it back anymore. I guess I outgrew that part of my life. I've been doing hard work—man's work—since before I was ten years old.

❊ ❊ ❊

I take a bath and wash my hair. This is a special treat. My entire family shares a bathroom and taking baths are usually only a once-a-week activity and they never last more than a few minutes. I think I stay in the hot water for an hour, the water is already cold by the time the knocking on the bathroom door drives me out.

"All right, already!" I yell at the obnoxious perpetrator. "Give me a break, already. And give me a minute to dry off."

I slick back my not-quite-black hair, like the Mob guys do. I use some greasy pomade I have. My dark blue suit is cut broad across the shoulders, like what's in style, and my pants are tapered. I wear my best white shirt and red paisley tie. I slip on my two-toned Oxfords. Me, Thrill and Naughty have started dressing better now that we're older and don't run the numbers, but tonight I have on the best clothes I own. I see myself in a mirror—I look like I'm twenty years old.

My mom is all compliments about how handsome I look. My older brother is jealous. The little ones, Frankie, Glory and Norma—still no nickname—are all ooohs and aaahs. My father, who happens to be home, doesn't say much.

"Look at mister high and mighty," he finally chimes in. "Mister important down on The Block."

I mutter, "More important than you." But not so loud that he hears me say it. The last thing I want is him getting in my face.

"You have a good time tonight, Paul," my mother says as she kisses my cheek.

"I will, Mom. I'll see you tomorrow."

We walk in the Two O'Clock Club at exactly nine. The place is packed, but Beans is easy to spot. He's always the loudest guy around, and I think he looks at tonight as a special night for him, too. He calls us over as soon as he spots us walking toward the bar.

"Here they are now!" he yells. He's got a bottle of champagne in his hand. "Drinks are on the house tonight, boys, so drink up."

We start with champagne, switch to beer, and then whiskey

and soda. At the pace we're drinking, we won't last an hour. I see Mob guys everywhere—made men, associates, soldiers—you name it. Sal the Shovel and Willie the Mechanic even come over and shake my hand; they're made guys. It doesn't take long before Beans starts his speech about the three of us. He drones on and on about how he took us under his wing, trained us and how he expects big things from us.

Then he says what we have been waiting all night to hear. "You guys are in."

The crowded room erupts in applause. Glasses are clinking together in toasts all over the bar. Beans shakes our hands, pulling us into a four-person bear hug.

That was it. We are in—as in the family—in the Mafia. And it's for life.

❈ ❈ ❈

This is when I find out what the "Mob" really is. Baltimore is not a big city. Take away the waterfront, the port and the docks, and there's not much to the city. Organized crime, like in New York and New Jersey, or even Philadelphia, didn't really take hold in Baltimore. Nonetheless, the Mob is involved in most everything—much more than what I know or do. I just know the numbers and a little about the gambling. The group of Mobsters I'm associated with is affiliated with the Mafia out of New York and the Gambino Crime Family. They call themselves the Baltimore Crew. They're affiliated only, meaning they pretty much run their business however they want as an independent organization. So, I would say we're like the local Mob. The Crew's boss is Patsy Corbi— he's one of the most important people in all of Baltimore. Mr. Corbi and his brothers have been in charge for a long time. He comes around often, from what I hear, but I've only seen him a few times.

Interestingly, most of the night clubs on The Block are owned by Jewish men. Mr. Goodman bought the Two O'Clock Club a few years ago and Max Cohen owns the Oasis and a few more. Hon Nickel owns the biggest burlesque theater around, the Gayety Theater. I work in all of them, but I don't work for the owners. I guess the Mob and the club owners work together.

I know Beans and his friends keep an office of sorts in the basement of the Two O'Clock Club. I've been dropping off money bags and numbers bags and gambling sheets in his office forever. I also know that most of the gambling, outside of the bookmakers on the street, is run in the basements of the various clubs on The Block. Mob guys are always coming and going, it's always hopping with action.

Me, Thrill, and Naughty just play a small part in the scheme of things. So much more is going on behind-the-scenes that we know nothing about. But you know what? I'm perfectly fine with that, I don't want to know more than I need to. I only need to know what Beans tells me to know.

# Chapter 6

# WATCHING

"I want you guys to watch. That's it for now—just watch what's going on. You're my new watchers," Beans says the next day. "You see something, you find someone and tell them."

I'm struggling to concentrate, and my head is pounding from my hangover, but I manage to say,"Watching what, Beans?"

"Haven't you been paying attention? The clubs and the girls, stupid," he says.

The three of us—me, Thrill and Naughty—will be a team, always together. Our job is to make sure no one's casing the place, cheating the place, stealing from the place, looking for a fight, or bothering the girls on the floor. If anything gets out of hand, we call in the heavies—the guys who bust heads. Beans says we don't have enough training to be head-basher. We keep an eye on everything. We learn by on-the-job training because no one has the time to teach us what we're looking for.

We have five clubs that we work, all of them on The Block —The Oasis, The Flamingo, The Gayety, the Two O'Clock Club, and the MM Club. Beans says we won't work the same club more than two days in a row, three tops. He doesn't want us to get too familiar with the same faces; we need variety, that's why he keeps switching us. Our shift is from eight at night to two in the morning, or whenever they decided to shut the club down for the night. All the clubs are different, but still the same in many ways. They all have lots of men, and drinking, gambling, and of course, lots of beautiful women for entertainment.

The Gayety has a high-class burlesque with dancing show girls on the main floor, a bar with strip-tease in the basement, and a pool hall upstairs. The Two O'Clock Club is the most respectable cabaret and bar on The Block, and The Oasis is a night club that has it all. The Flamingo is a strip-tease bar, and The MM Club is a brothel and night club that's next to the Two O'Clock Club. The two clubs share a common wall.

The Block, Baltimore's red-light district, has been around for a hundred years, but after the great fire of 1904 burned most of the buildings, the re-built Block, rising like a Phoenix from the ashes, has achieved celebrated fame. At one point, the boundaries had spread all the way to Fells Point, but now it's concentrated around Baltimore Street for six or so blocks. The Block is legendary throughout the nation for its risqué shows, beautiful show girls, and night clubs. And for an anything-goes attitude. The back-of-the-waterfront bawdy entertainment district never sleeps—even after the booze is legally supposed to stop flowing at two in the morning. With a never-ending stream of customers from the waterfront—sailors, seamen, dock workers, longshoremen, and industrial workers like my father—why would the clubs ever close?

❋ ❋ ❋

Watching people is an art form. The subtleties are an acquired skill. Much like when I first started running numbers as a bag boy, I have no clue what I'm doing. I'm seeing things happen without knowing what I see. Understanding peoples' behavior, the nuances, and their reactions takes time. I don't have the time—I'm expected to know what people are thinking starting on day one.

The first rule in people watching is not to be obvious. If someone knows they are being watched, they alter what they do, they hide their intentions. I become very good at seeing out of the corner of my eye, and seeing multiple goings-on at the same time. I can stare straight ahead, but watch something across a crowded room in a corner of the club. The clubs are always crowded. I have no idea how I'm supposed to watch hundreds of people jammed into a confined space, and most of them are either drunk or halfway to being drunk.

The second thing I learn is to listen. I listen to boisterous conversation and strain to hear whispered secrets. I learn how to differentiate between an animated conversation between friends and a loud discussion escalating into a heated argument. Body language is sometimes the most telling aspect of a conversation. Relaxed people seldom fight, but they do steal or cheat, if they are good at hiding their intended purpose. On the contrary, clenched teeth and a rigid jaw almost certainly means a fight.

It's a rare occasion when something doesn't happen during my nightly shift.

❊ ❊ ❊

"Each of you guys stands in a different spot," Beans tells us. "Kinda like dividing the room up, know what I mean?"

"Yes, Beans, we know what that means," I say.

"You guys look nice," he compliments. "I was afraid you'd come in tonight looking like bums."

"You said for us to dress nice, remember?" Thrill says.

"I remember, but who knows with you guys?"

I know he's not being serious, just ribbing us. The three of us have slacks, button-down shirts and jackets on, but no ties. Besides Beans and the other Mobsters, we're the best-dressed men in the place. The club has a main stage and two smaller stages to either side. The main bar-top runs almost the length of one wall and bows outward in the middle; smaller bar-tops are on the sides of the main top. The floor has tables but also some open space. Hundreds of people can fit in the club.

We each take a third of the room at the Two O'Clock Club our first night. I've always been an observant person—running the numbers made me notice and remember things most people wouldn't. After a few minutes of standing around, I decide to walk my portion of the room. It's loud and crowded, and a burlesque show is on the main stage. Most of the men are watching the girls. I don't blame them, the girls are practically naked, and they're gorgeous.

I've been hanging around clubs for a long time. I've seen plenty of strippers, show girls, and dancers, but I've never watched them. They have always just been part of the scenery. It's hard to explain. I know Thrill and Naughty have also seen plenty of beautiful show girls and dancers, but tonight is the first time it's our job to do nothing, really, except watch them. I've also seen naked girls before. The girls from The MM Club, who also work the Two O'Clock Club, have paid me night-time visits in the past. They're never shy about showing their bodies. I haven't told my friends about what used to happen to me. Only Mrs. Russell knows.

Eventually, I make my way back to where Thrill and Naughty are standing.

"Holy cow, will you look at that one!" Thrill exclaims.

It's Sarah Gilbert, my favorite. She's the most beautiful girl I've ever seen. I want to brag to my friends about the night she and her friends attacked me, but I'm too embarrassed.

"And what about that one!" Naughty says while pointing at Mary Kelly.

"I can't believe our job is to watch beautiful girls," Thrill says. "Thank you, God."

"You should thank Beans," I say, "God's got nuttin' to do with it."

"Thank you, Beans," Thrill adds with a chuckle.

"Don't let on that we like it so much, he'll probably make us do something else if he finds out," Naughty chimes in.

I decide to spoil the fun, "We're not supposed to just watch the girls, you know, we're supposed to watch out for other stuff, too."

"Don't be a party-pooper," Naughty says.

"Yeah, Funeral, shut up, why don't ya and watch the show," Thrill adds.

I smile and look away. They're so immature. "Well, I'm gonna move around the room," I say. "Don't let your eyes pop out from staring so hard." I couldn't help but add a parting jab.

❀ ❀ ❀

At first, I don't notice what he's doing, except that he's the only guy at the bar not watching the girls. Every so often, he slides down the bar a few feet and inadvertently blocks my view. Then he moves to another spot and does the movement again. The third time I'm in the right position to see what he's up to. He waits for someone at the bar to leave his change behind. He slides down the bar, moves his body so the unsuspecting victim is blocked and can't see what he's doing. He shoots his hand up and grabs the money and is gone in a second. He's so fast that I missed what he was doing the first couple of times.

"How's it going tonight?" I ask him.

"Mind your own business, kid."

"You are my business."

"Bloody hell, bugger off you little punk or I'll brain ya!"

"If you give the money back, I'll let you leave the club without any trouble," I tell him.

He stands up. He's two or three inches taller than me, but he

79

has a gut, a big pot-belly. I can pummel the guy if I must. He gives me a shove and tries to move past me.

"I can't let you leave with the money you stole," I say as I grab his arm.

"Get out of my way!" he shouts, loud enough for others to hear.

Within two seconds one of the head-bashers is standing next to me. "Trouble?" He asks.

"Guy's been stealing other people's change," I answer.

"Like hell I've been!" the guy yells.

"You've got two choices," the head-basher says. "Both involve you leaving the money and getting tossed out of here on your arse. Choose wisely."

"Actually, that sounds like one choice," he wisecracks.

"One is you leaving the money and not getting your arm broken, the other is me breaking your arm and taking the money from you," the head-basher says.

The guy pulls out a couple of bucks and throws them on the bar, and turns to leave. The head-basher looks at me. I shake my head no.

"Why do they always choose number two?" The basher says.

He twists the guys arm into a pretzel and pushes him onto the floor. The guy screams in pain. I doubt anyone even noticed. The basher—he's a big Irish guy named Mike—motions for me to check his pockets. I pull bills and coins out of every pocket the guy has. Then I hear the bone break in his upper arm. I can't look, I turn away. The guy passes out and Mike drags him to the front door and throws him out on the sidewalk.

"Nice job, kid," Mike says when he gets back to the bar. Then he adds, "You're the one they call Funeral, right?"

"I am."

"I'm Mike Sullivan, ain't got a nickname."

"I'll call you Bones," I say off the top of my head. "That is, if you want a nickname," I quickly add.

Big Mike Sullivan practically falls on the floor he's laughing so hard. "I love it!" he finally yells. "Bones Sullivan it is."

It's not long after and Bones comes to my rescue again. I've been watching the same two guys bantering back and forth for over ten minutes. When two hard-drinking, hard-looking men stay at each other for more than a few minutes, you know trouble is brewing. I can't make out exactly what it is they're disagreeing about from the distance I'm at, so I move closer. The discussion is about work and money. The subjects are frequently discussed as most men don't have enough of either. One guy isn't satisfied with the work the other guy did and isn't paying. I'm able to catch bits and pieces only.

"You owe me…"

"I owe you nuttin' until it's done right…"

"No-good cheapskate…"

"You're a lazy bum…"

I make my move just as the lazy guy starts to throw a punch at the cheap guy. I catch his arm at the elbow and slow his punch down. The cheap guy seizes the moment and clobbers the lazy guy right in the jaw, sending both of us crashing to the floor, him landing on me. Bones Sullivan is on the guy that threw the punch faster than I've ever seen a 200-pound man move. Cheap guy, the punch-thrower, is on the floor begging for mercy in less than a second.

"We don't allow fightin' in the Two O'Clock Club. No sir, we don't," Bones Sullivan says with a bit of a brogue.

This commotion does bring the club to a partial standstill.

Everyone likes to see a fight—encourages them, even. That's why the head-bashers, or bouncers, clear the fights as fast as possible. Two more large men help Bones Sullivan carry the two would-be brawlers out the front door. I'm still lying on the floor when Bones offers his hand. I grab hold, and he pulls me to my feet.

"You're going to love this job, Funeral. Never a dull moment," Bones Sullivan says.

I couldn't agree more. I already love it.

❄ ❄ ❄

My second night I'm reminded what the number one priority is—the girls. My most important job is to watch the girls. No one can harass the girls beyond what is deemed acceptable, and deems acceptable is a fine line and every girl has her own version, and that version changes continually depending on who is paying attention to her. An attractive man or a wealthy man can get away with much more than an unattractive or poor man can. It's considered a touchy-feely business to begin with, but every girl draws the line at something.

It's been over two years since I got my surprise birthday present from the five girls in the bedroom at the MM Club. All five girls are still around, working the club floor or dancing in the shows. I've become very close to all of them, in a brotherly way, of course. Sarah Gilbert attracts a lot of attention, but she still seems very innocent and naïve to me. And I know that Mrs. Russell doesn't let her take guys upstairs into the private rooms.

Close to the girls in a brotherly way is hard to explain. I can't help but be attracted to them, they are all very beautiful, and I'm a teenager. If they started to visit me in the middle of the night again, I'd have a hard time resisting. I'm closer to the girls who work at the Two O'Clock Club and the MM Club because that's where I spend most of my time—the sneaking into my room a couple of years ago by the girls notwithstanding. I know most of their stories, how they ended up working here, working on The Block as dancers or as other things, and I'm knowledgeable about what the girls do when they leave—they mostly just go home and live like everyone else. The girls are very normal people, with parents and families. Some do live at the club, in the spare rooms on the top floor and still others live together as roommates. Some have boyfriends, who can sometimes be jealous and cause problems. I know what most of their dreams are. Many dream about starring in big shows, or going to New York or Hollywood and becoming famous. Some use their time on The Block as a stepping stone. Most of the burlesque shows are innocent, aside from the girls dressing provocatively. Most of them don't bring men upstairs at the MM Club; some do, of course, and I don't hold it against them.

Sarah's story isn't that different from most. She started as a dancer, got discovered at an early age, moved to the city at seventeen, and did whatever it took to make it. I don't know what happened with her parents, she doesn't talk about that, but I'd bet they're poor, living out in the country. I'm sure they miss their daughter but have no means to visit her. Mrs. Russell took her in and lets her live at the club. I know she's protected. Sarah is almost twenty now, but still an innocent looking beauty to me.

"Please don't touch me there," I hear Sarah say. I've been watching her walk the club floor for a few minutes before the cabaret show she's in starts.

"I'll touch you anywhere I want, little missy," I hear a drunk guy slur.

He's older, probably forty, balding, and fat. Not someone

who would be considered attractive by any stretch of the imagination. Most likely works down on the docks and blows off some steam every night on The Block.

"Ow! That hurts. Please don't pinch me," Sarah yells.

I watch as the guy pulls Sarah down on his lap. His hands are all over her. His friends egg him on. I look around for Bones Sullivan or one of the other head-bashers. The place is too crowded, I can't see anyone, but I also can't let this go on. I move behind the guy's seat.

"Everything all right, Sarah?" I ask.

"Oh Funeral, can you please tell this man to let me go?"

Even some of the girls call me by my nickname.

"Funeral?" he bellows. "What are you, a killer?"

The three men at the table with him erupt with laughter from their seats.

"A real tough guy, eh?" one of the friends shouts.

"Mister, let her go," I say. "If she doesn't want you hanging all over her, let her go. Them's the rules."

"What could you possibly do about it, pipsqueak?" he asks through his drunken laughter. "Huh, Funeral?"

My movement is so sudden, it takes him by surprise. I take a step to the side of the chair and grab Sarah by the wrist, pulling her out of his grip. From his expression, he's astonished by my strength. He quickly recovers, though, and jumps to his feet. I push Sarah out of the way just as he starts to throw a punch. Like most men, he's got a height and weight advantage over me, but I easily duck under the punch and start to back up, trying to create some space.

Unfortunately, I back up into the arms of one of his friends; he grabs me around the chest. This type of double-team is nothing new to me; I know exactly what to do, and they never expect it. I throw my head back and blast the guy in the chin while simultaneously stomping down on his foot—one guy out-of-action.

The original guy, the one who was groping Sarah, is now right in front of me cocking his right arm. I almost feel sorry for him. He's so slow I think I can avoid the punch without even moving. He misses by a mile and leaves himself wide open for a counter-punch, just like Killer Marino taught me. I punch the guy square in the nose. I watch the blood spurt, knowing I can stop now, the fight is basically over. But, why should I? I hit him again, and then again with another right hand, followed by a left uppercut. The guy hits the floor with a bang.

"That should pretty much end it, boys, don't you think?" Bones Sullivan says as he walks up, surveying the damage. "Go on, pick your friends up and show yourselves to the door."

Sarah falls sobbing into my arms. "Thank you, Paulie," she whispers into my ear. I like it when she uses my real name.

"I'll always look out for you, Sarah," I say as I wrap my arms around her. She's shorter than me, and fits perfectly under my chin if I lift my head. I feel her body against mine.

A dozen people start applauding, including Bones Sullivan. He says, "Very nice work, Funeral, very nice indeed. I'd say you've got a future as a head-basher in the not-too-distant future. Yes, sir."

"He was drunk. And slow," I offer.

"Maybe so, but I bet you've had some training and I suspect quite a lot of experience at fighting, too. Am I correct, Funeral?"

"You're right, Mr. Sullivan. I've been fighting for Beans since I was ten."

"Ah, Beans does like to start 'em young," Bones says as he

walks away.

Both Thrill and Naughty caught the tail end of the short, but sweet, brawl. "Damn, Funeral, you should have called us over," Naughty says. "That looked like fun."

I'm cracking myself up at this point, but manage to say, "It sure was!"

❊ ❊ ❊

"I couldn't have chosen better myself, Paul," Mrs. Russell says to me later that night. "You are absolutely perfect for watching out for my little babies."

It's late, a few minutes past two in the morning and the Two O'Clock Club is closing for the night. I'm beat, it's my second late night in a row, plus I'm working at seven in the morning at the lumber yard.

"Can I get you something to drink, Mrs. Russell?" I ask from behind the bar, helping to clean up.

"I'll take a whiskey, neat," she says. "Pour a beer for yourself and come and sit with me."

I pour her whiskey in a snifter glass, not chilled or with ice, and move out from behind the bar with a beer in hand.

"Sarah told me what happened tonight."

"I'm just glad I was nearby and could help."

"My, have you grown up—you're practically a man," Mrs. Russell says with a sigh. "Do you remember that first day I taught you how to play cards?"

"How could I forget?" I answer. I'm still the best blackjack player in the neighborhood, thanks to Mrs. Russell. "I should be splitting the money I make with you since you taught me how to play so well."

"I'm grateful that you are in my life, Paul, and still find the time to visit with me."

I spend at least one afternoon a week playing cards and reading with Mrs. Russell still to this very day. I wish I could express to her how I feel about her, but I don't know how. I'm not even sure myself, how and what I feel toward her. She shows me more love and compassion than either of my parents—my mother because she has lost the ability to show love and my father because he hates the world.

"I'm grateful, too, Mrs. Russell," I manage to say.

"Please don't grow up anymore. Can you promise me that?"

"But I want to grow up."

"Then promise me that when you do grow up, you have a normal life," she says. "This is no life for you, Paul. You are better than this. You are too smart for this kind of life—smart enough to go back to school. You could even go to college someday."

"I need to work to support my mom and the kids."

I know she is just dreaming. A dream where I go to college, become a lawyer or something similar, and marry a beautiful, innocent girl completely removed from the girls who work on The Block. Marry a girl the opposite of her. Perhaps she is talking like this because she is getting older and feeling nostalgic.

"Of course, you must work, dear," she says after a long period of silence.

I watch her take a sip of whiskey, her age starting to show around the corners of her mouth and around her eyes. She has a full figure; her hair is auburn and her eyes are a blue like I've never seen before. Dark blue like a stormy sky. When I think about it, I really don't know that much about her, even though I have spent many hours in her company. I know that she doesn't have a husband, but I don't know if she has ever been married.

I ask, "Have you ever been married, Mrs. Russell?"

She puts her glass of whiskey down on the bar-top and looks at me with a peculiar look. "Why on earth do you want to know that?"

"I'm curious I guess," I say. And then after a pause, I add, "No, that's not it, Mrs. Russell. What I mean is you're better than this, too. You're better than me. You're a lot better person than me. You deserve better than this."

She's staring at me now. A tear is forming in her eye.

"This is just where I ended up," she says. "And yes, I was married once a long time ago. But it only lasted less than a year before he ran out on me."

"I'm sorry, Mrs. Russell," I offer lamely. Am I getting to personal with her? Have we started a conversation that neither of us wants to have?

"I had dreams when I was your age. I wanted to dance on Broadway, dance in real shows," she tells me. "After Johnny left me, I had nowhere to turn. I ended up working as a show girl, then doing whatever it took to survive. Mr. Goodman took me in and I've been here with him ever since."

Mr. Goodman is one of the Jewish guys who own clubs on The Block, including the Two O'Clock Club.

"Why don't you get married again?"

"Bless your heart, Paul, but who would want an old show girl like me?"

"I think you're beautiful."

She reaches over and kisses me on the cheek. "Thank you

88

for thinking so. But I know better. Once upon a time, maybe."

Mrs. Russell's job is kinda like mine in a way. She watches out for the girls, just like me, making sure nothing bad happens to them. I guess she's their manager. Maybe it's more like the way Beans is with me, Naughty and Thrill. Only she does love the girls that work for her. Just like she considers me her son, she considers the girls her daughters.

"The last thing you want to happen, Paul, now listen to me, is to wake up one morning fifteen, twenty years from now and find yourself still in a place like this."

I let her words sink in. I can't even imagine what my life will be like in a year, let alone fifteen years from now. I'm only fourteen years old, why should I be worried about the future? Heck, I'm just happy not to be working on the streets anymore, not running numbers, running bets, running money all over the place. I'm in the clubs now; I'm in the big time. I'm where all the action is. This is what's important to me. Watching the girls to make sure nothing happens to them. I'm essential to their well-being. I'm taking care of them, watching over them, just like Mrs. Russell.

I feel a hand on my shoulder, it's Thrill. "Hey, me and Naughty are heading home, you coming?"

"I think I'll stay and finish my beer with Mrs. Russell."

"Okay, buddy, see ya tomorrow," they both say as they turn to walk away.

Me and Mrs. Russell sit quietly sipping our drinks, enjoying the silence and each other's company. We are comfortable with each other like old lovers are. Neither of us needs to talk, neither desires to have our thoughts interrupted. Where will I be in ten years? Fifteen years? These are my thoughts. I can't imagine what she is thinking about.

"Do you mind if I find a room at the MM?" I finally ask.

"No, I don't mind," she answers.

I kiss her cheek and walk out the back exit and up the staircase to the MM Club. I use the key Mrs. Russell gave me. A few minutes after I settle into bed, Sarah Gilbert quietly enters the room. She climbs into the bed.

"Goodnight, Paul Signori," she whispers in my ear.

We are both asleep a second later.

# Chapter 7

# FIGHTER

It's the spring of 1938. The baseball season is about to start. The gamblers will be out in full swing, betting on every game. I don't have a team I follow; I'm not all that interested. Horse racing is a completely different story. I'm very interested. Last year, 1937, the greatest horse of all time, War Admiral, won the Triple Crown. War Admiral trains at a horse farm in Berlin, Maryland, across the Chesapeake Bay called Glen Riddle, and he's trained by the great George Conway. My friend Jack O'Donovan talks about riding at Glen Riddle and working with George back in the day. Seabiscuit is another famous racehorse. The Kentucky Derby is only a couple of weeks away, and again, the gambling and the betting and the money will be prodigious.

Then there's boxing, and everyone bets on boxing. The matches never stop, the money never stops flowing as boxing is a year-round sport. Joe Louis, the heavyweight champion, is everyone's favorite boxer.

I don't pay much attention to the news. I know we're still in the Great Depression—at least it's finally got a name—but I don't care. I'm working days at the lumber yard making decent money, most of which I give to my mother, and nights for the Mob. The money the Mob pays me, I keep most of that, but I always have a stash just in case my mom needs extra. I simply don't have the time to worry about things happening outside of my own world, although, I do admit that most people seem more optimistic—at least more so than last year.

One way I can tell that things are getting better is that most people now own cars, which makes Uncle Marco very happy. I see traffic jams on the busy streets. A few years ago, I don't remember seeing hardly any automobile traffic. There's also talk about a coming war in Europe and some German guy named Hitler, but I'm not paying much attention to that, either. If he wants to conquer the world, let him—as long as he leaves Baltimore alone, that is.

✳ ✳ ✳

Despite my new, elevated position as a watcher in the clubs, I'm still forced to fight. At fourteen, I'm not full-grown by any means but I'm tall for my age. I also have my father's uncommon strength. My strength, coupled with years of hard work, has produced the physique of a boxer; I'm all hard muscle. If I fought in the ring, I would be a welterweight, about 140 pounds. I'm quick, lightning fast, and I hit like I have hands made of cement.

"I heard about the other night, Funeral," Beans says. "Two guys? That's a record for one of my watchers."

"Just doin' my job, Beans."

"I've got something lined up for ya. He's eighteen, I think, and a little bigger than you, but you can take him."

"I'm not sure I'm following you, Beans."

"A fight, Funeral," he says. "What, do I have to spell it out for you?"

"A boxing match? In a ring?"

"No, not a boxing match—bare-knuckles in an alley. This is the real McCoy, Funeral, a real fight with betting and everything."

He wants me to be a bare-knuckle street fighter, which I kinda already am, so he and his friends can gamble on my fights. It seems I never can stop thanking Killer Marino. Now, it's because of my very tough knuckles, thanks to him. In all the fights I've had, I've never cracked a knuckle or broken a hand.

"Do I have a say?"

"What do ya mean, Funeral? Of course, you're gonna do it, I'm even gonna pay you," Beans says. "Besides, you're the best of the three of you."

I look at him kinda funny, and say, "Huh?"

"You're a better fighter than Naughty and Thrill. That's why we picked you."

And that's how it starts. He tells me I'm fighting someone, probably some guy who's been bare-knuckle boxing for years. It's for money, he tells me, like that makes it all right or even different. I guess the difference is this fight is scheduled and I have an opponent, not some random guy on the street.

"When?" I ask.

"Tomorrow afternoon, before you start your shift."

"Thanks, Beans, for giving me a whole day to get ready."

"You don't need a day, Funeral, you's born ready," he says. Then he turns to his friends, Bats and Fish, and says, "Am I right? He was born ready."

"Kid looks ready to me," Fish says.

"As ready as he'll ever be. Maybe we move it up to today," Bats adds.

The three of them have a hard time controlling themselves, they're laughing so hard.

"No, tomorrow will be just fine. Ain't that right, Funeral?"

Tomorrow can't come fast enough.

❋ ❋ ❋

I look the guy over for a few moments. He's tall and lean, four or five years older than me. By appearance alone, it looks like he could kill me, and I should assume he knows how to fight. I'm sure he does, as a matter of fact, or why would he be here in the first place? I've had a day to think about this fight— longer than any other fight I've had. I can't help but admit that I'm a little afraid.

We're in the alley behind the Two O'Clock Club. Trash cans and filth is everywhere and I'm surrounded by walls. It always stinks back here. We circle each other a few times, looking into each other's eyes. It seems neither of us wants to make the first move. I don't know what he's waiting for. I want to look at the crowd of men encircling us but I refuse to take my eyes off him. I can hear Beans shouting something in the background of my mind. There's lots of excitement, shouting and yelling, but I block it out.

In the blink of an eye, he's on top of me, grabbing around my neck. Punches from close range are connecting with my head and face. He's swinging with his right hand and holding me in a head-lock with his left. Luckily, his punches are not doing much damage. I taste blood. Thinking fast, I cock my left hand and blast him in the nuts. He loosens his grip around my neck as he doubles over and I'm able to push myself free. We're back to circling again. I pause briefly to wipe away a trickle of blood from my mouth. I can taste its saltiness on my tongue.

I wait for him to make his move again, but this time I shift to the right at the last second and land two quick lefts to his face. Neither has much effect. I'm better with my right hand, being as I'm right-handed, but I learned to use my left long ago. He recovers and throws a straight right that I see coming from a mile away. As his right flies by the side of my head, I connect with three more quick punches, this time drawing blood.

I'm quicker than my opponent, but he's bigger and stronger. I'm the better boxer—thank you, Killer Marino—but I suspect he's a good street fighter. I'm not half bad of a street fighter, either when I think about it. He forces his way in close again, and despite jabs with my left, he's got a grip on me. I stomp his foot and he howls in pain. I grab his hair and try to force his head down into my knee, but he's strong and gets free. We're both breathing hard. I see his head coming, but I can't get out of the way, he's too close. I think my nose is broken, blood is everywhere, but no one stops the fight.

I then feel an anger rise up in me like I have never felt before. I'm back in his face throwing punches in a split-second; he certainly didn't expect me to recover this fast. I pummel the guy relentlessly, right hand to his face after right hand. I can't stop. He's on the ground trying to cover up, but I won't let him. My left hand grabs hold of one of his wrists and pulls his arm away. My right hand, balled into a fist, smashes away.

I feel several hands on me, pulling me off the guy. Beans is standing in front of me; his expression is blank. I have to believe he is almost in a state of shock, as is everyone else who watched.

"He shouldn't have used his head, Beans. He shouldn't have used his head. Heads ain't fair," I say between gasps of breath, my nose still pouring blood.

I think I hear someone say, "Anything goes in a street fight." It might have been Beans himself because he said that very thing to me once upon a time.

"All that matters now is that you won," he says, finally flashing a smile.

I think the shock is wearing off. I think he had no idea of the fury I'm capable of. He pulls a hanky out of his back pocket—it probably has his snot all over it——and holds it over my nose. I watch as Bats Battaglia collects wads of cash from the men who backed the guy I beat. It looks like I made them a bunch of money. I should have stayed down after the head-butt. Maybe I wouldn't have to fight again if I had. I watch as the other guy is carried off. I should probably feel something, remorse or pity, but I don't. If he had the chance, he would have beaten me as badly.

"Let me check your nose, Funeral," Fish Fischetti says as he pulls the snot-rag away. "Yeah, that's what I thought. She's broken. I'm gonna have to set it. This'll hurt."

He sets my nose back into place using the sides of his hands, pushing and twisting simultaneously. I wail in pain. He hands me Beans' hanky.

"Looks as good as new," Fish says. "Well, almost."

My nose is swollen and my eyes are both black within the hour despite having a piece of raw meat draped over my face. But on the bright side, everyone at the Two O'Clock Club is patting me on the back and handing me free drinks. I try to drink the pain away. Bones Sullivan is very impressed. He thinks it's only a matter of time before I'm working with him.

I notice Mrs. Russell and a few of the girls watching me. She doesn't look pleased; neither do the girls that I'm charged with protecting. Especially Sarah Gilbert, she looks to be crying. Is she crying because of me? Because I fought some guy in the street for money or because I broke my nose? At least Thrill and Naughty don't hate me now. I don't think I could do anything that would jeopardize our loyalty to each other. Besides, they've seen me look this bad before—plenty of times—and me them.

Beans gives me the night off, very generous of him, I think. Oh, and my cut of the profits is almost a hundred bucks. Not bad for ten minutes of work and a broken nose.

My next fight for money is a couple of weeks later. The guy's my age. He doesn't stand a chance. It only takes me two or three minutes to knock the guy out, but he does land some punches. My face has a few bruises.

❊❊❊

I don't know what I would do if I didn't have the stables. No one knows where I disappear to, and I like it this way. I doubt they would understand. Anyway, this is my place—my place to think about nothing except riding a beautiful animal.

"Why do you always look like you've been in a fight?" Jack O'Donovan asks me as I'm saddling Suzy.

Why is Jack bothering me with this today? Two weeks ago, after I broke my nose, I looked a lot worse. "Because I probably have been in a fight," I answer.

"Why do you fight? Do you like it?"

These are tough question to answer, and I really don't want to answer them. But, no, I don't necessarily like to fight, but do I really have a choice in the matter? What would Beans and the rest of them say, or do, better yet, if I refused to fight?

"No, Jack, I can't say that I like to fight," I say.

"So, why do you fight, and it seems like you fight all the time because almost every Saturday you come out here you've got bruises on your face?"

I suspect that he has an idea of what I do, but he's never asked and I've never told Jack that I work for the Mob. The man is not stupid and he certainly has been around the block a few times, so to speak. Not the famous Block, which I'm also sure he has been to, but the proverbial block.

"Jack, can you keep a secret?" I ask.

"Sure, I can."

"A couple of months ago, the Italian Mob down on The Block made me part of the family. I work for the Mob. I used to be a bag boy, running the numbers. Was doin' that since I was eight. Now, I'm a watcher. That's what they call it, a watcher. I keep an eye on everything, you know? I watch the people in the clubs and look out for the girls."

"So why the bruised face, Paulie?" he asks again. "You have to fight when you do this new job?"

"That's different. The fighting, I mean."

"Well, go ahead and tell me about it."

Jack O'Donovan was phlegmatic, but also perceptive. He knew something was always bothering me, but his stoic personality stopped him from inquiring what it was—in the past, that is. Apparently, he has seen enough. I've been going to the stables since I was ten. Three, maybe four, times a month for four years I trek the almost eight miles to the stables—eight long miles away from my normal routine, and spend two hours riding Suzy. Jack and I have had many conversations over the years—sports, horse racing, girls, the weather, you name it— but he never asked me what I did the other 166 hours a week that he didn't see me.

"They ask me to fight people on the street," I tell him. "Lately, it's been for money."

"Ask or demand?"

Always the perceptive one, that Jack. "I guess they demand that I fight people on the street," I answer.

"And you never say no?"

"No."

"No, you never say no?"

"I never say no."

"And what do you think would happen if you did say no?" he asks.

I stop and think about what would happen.

"I'm not sure," I finally answer.

"So, you do like to fight people on the street," he says. "Otherwise, you would say no and find out what happens when you say no."

Why does this old man have to make me think? Make me justify what I do? "I'm only fighting a couple times a month now. It's not a big deal," I try to justify. "And like I said, they bet on the fights and pay me."

"Oh, I get it, you're their street fighter," he speculates.

I've been their entertainment for as long as I remember. All the way back to when Beans first told me to fight some guy and I got my head beat-in when I was ten.

"You don't understand," I say.

"Explain it to me."

"I can't say no to these guys," I explain. "I'm in too deep, I guess. They made me part of it, part of the family."

"Part of the family for life, Paulie, it's always for life," he says. "And life can be a very long time."

This is the first time I think about that particular revelation—for life. Life can be a long time.

"This is what I want to do, Jack. I like working for them," I say, but I'm still searching for the right explanation. "Do you know how old I am?"

"Fourteen. You turned fourteen not too long ago."

I could see Jack was putting some things together.

"You turned fourteen and they brought you into the family, so to speak," he finally says. "I bet you come from nothing, Paulie, right? Your father is probably a drunk. You've been working and not going to school for years, I bet. I bet you think working for the Mob makes you important, don't you?"

How does he know all this stuff about me? "I am important," I finally say.

"I'm sure you think they think you're important."

"They wouldn't have given me the job as a watcher if they didn't think I was important. And if they didn't trust me."

"Say no to them and find out what happens to you."

"What makes you such an authority on the Mob?" I ask.

"Who do you think runs the horses?"

It had never occurred to me that Jack had dealings with the Mob in the past. The light bulb went on in my head. "Did you get screwed over by the Mob when you were a jockey?" I ask.

"Not me so much as the horse, and the horse's owner."

"Did Suzy get screwed over?"

Jack won't answer the question, but I know it's true. He knows how much I love Suzy and he doesn't want anything to spoil that.

"We're talking about you, Paulie, not some old used-up man like me. Trust me when I say the Mob uses people. Just when you think nothing can touch you, you're too important, they shoot you down," he says with melancholy in his voice. "Try to stay on the outside as much as possible. Don't let them suck you in any more than they already have."

I've got no ambition to be anything more than a worker for the Mob. I don't want any responsibility, I don't want people under me, I don't want to give orders. I'm happy just working with Thrill and Naughty.

"Don't worry, Jack, I'm still just a kid," I say. "No one takes me seriously."

I sense that the somber talk is winding down. Jack has given his advice, something he probably doesn't do very often, outside of giving advice about riding a horse.

"Are you any good?" he asks after a long period of silence. "At fighting, I mean."

I smile. I am good. I can easily train to be a real boxer.

"I am."

# Chapter 8

# TIMES ARE CHANGING

I'm fifteen and a half going on thirty. I was grateful to be off the streets at one time, not running numbers as a bag boy, happy to be in the clubs where the action is. I miss those days now, the days when I was eight and carefree, when running numbers was like a game. I was an innocent boy learning how to be street smart. I'm far from innocent now. Now, I'm an enforcer, a watcher of beautiful young women, the only life-line of protection they have. I graduated from floor watcher a long time ago. I now watch as the ladies bring their tricks, their numbers, their men—whatever adjective they use—upstairs.

If the light stays off after the door is closed, the girl is okay. If the red light comes on, it's a whole different story.

❈ ❈ ❈

Despite my aversion to current events, I can't help but notice the headlines on all the newspapers. It's the first of September. The year is 1939. The *Baltimore Sun*, sitting on the bar-top at the Two O'Clock Club, our favorite hang-out joint, is proclaiming "Nazi Army Invades Poland" in a bold headline. Lots of Mob guys are talking about the invasion. I overhear one of them saying that Italy and Germany signed something called the Pact of Steel a few months back, meaning they would join forces in the event a war was started. I already know that the Mafia in Sicily—they control the Mafia here in the States—does not like the Italian leader, Mussolini. He's a fascist, whatever that is, and he wants to destroy the Mafia because he can't control them and they're too powerful.

Here on the waterfront in Baltimore, the local Mob controls the docks. The Mob controls the unions, the dockworkers, you name it. The Mob guys I know all hate this Mussolini, and although it doesn't seem possible since they operate outside of the law and the government for the most part, these guys love America. They fly American flags, celebrate the Fourth-of-July and thank God they live here in the United States of America. I guess I'm more patriotic than I let on because deep down, I too, love America.

"We live in the greatest country on God's green earth, Funeral, don't ever forget that," Beans says to me when he sees me reading the headline. He has a young girl hanging off one of his arms.

"What do you make of this Nazi stuff, Beans?" I ask. "And who's the kid?"

"This is my daughter, Funeral. Little Thea, I want you to meet my friend Funeral," he says.

"Nice to meet you, Thea," I say. She squirms around his back. This is my first glimpse into the man I know as Beans' family life after all these years. "I didn't even know you were married."

"Come on, Funeral, of course I am." With that statement, the subject of Beans' family life ends.

It's amazing when I think about it, but I know so little about a man I have known for such a long time and someone who has been such an influence on my life. He's married and has kids—or at least a kid. I wonder where he lives. I guess I'm not really all that interested because I decide not to pursue any more questions after his last statement—of course I am, like I should already know that fact.

"Okay, so what about the Nazis?" I ask, back to the original subject.

"The Nazis is bad eggs, Funeral. Very bad," he says. "You mark my words—we'll be fightin' them before long."

"Do you think America can take the Nazis?"

He thinks about this for a while, finally saying, "I think so,

Funeral. We's the greatest country ever, we can do anything if we have to."

Both of us are quiet, deep in thought—at least I am. I conclude that if America goes to war, I'm joining. What also has me thinking, after reading this headline and hearing all the talk, is that Beans is right, America will join this war at some point.

Two days later, Sunday the 3rd, I see another newspaper on the bar-top at the club, its headline: "England, France Declare War!"

America is friends with both England and France. I'm now positive that we will end up going to war.

❀ ❀ ❀

I can only ponder what's happening around the world for so long. My schedule is packed with work, with little rest or downtime. I stopped working at the lumber yard a while back and now go to my Uncle Marco's office six days a week; we have Monday off. He hired me as his assistant, teaching me the automobile title business. Everyone owns a car now it seems. Cars are everywhere in the city, and they all need to be registered and licensed. Finally, I don't have to use my hands and my brawn; I now get to use my mind. I find business to be fascinating. Helping people, the customers, solving their problems is more rewarding than I ever could have imagined. People come to us frustrated and sometimes angry, and we help them and they leave pleased with what we have done for them. My uncle charges a small fee, of course, but that's the business part. He makes good money because he has so many customers. Together we can hardly keep up with the demand. He's also teaching me the bookkeeping part of the business—

another skill I never thought I would, or could, acquire. I cannot express my gratitude enough for the opportunity my uncle has given me.

When I thank him, he usually turns the compliment, and thanks, back at me. "I wouldn't know what to do without you, Paulie," he says all the time.

Baltimore has a government office for the Motor Vehicle Administration, which is a somewhat new organization. People get license plates for their cars and a driver's license, which, by the way, doesn't even require a driving test from the MVA. Standardized driving courses are just beginning, so most people are taught by a relative or friend. My uncle taught me years ago. I've been driving for more than three years. People buy cars—new or used—from car dealerships, but the dealership doesn't help with the paperwork of getting the title or registering the car. My uncle's business, working with the local dealers, helps people get their cars titled so the MVA can get them their plates.

I'm surprised by the number of people who can't read or write, or in our neighborhood who don't speak much English. Without help, I don't think they would have a clue what to do after they buy a car. I get compliments every day about how helpful and smart I am and how nice my handwriting is. It wasn't all that long ago, before Mrs. Russell's help, that I could barely read and write myself. I've come a long way in five years, and coming to the realization that other people think I'm smart is gratifying.

I'm also a feared street fighter. I am not sure how to balance these two professions in my mind. I try not to think about it too often; it's just what I do. I try to take the emotion out of the act of fighting and make it like a business. In a way I'm providing a service, and I get paid very well for it. My fights are now always scheduled, and they're usually planned many days in advance. And believe it or not, I have a say in who the opponent is and when I fight. I think I can say no and quit altogether if I push hard enough. In a way, though, I do look forward to the fights. I believe that if you're good at something, you might as well do it. And I'm good at fighting.

I can also put my bookkeeping knowledge from my uncle's business into practical use. I've always had an appreciation for money and have always found ways to make it, but now I understand the real value of money. Before, I would earn money one way or another and give it to my mother who would in turn pay off bills and buy food. Now I can save money, make a budget for my mother's needs, and take care of whatever needs I have. Earning money from my uncle, the Mob, and from street fights has left me in good financial shape for a kid my age. I'll be able to buy a car when I turn sixteen.

My opponents are usually older, but only by a few years as most are closer to twenty. I think Beans and the Mob try to keep it fair by not putting me up against man twice my age. I fight all types, shapes, and sizes of challengers. The size of a man doesn't bother me in the least anymore. It did when I was younger and small, when I was afraid to fight and never wanted to fight people who were bigger than me, but I've had considerable training and even more experience. I haven't tried to count the number of fights I've had, dating back to the first when I was ten and Beans told me to go fight some guy across the street. I think back on that fight often and what has transpired since. I wouldn't be surprised if I've been in 200 fights. I have won more than I lost, but believe me; I used to lose my share. Not anymore. Now I only fight to win.

I'm not afraid of Beans and his friends anymore, either like I used to be, and now that my street fighting has progressed into more like a business with me sharing the winnings, our relationship has once again changed. I wouldn't say we're on equal footing, not by any means, but I am treated differently.

I'm also older—not a kid anymore—and more is expected of me. Maybe I perceive it wrong, but I feel like they consider me an adult and treat me accordingly. I would never entertain the thought of fighting with Beans or any of the other Mob guys, even though I could take just about any of them. It's unfathomable—it simply would not happen. I value my life too much. I haven't seen it for myself, but it's common knowledge that serious transgressions against the Mob are dealt with in the harshest way—like you're dead. I've never been part of a Mob payback; I don't know what I'll do when—or if—they tell me to participate. If it does happen, it will not come in the form of a question. In other words, they won't ask, they'll tell.

❀❀❀

"They say this kid has never lost," Beans is saying to Fish Fischetti. I don't think he wants me to hear, but I'm good at listening. I hear lots of things I'm not supposed to. Another of the many tricks—skills—I've learned on The Block.

"Maybe we hedge our bets?" Fish replies.

I laugh to myself. Hedge their bets—in other words, bet on the other guy. Such a vote of confidence, but I don't blame them. The kid looks like a beast at 200 pounds, probably more, and over six feet tall. I'm at best a middleweight myself I'd say, maybe around 160 pounds. I'm also a couple of inches shy of six feet, so I pack a good amount of muscle weight on my smaller frame. I usually use my height and frame to my advantage by coming in low, under taller guys' reach, and hit with real hard gut punches to start a fight. This takes the wind out of them.

"See what odds they're laying on their kid first," Beans says.

I'm not paying attention when Fish comes back so I don't

hear what they plan on doing. As for me, I plan on taking this kid out, and quick. I have no fear of being hit. No fear of being knocked out. And I'll do anything to win.

I'm standing by myself, watching him go through all kinds of warm-up moves and shadow punches, when I notice a familiar face in the crowd. I flash a great big smile at my friend and signal for him to come over.

"What are you doing here?" I ask.

"Oh, I thought it was about time I saw for myself," Jack O'Donovan answers. "You're fighting that kid?"

"You ask that like you've got some doubts," I answer.

"He certainly is big enough."

"The size of the other guy never concerns me, Jack. Kinda like when Seabiscuit beat War Admiral," I say.

"Point taken," Jack acknowledges. Seabiscuit is a small horse when compared to the massive, powerful War Admiral, but Seabiscuit beat him.

"Besides, I've fought all sizes. They all react the same when I hit 'em and they start to bleed."

"What about when they hit you?"

He makes me laugh. If he's trying to boast my confidence, he's doing a bad job. "Sometimes it hurts," I answer.

"Well, you're probably quicker anyway."

I ignore him as best I can, but I do want him to do something for me—something I've never done before. "Jack, listen, I want you to place a bet for me." I pull $200 out of my pants pocket. I'm wearing street clothes: a pair of work pants and a tee shirt. "Get the best odds you can—should be at least five or six-to-one against me."

I can't tell from Jack's expression what he's thinking. Then he says, "Is that legal? Betting on yourself?"

"Of course, it's legal. Betting on the other guy would be a problem, don't you think?"

The big kid does exactly what you'd expect. Secure in his confidence because of his size, he comes right at me. Slow and predictable, I sidestep, avoiding his big right hand and drop down below him, almost in a crouch. I love to hit from this position because I can use my legs. I spring out of the crouch and nail the kid right in the solar plexus, right below his sternum and his heart. This takes the wind out of him. My next punch is from a perfect position, an upright position with balance and my weight behind it—just like Killer taught all those years ago—and it's right on the point of his chin. The guy is out before he hits the ground. I casually walk back to my group of supporters, awaiting some sort of congratulations on the fastest knock-out of my career. But it doesn't come. They had hedged their bets all right and lost. By them losing, because they bet against me, I don't get a cut of the profits as there won't be any. Had I lost, they would pay me from their winnings.

Lucky for me, Jack showed up to watch. I can see him now, waiting to get paid. He's smiling ear to ear. In the process of betting, my line got worse and the other side was very happy to take Jack O'Donovan's $300 bet. And the odds were six-to-one against me! The $300 became $1,800—my biggest score ever! I split the proceeds evenly with Jack after he tells me he laid $100 on me also, which is why he bet $300, not $200. I figure if he's that confident in me, he deserves an even split. My cut of $900 more than doubles my secret stash, and I know exactly what I want to do with some of my winnings. I'm going to invite my mother out for an expensive dinner, and I'm going to buy her a new fancy dress. I'll ask Mrs. Russell to help pick it out. I'll even invite Jack to join us for dinner.

"I know the first thing I'm doing with my share, Jack. What about you?"

"You first," he says.

"All right, I'm buying my mom a dress and taking her out on the town. Dinner, maybe some dancing—and guess what— you're invited."

"You got yourself a deal, partner."

"Your turn, Jack. What are you gonna do?"

"Oh, I don't know. I don't have much need for money anymore. I live at the stables and I eat for free. I already got a car. I really don't know what I'll do," old Jack O'Donovan says.

I find out that he gives most of the money he won away— gives it to a struggling young couple who works at the stables.

I pull a few strings and get a table for three at The Chesapeake on Saturday night, two nights after the fight, which is just about impossible unless you know someone. Luckily, I know people, and Beans gave me the night off. Before I drive out to get Jack, I spring the surprise on my mom.

She sees me carrying a box wrapped in wrapping paper and asks, "What in heavens name do you have there, Paul?"

"It's for you, Mom."

"Well, what the dickens is it?"

"Go on, open it."

Once opened, she gasps, "It's beautiful, Paul. For me? Why?"

"Because, Mom, I'm taking you out tonight, and it's gonna be only the best, all night," I tell her.

The Chesapeake is Baltimore's best restaurant by a long margin. My steak is so perfect I can cut it with a fork, just like their motto says. I've never seen my mother happier. The dress Mrs. Russell picked out is beautiful. She's beautiful—my mother is an attractive woman—and after the girls from the club got done with her, she could've been one of the dancers. I watch her eat, smiling the whole time. Why didn't I do this sooner? She deserves better than the life she's stuck with.

I find it rather amusing that she, still to this very day, never asks me where I get my money. She knows I have a job and that I give her money to live on, but the extra cash I have, she never questions. I imagine she does know what I do, but she doesn't question me, or ask how I get the bruises or black eyes.

Sometimes, not knowing is better.

"Paul, I want you to pay close attention to Mary. She's got a really bad number tonight," Mrs. Russell says. "She gave me a signal that there might be trouble."

"I won't let anything happen to her," I assure Mrs. Russell.

This is what the last five years of my life has been for—the training, the experience, the fights—all of it. I won't let anything happen to her. I'm distracted by what Mrs. Russell told me for the next hour as my eyes stay focused on the room Mary is using. Mary Kelly is Mrs. Russell's number one girl I recently found out. She's the most sought after, and because of that, I must watch out for her more often than any of the other girls. This also makes her the most experienced and less likely to take any trouble from a man. But she emerges from the room and is all smiles. I guess the guy wasn't that bad after all.

Sadly, this isn't always the case. The girls are supposed to collect the money up-front, as soon as they get their customer in the room, but most wait until after the deed is done. I think they're hoping for a bigger tip. That's why they wait, but waiting to get paid can lead to trouble when the guy doesn't want to pay.

I watch as another girl leads a young man upstairs. He's good-looking and probably no older than twenty. I don't know this girl, I think she's new. It's Tuesday night and not too busy, not much to distract me from watching the door. Monday and Tuesday nights are the slowest. The red light comes on; it's been about thirty minutes. Besides watching the girls, and their doors, Thrill, Naughty, and I always keep ongoing eye contact —two of us always respond when the red light comes on. I motion for Thrill to meet me at the stairs.

"I'll go in first and move to the right, you follow straight in," I tell Thrill.

"Sounds good. How do want me to grab him? Usual way?" Thrill asks.

"Yeah, grab his arm and pull it behind him and hold him up."

"Did you see what he looks like?" Thrill inquires.

"Young and looks like he's in shape."

"Think he'll give us trouble?"

"If he does, he'll wish he hadn't."

I take the stairs two at a time. Thrill is right on my heels. I waste no time bursting through the unlocked door and I move to the right. Thrill is directly behind me; my body partially obscures him from view, and this always surprises the man in the room. Thrill has his arm clenched and locked behind his back, holding him upright and hindering his ability to resist. I step directly in front of him. He's tall and well-built, and he's struggling to get free.

"What's the problem, Rebecca?" I ask the girl, remembering her name.

"Guy won't pay."

It's what I thought. This is an easy one. "Settle down," I say to the fellow. "No one's gonna hurt you."

He stops struggling and looks sheepish, trying to ingratiate himself. "It's not that I don't want to pay, I just haven't got it on me."

"Can you get the money?" I ask. Thrill has the guy pretty much locked up at this point, so I'm not fearful of him fighting.

"Yeah, I can. Can I come back and pay?"

"You married?" We make the married guys leave their shoes. No one wants to get home with no shoes on. That would be hard to explain.

"No."

"Okay, what can you leave behind as collateral?"

"Huh?"

"Anything valuable we can hold on to until you come back? Maybe your wallet?"

"How about my watch?"

He's back in forty-five minutes and pays up. As far as I'm concerned, this is a win. No one got hurt, especially Rebecca, and she got paid.

A couple of nights later, Thursday night, Naughty and I respond to a very quick red light. I see that it's one of the girls from the MM Club when I burst through the door. Betty is on the floor crying; the man is standing over her. It must have taken her considerable effort to get to the light switch. I hit him with a right to the kidneys, and he doubles over. Naughty then pulls the guy into a headlock. He's strong as an ox and breaks free. There's no time to try and talk him down, as the situation has rapidly escalated. He charges and tackles Naughty who didn't have any room to maneuver. I try to pull him off, but he weighs a ton.

"Get this guy off me, Funeral!"

"I'm trying!"

Next thing I know, he's pulling me to the floor with his free hand. Now both of us are under him. He pops Naughty in the face with his right, but because he let go of me to punch Naughty, I manage to get free. I nail him with a right to the side of his jaw that would have knocked anyone out cold. The guy is not fazed. But he's mad as hell and he's turning his attention to me.

"Settle down, mister, there's gonna be more of us up here any minute," I appeal.

He doesn't respond—he has yet to say a word—but instead grabs hold of me around the waist and lifts me off the ground, squeezing the life out me. I hit both of his ears simultaneously and he drops me. Naughty is back up now and laying into the guy's sides with kidney punches. Thrill must have heard the commotion because he suddenly appears in the room. It's now three on one. Just like all the times before, the three of us protecting each other's backs. The odds-makers wouldn't give this guy a chance against the three of us. But still, it takes several minutes of dogmatic persistence before we can get him out of the room. Bones Sullivan comes to our aid and with his help we get this beast of a man out of the club.

We're not through with him, though—he's hurt all three of us, and not just physically. He also succeeded in bruising our pride. We form a circle around him and take turns punching his face and gut, spinning him around the circle. This lasts for a good five minutes before Bones Sullivan ends it. "He's had enough, boys," Bones says.

We're breathing hard. Naughty and I are bleeding from

punches we received and Thrill's hand might be busted, so we don't need much convincing to stop the beating.

"He had that coming, Mr. Sullivan," Naughty says.

"He sure did, Naughty, now check his pockets. See if he's got what Betty's owed," Bones orders.

"He's got about twenty bucks," Naughty says as he pulls money from the guy's wallet.

"Thrill, get a cup of water and throw it in his face. We'll try and get this big lug off the sidewalk. He'll scare away the customers," Bones says.

"Let's drag him out to the alley and leave him," I offer.

"No, let's be civil about it. He's paid up and he's beaten up pretty good, too," Bones says. "Took all three of ya, huh?"

"He's like a bull, Bones," I say.

"You better get back inside, Funeral, and keep an eye on things. We'll take care of him," Bones announces as he throws the water Thrill brought into the guy's face, waking him up.

I hear our head-basher say, "Okay, mister, your fun's over for the night. Time for you to head on home to your wife and sleep it off."

I watch from the entrance of the Two O'Clock Club as the imprudent and badly beaten man stumbles down the street. My work is done—for tonight at least—but tomorrow night anything can happen.

That's why I love my job—never a dull moment.

# Chapter 9

# SIXTEEN

It's the perfect car. Mr. Pastorelli says I can have it cheap, probably because I worked all those years cleaning his embalming tables for so little money. The hearse, if you think about it, is the ideal car for a kid nicknamed Funeral. I count out $250 and give the wad of bills to Mr. Pastorelli, and he signs over the title. Luckily, I know exactly how to handle the transaction. I've bought myself a present for my sixteenth birthday. Thrill nicknames the car the "Funeralmobile."

My first trip in the Funeralmobile is out to the stables three days after my birthday, Saturday the 6th of April 1940. Occasionally, I would borrow a car from Uncle Marco to make the drive, but more times than not, I walked. I'll be driving to the stables from now on.

Jack O'Donovan can't believe his eyes when he sees me pull up. "Why on earth did you get a hearse?" he asks.

"It just fits, Jack. No other way to explain it," I answer.

"I guess it does fit, doesn't it, seeing as though your friends in the Mob call you Funeral," he says. "A bit sardonic, if I don't mind saying so myself."

"I would have thought you'd appreciate the irony, Jack. How'd you know about Funeral, anyway?"

"I'm not deaf, Paulie. I hear them calling you that at your fights," he says, "Oh, and happy birthday."

Jack became a regular at my street fights. We bet on a few more fights together, but never the amount we had wagered the first time, and there certainly were never any betting odds like that first time, either. Most fights are now always even money. Lately, he's been less enthusiastic about my extracurricular activities.

"I'm glad you still call me Paulie," I tell him.

Suzy is her usual excited self when she sees me. I set about at my routine of giving her a quick sponge bath and brushing her, and of course, giving her a couple of apples. I slowly saddle her, not in any hurry. I put my foot into the stirrup and climb on top of her. I realize that it has been six years. Suzy is the only horse I've ridden in six years. She's over twenty now according to Jack. But a well-cared-for horse like Suzy can live to be past thirty and ridden for almost as long. I figure I still have plenty of years left with her, but I take it easy now. She doesn't do much hard running anymore. We both seem content to accept this new arrangement of easier rides, enjoying an occasional gallop. The excitement of being up in the saddle has never diminished, not a single bit.

"Come on, Paulie, have a beer with me for your birthday before you leave," Jack says as I'm taking Suzy's saddle off.

"Give me a few minutes to finish up here first."

Jack has a couple of bottles of Gunther's Lager Beer waiting, both dripping with condensation. I grab one of the bottles from his little jockey's hand and drain half the bottle. I'd worked up quite a thirst. "Thanks, that hits the spot."

"Have you seen the morning paper?" Jack asks.

"No. Should I have?"

"You better start paying attention. The whole world is getting ready for war. In a couple of years, you'll be old enough."

"I've already decided. If America goes to war, I'm going."

"I thought you would feel that way," Jack says.

Jack and I sit in silence while we finish our beer, which doesn't take me very long. I've already stayed longer than I wanted, but Uncle Marco is much more forgiving about late arrivals than Beans had been, so I don't mind sitting with Jack.

"I should be going, Jack. But thanks for the beer, and you know, I will start paying more attention," I tell my old friend.

"Oh, I've got a fight next week, next Thursday. You gonna come?"

"Maybe, maybe not," he says, and nothing else.

I walk away, turning to wave to Jack when I reach the hearse, but he is nowhere in sight. I wonder what his problem is, I ask myself.

I can't stop thinking about what Jack said regarding the war, and how he was so abrupt and non-committal about my next fight. I think he's truly concerned about me. How does he view my life? Does he see me as reckless, or in control? I value his opinion and I know he wants me to stop fighting. That's the reason for the non-committal reply, and I know he doesn't like me working for the Mob. I try to explain to him that what I'm now doing is good—I'm protecting the girls, but he still doesn't like it. He thinks I'm getting deeper and deeper involved and may never be able to get out.

❋ ❋ ❋

I've had several days in a row with nothing much happening at the clubs. Beans keeps me and Thrill and Naughty at the Two O'Clock Club and MM Club most nights now. I bet it's because Mrs. Russell requests us over the other teams Beans uses. I only had one dead-beat guy not wanting to pay. Me and Thrill slapped him around a bit and made him leave his shoes —he's married—and go home and get the cash. He was back an hour later looking worse than when he left. His old lady must have socked him a couple of times, too.

I'm glad it's been an easy week. I'm a little nervous about my fight today. I overheard loud-mouth Beans talking about the guy I'm fighting. Supposedly he's some out-of-town talent. I know I'm good—at least good for around here—but there's lots of men better than me. It's been close to two years since I lost a betting fight—so long ago that I don't even remember when. Most of the local Mob guys have been cleaning up by betting on me. I admit, I'm feeling some pressure now. It's like I have to win. Too much money is riding on me and I don't want to let anyone down.

When I see the guy, I relax, but just a little. He doesn't look too tough. He's maybe twenty, twenty-two tops, and built much like me—tall, but not too tall, broad shoulders, and lean. I can take most men that are the same size as me. My biggest strength is my quickness. I can be real hard to hit, and when I hit people, they usually feel it. I can make a guy miss, and then I hit him four or five times before he's had a chance to recover.

We both start off slow, feeling each other out. I snap off a few jabs, looking for an opening but he bounces away. He seems quick and agile, so he'll be hard to hit. I don't foresee much grabbing and holding. I'm thinking way too much, losing my concentration. He's waiting for something, waiting for me to make a mistake. I move in for a combination—two jabs followed by a right and then a left. He dodges and I miss with all four punches. That's a first—my opponent is quicker than me. And that's what he's waiting for. He tags me with a right hand on the chin. My head snaps back and my legs buckle, just a little, but enough so that I'm off balance. He then lands three straight punches and I go down. From my knees, I look out at the men watching. I see Jack O'Donovan. There are a lot of shocked expressions. I lower my head. I know I can't beat this guy.

I last a few more minutes, going purely on guts, but the next time I go down, I can't get back up. The other guy is declared the winner. The Mob guys who back me are going to be paying out a bunch. I have no idea how much they bet, but I do know it's considerable. My only solace is the fact that I've won them much more money than they've lost. I catch a quick glance at

Jack. Our eyes meet for a split second, and then he turns and walks away. I know exactly what he's thinking.

❊❊❊

My life is unquestionably becoming more complicated, as is the world around me. It seems more and more people have expectations of me. With age comes responsibilities and I'm over sixteen, working two full-time jobs. Uncle Marco and I share the daily workload at his title company. He has put a significant amount of trust in me; I don't want to let him down. I don't want to let the girls in the clubs down, either. How I do my job directly relates to their safety. A man can do much damage to a defenseless young lady in a matter of seconds. In these situations, seconds really do matter. So far, in all the time that I've been protecting the girls, I've only had one badly hurt; I was about ten seconds late getting to her and she paid the price with a broken jaw. And I've got the Mob gamblers to worry about, too.

After my last fight, the one I lost, I turned down my next opportunity to fight a couple of weeks later. No one complained or told me I had no say in the matter. Maybe now is a good time to quit altogether. Or at least take a couple of months off. I know a few people in my life that would be glad. Mrs. Russell has been increasingly critical of the choices I've been making. She's not a big fan of the Funeralmobile, and she was never a fan of the street fighting. Jack wants me to quit the Mob altogether, not just the fighting part. If my mother knew the extent of my involvement, she'd want me to quit, too. I love how she continues to turn a blind eye to my activities, all the while accepting the cash I give her. At least she doesn't seem to mind the Funeralmobile.

Lately, I spend less time at my family's home. I've practically moved into a spare bedroom at the MM Club. It makes sense—the hours at the clubs are long and can be brutal, sometimes until three in the morning. I'm usually too tired to drive home, even though it's only a few minutes. The house on Albemarle Street is small and any noise at that hour is sure to wake someone up. I can only imagine what my old man's reaction would be to me waking him up at three in the morning. I don't think he'd try anything physical with me—he has surely heard about my street fighting, and he may even have seen me fight before. The crowds are deep with men and I'm concentrating on my opponent; he could be in the crowd and I wouldn't have a clue. He, of course, has never mentioned anything to me. We barely exchange any words about anything, not even when I help him with a side job. I don't do side jobs with him for the money. Despite everything he has put his family through, I still desire a relationship with him, and if the occasional building of a front porch is the only way to have one, I'll sacrifice a day or two.

After a long Friday night, the cup of coffee I'm drinking tastes great. The Saturday morning paper, the *Baltimore Sun*, is lying on the bar-top at the Two O'Clock Club. The May 11, 1940 headline screams in bold print that Germany has invaded the Netherlands, Belgium and France. It looks like the war in Europe is back on and in full swing. I don't know how I know, but I do—this war in Europe will someday play an important part in my life. The world around me is getting more complicated.

"What are you reading?" Thrill asks.

"Oh, nothing much."

"Come on, talk to me, Funeral."

"Okay, Thrill, I'm reading about the war. Germany has invaded a bunch of countries. Holland, Belgium, France," I say. "You know that we'll get involved in this war, right?"

"Yeah, I suppose so," Thrill agrees. "But when?"

"A year, maybe sooner, maybe longer."

"How old do you think you'll need to be to join?"

There has been much talk about a draft, like what happened during the Great War. The draft age was twenty-one for that war, but men could enlist at eighteen.

"You can join at eighteen," I tell him, "Might be able to join if you're seventeen."

"We'll all be eighteen in 1942."

"That's a long way away," I say. But that's not what I'm really thinking. We'll all be eighteen in the blink of an eye. I remember back to a late-night conversation with Mrs. Russell I had. I have no idea what I'll be doing in a year, or two years, or five years, I remember thinking.

"Not that long, Funeral," Thrill says. "If you had to pick one, would you join the Army or the Navy?"

"Navy," I say without hesitation. "What are you saying, that you're gonna join if we go to war?"

We live on the water, the Chesapeake Bay. All of us have been on boats and we all know sailors. I talk with sailors at the clubs every night. Most seem like good guys.

"Yeah, I'm gonna join. And it'll be the Navy, too," he says. "All three of us should join."

"Wouldn't have it any other way," I say. "Can you imagine the three of us on the same ship?" We both start laughing. Wouldn't that be something? The trouble we could get ourselves into.

"I like the way the Navy guys look in their uniforms," Naughty adds from behind my shoulder. I hadn't heard him come in the club. "That, and who wants to be on the ground gettin' shot at?"

"Where'd you come from?" Thrill asks.

"What do ya mean? I just walked in."

"Never mind, Naughty," Thrill says. "Me and Funeral are gonna join the Navy if we go to war, that's what we're talking about."

"Yeah, I heard. Me, too," Naughty says.

"Don't you guys have something better to do?" Beans chimes in. "It's like you's live here or something."

"I gotta head to work, Beans, so I was just leaving," I say. "Catch you guys later tonight."

"Yeah, see ya, Funeral," Thrill says. "Come on, Naughty, let's see what kind of trouble we can get into."

❀❀❀

Five weeks later, June 22, 1940, I'm reading the latest headline: "France surrenders to Germany. British forces barely escape back to England from a place called Dunkirk; Great Britain now stands alone against the Nazis."

Time is flying by, every day no different from the one before it. It's as if we're rushing to some important date in time, the future, but not knowing what it is. The headlines from September proclaim the "Selective Service and Training Act: Every man, age twenty-one to thirty-six, has to register for the draft, the first peacetime draft in our history." I don't think anyone is naïve enough to think that peace for America will last much longer. Some of the guys I know who are eighteen or nineteen have joined the local National Guard, but that's the Army, so I'm not all that interested. A month later the draft begins, as well as the federalizing of the National Guard into the regular Army. The papers are calling it the Mobilization of

130

1940. Everything is moving at the speed of light.

Another change that has gradually taken place, besides having less and less street fights for money, is all but one of the original five girls from the MM Club are gone. The girls that work at the clubs come and go at an alarming rate. Some get discovered, in a way, and move on to greener pastures, while others simply move on. Dancing in the shows can be a cutthroat business with dancers stepping over each other to get ahead. Then, there are the girls that take men to the private rooms. It doesn't take much imagination to figure out why these girls move on. When Sarah Gilbert moved—she was apparently discovered again—to New York, I was sad to see her go. She gave me a hug and kissed me on the cheek. She thanked me for looking out for her and I wished her luck.

I have not become close with any of the new girls I watch. I will even admit that I have a hard time keeping track of their names. I think it's better this way. There is no reason for me to have personal relationships with the dancers, show girls, and strippers I protect. I care about them, don't get me wrong, and I'm always nice and friendly, but nothing more. I don't want to be involved in their lives outside of work. I look at my job as a Mob enforcer much the same way I look at fighting for money—completely take the emotion out of it. This way I can live with myself if something horrible should ever happen to someone I'm supposed to protect.

"Do you miss the girls, Mrs. Russell, when they leave, I mean?" I ask after another late-night shift. This seems to be the only time we get a chance to talk anymore, after the club closes.

"Why do you ask? I would assume that you know I do," she says. "I was sad to see Sarah leave, as I suppose you were, too," she adds with a wink.

"You're right, I was sad she left," I say as I think back on our strange—for me anyway—and unfulfilled relationship. "What about me? You gonna miss me if I leave?"

"I didn't know you were planning on going somewhere. Is there something I should know about?" Mrs. Russell asks. I have her undivided attention.

"I've been thinking a lot about the war in Europe lately," I say. "I'm gonna join the Navy if we go to war."

"You know that I'll be against you going, but that's just because I couldn't bear to have anything happen to my boy. Anyway, I don't see that happening for a long time, if at all. There is a movement in America called isolationism. Most people do not want America to get involved in foreign wars," she says. "As of right now, I'm one of them."

"I've heard about the isolationists, Mrs. Russell," I say. "But I don't think America will have a choice. I bet we'll be forced to join."

"I'm hopefully optimistic, Paul, that will not happen."

Time is indeed flying by. I can't believe I'm celebrating the New Year, 1941. I'll be seventeen in a few months. Where I'll be in a year, or two years, or five years, I don't know.

# Chapter 10

# INFAMY

"Turn the radio up, Paulie!" my uncle shouts.

I'm not really listening. Some news update from WCAO, CBS' affiliate here in Baltimore, has come on and the music, *Green Eyes*, by Jimmy Dorsey is cut off. It's easy for me to tune out noise; I hear so much nonsense and noise at the clubs that turning a deaf ear takes on a whole new meaning.

"Sure thing, Uncle Marco," I shout back. I turn the radio up a few notches and start to listen. It sounds like something important is happening.

"Did you just hear that, Paulie?" Uncle Marco yells. "We're under attack!"

It's Sunday afternoon on December 7, 1941. I'll be eighteen in four short months. Me and Uncle Marco are the only ones in the office, getting caught up on paperwork. I look up from my desk and turn toward the radio. I'm giving the broadcast my full attention as I listen to the frantic voice of a news reporter. He's describing the scene from a place in the Hawaiian Islands called Pearl Harbor. Uncle Marco is right, we are under attack.

The radio guy is yelling, barely able to control his emotions. "The United States of America is under attack from the Imperial Navy of Japan!"

❀❀❀

I waste no time. I race out of the office toward The Block. I need to find Thrill and Naughty. I need to be with my friends. This is the moment we have been talking about for the last year. The question of when America will be going to war has been answered. I find them both listening to a radio in the Two O'Clock Club surrounded by people.

"Funeral!" Thrill shouts as he sees me run into the club.

"Have you heard the news?"

Monday morning, I'm standing in a line about a mile long. Thrill and Naughty are with me, as well as hundreds of other men. Me and my friends are silent; we did all our talking last night. If it were up to us, we'd be on a ship heading toward Japan today. Those lousy Japs pulling off a sneak attack on us like they did. I'm finally almost to the front of the line.

"How old are you, son?" the sailor behind the desk asks.

"Seventeen," I answer.

"Why don't you come back when you turn eighteen? That way, we don't need your parents to sign a consent form."

"But I won't be eighteen until April."

"Trust me, the war will still be going on."

❊❊❊

It's been a long four months, but the waiting is finally over. I have no desire to celebrate my eighteenth birthday. Instead, I'm heading to the Navy recruitment office across the harbor. I watch as the man in a Navy uniform stamps "Rejected" on my paperwork.

"Sorry, son, but the United States Navy can't use you."

My expression is blank, my eyes can't leave his. "What?" I finally manage to ask.

"You've never had your eyes checked, have you?"

"No."

"You're far-sighted. Isn't everything blurry, out of focus up close?"

"Sometimes, but it never bothers me. I see just fine."

"Well the Navy doesn't want you because of it," he says. "Look around you, son, there's hundreds of men here who want to join the Navy, and this is only here in Baltimore. We have recruiting stations all over the country. Give it a few months and try the Army. I'll bet they'll beg you to join."

I feel like I've been gut-punched, sucker-punched. I couldn't have imagined something like this happening to me in a million years. How could I, Funeral, Mob enforcer, street fighter, all-around-tough-guy get rejected by the Navy?

"I don't understand."

"Look, kid, I've got a lot of other candidates to evaluate, so I need you move on."

My first reaction is to punch this guy's lights out—it's what I do. But I come to my senses. "Please mister, could you please reconsider?"

"Like I said, try the Army in a few months, I'm sure they'll take you."

I know I need to move, but I'm paralyzed. I feel some guy push me from behind. My blood is boiling and I want to lash out, but I breathe deeply and close my eyes. I think about riding a horse. I think about Brown Eyed Suzy. I walk away from the man with the clipboard and his rejection stamp. I walk for miles, alone. I've left Naughty and Thrill at the recruiting depot. I end up at my Uncle Marco's office.

"I don't get it, Uncle Marco, just because I don't see perfect? They won't take me because of that?"

The requirements this early in the war are still very strict. Millions of men are trying to sign up, signing up as fast as they can. This mean the Navy can be as picky as they want because most of the men are trying to join the Navy. The Army on the other hand is drafting men, twenty-one and older, and putting them where they want, mostly into infantry units.

"I'm sorry, Paulie, really I am," Marco says. "But like the man said, maybe the Army will have you."

"The Army's drafting twenty-one-year olds, Uncle Marco," I say. "They won't take an eighteen-year-old the Navy rejected."

"I think this is going to be a long war, Paulie. No need for you to rush into it."

I meet up with Naughty and Thrill at the Two O'Clock Club—turns out the Navy rejected them, too. Thrill has clubfoot. We already know this, but it never bothered him or caused him any problems as far as I know, but the Navy said no, and so will the Army because he can't march like a normal person. Naughty was rejected because he had tuberculosis as a kid.

It doesn't seem fair that three guys who want to fight for their country get rejected, but whoever said life was fair? When has my life ever been fair? I guess it's only fitting that I get this slap in the face.

❋ ❋ ❋

Five days later, I'm working on the assembly line at the Glenn L. Martin Aircraft Company, working on the plastic bubble canopy for the rear gunner on a B-26 bomber. Since they won't let me fight, I figure this is the next best thing. Uncle Marco is sad I'm leaving him, but he understands. He says anytime I want to come back he'll have a job for me. I know that sooner or later I'll either try to enlist in the Navy again or I'll enlist in the Army, and I won't take no for an answer.

In early May 1942, a month later, the United States Navy fights Japan to a draw in the battle of Coral Sea.

On the fourth of June, the Navy wins decisively at the Battle of Midway against the Japanese.

On August 7th, the United States attacks Guadalcanal in the South Pacific.

The war is raging all over the world. The Nazis have conquered most of Europe. Only Britain remains. Germany invaded the Soviet Union over a year ago, and now is at the gates of Stalingrad. The Battle of Guadalcanal is the focal point of the war against Japan. If Japan wins and controls the Solomon Islands, Australia will be invaded.

The original plan when the Mobilization of 1940 began was to build an army of 900,000 soldiers. At that time, the draft age was twenty-one to thirty-six and there were 17,000,000 men to choose from. The Army only took the best—the men that were deemed the healthiest and most trainable. In 1942 the need for a much larger army became obvious. Consequently, the criteria for rejection due to physical ailments were greatly reduced. In September Congress passed the Burke-Wadsworth Act, lowering the draft age to eighteen. The law would be enacted in November. Once the new age requirements were in place, it was rumored that all voluntary enlistments would be ended. All eligible men would enter service through the draft, and if you were drafted, the United States would determine where you would serve, most likely in a front-line combat unit if you didn't have a unique or special skill.

21 October, 1942:

"Welcome to the United States Army, Private Signori," the Army sergeant says. "Now, since you're volunteering, I'll give you the choice, as long as its combat-related."

"What are my options?"

"Most common is infantry," he says. "Those are the guys who carry guns and fight on the front lines."

"What else do you have?"

"Well, let's see, you could join the combat engineers. You could clear minefields, or be a forward observer for the artillery. You could join the armor, be in a tank. There's also the cavalry, but that's reconnaissance and most don't choose that."

"Tell me about it. The cavalry I mean," I say.

"They get to go out and find the enemy—very dangerous," he says. He pauses for a few seconds as he's flipping through some pages. "There's also the Horse Cavalry," he adds as an afterthought. "I didn't think they still existed."

"I'll take it," I say without hesitating.

"The Horse Cavalry?" he asks. "You even know how to ride a horse?"

❖❖❖

The Army gives me all of five days before I ship out to a place called Fort Riley in Kansas. I don't think they want to give me a chance to change my mind. I'll be leaving by train out of Baltimore with a one-way ticket to Kansas.

On my last night in town, a party is happening in my honor at the Two O'Clock Club. I've only been at the party for a few minutes and already people are crowding around me. I had no idea I was so popular, but there is one person I want to see before anyone else. I push my way through the crowd towards her. I know she's been waiting for me to arrive.

Mrs. Russell greets me with a long, emotional hug. I know my leaving is hitting her hard. She was overjoyed when the

Navy rejected me, claiming it was a sign from God that I was not supposed to go to war. I didn't see it that way. I saw it as a temporary obstacle, a setback, one that I would eventually overcome. She doesn't understand, and I can't explain it to her, but this is something I must do—I have to go and fight in this war. Starting ten years ago, when I was eight, I have been training, in a way, for this exact eventuality. Everything I've been through has taught me how to survive—running numbers, being street smart, all the fights, protecting the girls, everything I've done. I'm the most reliable and resourceful guy around. Beans and his friends are always saying so.

"Paul, my wonderful little boy all grown-up now, please be safe." It sounds like such a cliché, especially from someone as sophisticated as Mrs. Russell, but I know she means it— please be safe. Through her tears, she adds, "Come back at least once before you ship overseas. I couldn't bear to never see you again." She hugs me and then plants a kiss right on my lips.

"You know I will," I say, blushing.

"You could have waited to be drafted, you know," she adds after composing herself.

"By enlisting like I did, I got to choose how and where I serve."

"But why the Horse Cavalry?" she asks, confused like everyone else.

"I'm going let you in on a secret. Promise you won't tell," I say.

"I promise."

"See that little fellow over there talking to Naughty?"

"Yes, who is he? I've never seen him before."

"I've been riding horses with him since I was ten at the Colonial Stables. His name's Jack O'Donovan. He used to be a jockey."

"Riding horses? You?" Mrs. Russell looks bewildered. "But how? I mean when?"

"I've been going most Saturdays for as long as I remember. It's been my secret, and now it's yours, too. Come on, I'll introduce you."

I take her by the hand and lead to where Jack and Naughty are talking. "I hope he's not boring you with his old stories," I say to Naughty. "Jack, this is my dear friend, Mrs. Russell."

"Pleased to make your acquaintance," Jack says as he bows and kisses her hand.

"My, quite the gentleman," Mrs. Russell says.

Jack is in heaven. He can't take his eyes off Mrs. Russell. She's probably the most beautiful woman he's ever seen. I grab Naughty and head to the bar, leaving the two of them to chat.

"I'll take a beer," I say to the bartender, a guy named Marty.

"On the house, Funeral," he says. "You know somethin', I'm proud of ya." I've known Marty for years. He's been a fixture behind the Two O'Clock Club bar.

"Thanks, Marty, appreciate that," I say as I'm shaking his hand.

I grab a seat at the bar. People are starting to come up to me to wish me luck and tell me to be safe. Bats and Fish and all the local Mob guys are coming over to me to pay their respects.

I don't know what to say in response besides, "Thanks and I will."

Even though the war has been going on for over ten months, I doubt I'll be joining it anytime soon. Besides a train ticket to Kansas, the Army hasn't told me anything. I assume I'll start my training when I get to Fort Riley. And after that I'll be assigned to a unit, and then maybe ship overseas, but I don't know. I don't know if I'll be fighting the Japanese or Germans. Germany declared war on us right after Pearl Harbor, so America is fighting a two-front war, although we have yet to start fighting the Germans. American forces are about to invade North Africa. That's where we'll begin our fight against the Nazis. I wonder if the Horse Cavalry can fight in Africa.

"Funeral!" Beans shouts from across the bar. He's the last of the Mob guys to come to me. He probably waited to be last to say his goodbye on purpose.

I stand to greet him. He pulls me into a bear hug. He's got tears in his eyes. "I'm gonna miss you, Funeral. Miss you a lot."

"I'm gonna miss you too, Beans," I say, realizing that I would miss him. He has been a constant in my life for over ten years.

He hugs me all over again. "You've been like a son to me," he says. "I never told you that before, but you have been."

Now I'm getting emotional. Maybe he does love me after all. He's almost forty, certainly old enough to be my father.

After Beans, I'm pulled into another bear hug, this time from Bones Sullivan. If Beans thinks of me as a son, Bones likens me to a younger brother. Over the last couple of years I've spent protecting the girls, and many of the nights spent with Bones, we've knocked our share of heads together.

"You know Funeral, I'm not worried about you in the least. If there's anybody out there that can take care of himself, it's you," he says. "Those lousy Nazis better watch out with you coming at 'em. Or maybe the Japs. Don't matter which one, they both better watch out."

"Thanks, Bones," I say. "You know something? I'm not worried, either."

I do mean what I've just said—I'm not worried. The prospect of going into combat doesn't worry me or scare me. I think it's supposed to, but it doesn't. Whatever happens is gonna happen; I'll be ready for anything. Before long, there's a line of show girls, strippers, dancers, and cocktail waitresses wanting to give me a kiss goodbye. There must be fifty of 'em and they don't leave a spot on my face that doesn't have lipstick on it.

I end up spending most of the night with Thrill, Naughty, and Jack. Jack was a hoot after about five beers, telling stories, laughing, and carrying on. I made sure he had a room to sleep in for the night. I end up watching the sun rise over the harbor with Thrill and Naughty, sharing a bottle and never going to sleep.

"Come on Funeral, we'll walk you to train station," Thrill says after the sun has risen.

"Yeah, okay, I'm meeting my family there at eight," I say. "Oh, and by the way, you guys can have the Funeralmobile." I hand Naughty the keys.

"Thanks, Funeral," Naughty says.

"We'll take good care of her," Thrill adds.

"Another thing. You guys know where my stash of cash is. I want you guys to make sure my mom gets enough money each week. Promise me."

"Don't even think about it again, Funeral," Thrill says.

"Yeah, and if you run out, we'll give to her out of our stash," Naughty adds.

"Don't take this the wrong way, but I love you guys," I say.

They both say, "Ditto."

We walk in silence the rest of the way. We're tired and a little hung over. My stomach is rolling. I need to eat something. Hopefully the train has breakfast.

144

Up ahead at the train station I see my brother Nicky. We wave to each other. He's almost twenty-one, but because of his hand, he can't serve. My mother and father are with him. I haven't spoken to my father in about a week. We occasionally pass each other in the house on Albemarle Street. I'm not going to miss him, but I will miss my mom. I stop by the house most days to give her money or just to say hello and see how she is doing. My little sister Norma, still no nickname, is running towards me. She's ten now and not so little, but that doesn't stop her from jumping into my arms. We spin around and around together before I put her down. Glory gives me a long hug and a kiss on the cheek. Frankie is fifteen and almost as tall as me; he's trying hard not to show emotion, but he breaks down and starts to cry a little. We shake hands, like men.

When I reach my mom, she's crying. I gather her up in a hug, kiss her cheek, and tell that everything is going to be okay. She nods her head, but I can tell she's worried. I don't blame her for worrying. She's a mother, she's supposed to. Nicky shakes my hand and pats me on the back.

"Take care of yourself, Paul," my father says. "Be careful." This is the first time he has used my name in years. He shakes my hand. His are rough and cracked. At this moment, I realize that this man—my father—has been one of the greatest influences in my life. Some bad, many of which are obvious, but there are also some good. Because of him I understand the concept of hard work. I worked side-by-side with this man for years and never saw him once leave a job unfinished or not have given his absolute best effort. He taught me pride in my work but not in a boastful way. I only wish he treated us better.

"I will, Dad."

In a strange but profound way, I know he's proud of me— much like he's proud of his work and when his customers are overjoyed with the finished product. Perhaps he sees me as his finished product, and I'm successful in life because of him. He doesn't say it, but I feel his love when we shake hands.

I turn to Thrill and Naughty and we hug each other. My train has arrived and people are boarding. I gather up the duffel bag my mother packed for me, turn, and walk away.

I look back at the small group of people watching me and wave goodbye.

# Chapter 11

# TRAINING

29 October, 1942:

It hasn't been ten days since I joined the Army and I'm already on an Army base. No one here knows who I am. No one knows what I was, what I did, who I worked for. It is liberating not having a past. I am no longer Funeral, the Mob enforcer, the watcher. I'm just another GI, another soldier, another guy from somewhere else. I can re-invent myself into anyone.

"Welcome to Fort Riley, home of the United States Cavalry," a sergeant says by way of greeting. "You boys are going to be part of dying breed; you boys are going to be horse soldiers. I can't tell you for how long, but for now, you're in the Horse Cavalry."

I know nothing about being a soldier, but I know I'm in the right place. Some of the men around me have peculiar looks on their faces. I volunteered to be in the cavalry when I joined, and I made sure it was the Horse Cavalry. The group of new recruits I'm with is sixty men. Many of us arrived at the train station outside of the army base at the same time and boarded trucks when we heard our names called.

The ride to the camp was all of ten minutes, and now, about an hour later, I'm assembling together with the other men on what looks like a parade ground. During that hour, I was issued my uniform, boots, and other supplies, all of which have been dropped in front of my new home, the barracks. I also got my hair cut short.

"You men will eventually become part of Troop C, 1st Squadron, First Training Regiment of the 7th Cavalry. Each platoon in the troop will have twenty men. That means there'll be three platoons. The troop will be led by a captain and his first sergeant. Each platoon will have a lieutenant in charge and he'll have a sergeant and a corporal, all experienced horse soldiers. I'm 1st Platoon's sergeant, Sergeant Hood."

Sergeant Hood stops talking and starts to pace back and forth in front of us. Another sergeant joins him. They chat for a few seconds.

"How many of you men are familiar with horses? How many of you can ride a horse, or have ever been on a horse?" Sergeant Hood continues. He seems like a nice enough fellow, not what I was told to expect. I'd been warned about nasty and demanding drill sergeants.

I'm in the third row of five rows, right in the middle. I only see a few hands go up around me. There's no reason not to admit that I know how to ride a horse, so I raise my hand.

"I want you men with experience to step forward. Since we don't need to teach you how to ride, we'll start teaching you how to be soldiers."

Fifteen men out of sixty come forward. I can only assume that the other men either didn't realize they joined the Horse Cavalry or the Army randomly assigned them here. Regardless of their situation, I can't help but think back to my first time on a horse. I was ten. The thrill, the excitement I felt that first time still resonates. I wonder if it will be the same for the men who have never been on horse.

"The rest of you are gonna learn how to ride horses first," Sergeant Hood continues. "Then we'll teach you how to be soldiers."

❈ ❈ ❈

"You troopers, follow me," the other sergeant says.

I fall-in with the fourteen men with experience and follow the sergeant. I'm surprised by the lack of discipline and urgency. The new sergeant—he has five stripes, three up and two down with a diamond in the middle—looks old and out of shape, probably been in the Army for years.

"I'm First Sergeant Potter, top sergeant in the troop you guys are assigned to," he says. "I'm gonna let you men in on a little secret. You won't be staying here very long and the neither will the Horse Cavalry. Not much use for horses in this war."

"What's gonna happen to us?" one of the men with me asks.

"Mechanized Cavalry," he answers. "But in the meantime, why don't y'all pick a horse?" He spreads his hands out in front of him as we overlook a fenced-in pasture full of horses. I have no idea what he's referring to when he says Mechanized Cavalry. I exchange glances with the men around me, none of them seem to know either. The man who asked the question walks to a gate in the fence and opens it. The rest of us follow him through the gate and into the pasture.

At least fifty horses are grazing on grass, appearing to have not a care in the world. I make my way around the animals, checking their eyes and their mouths. Jack O'Donovan taught me well; I can determine the age and health of a horse within minutes of an examination. On the whole, the horses seem rather healthy, well-fed, and cared for. Most of them are around three or four years old, not quite fully mature, but having been under saddle for a couple of years.

After about fifteen minutes, I find the horse I've been looking for. She's perfect—a beautiful, dark brown thoroughbred, not all that different from a horse I know back home named Brown Eyed Suzy. I estimate her age at four and her health as perfect. I wish I had an apple to give her.

"Aren't you a beauty?" I whisper into the horse's ear as I rub her muzzle. "If you haven't a name, I'll call you Suzy Two."

All the horses have a halter and lead rope attached. We're ordered to lead the horse we choose to the stable.

"Go on and get a saddle and saddle your horse," Sergeant Potter says.

"Do the horses already have names?" I ask.

"They do not, Private, so go ahead and name 'em if you like."

I'm the first one finished saddling my horse.

"Where'd you learn about horses, Private?"

"Baltimore," I answer, unsure how to address him.

"A city boy? And you know about horses?" he asks. "I would have thought you'd be a farm boy."

"I've been riding since I was ten," I say. "I had a good teacher. He taught me to treat a filly like a lady, Sergeant."

"I see you picked a good horse," Sergeant Potter says as he gives Suzy Two a quick check. "What do they call you back in Baltimore, Private?"

I almost say Funeral out of habit. "People just call me by my name. Paul Signori."

"Siggy," he says, "I'm assigning you to Sergeant Hood and 1st Platoon. That's where we usually put the best men."

As quick as that I have a new nickname. Almost as quickly, I become one of the best horsemen in our platoon. Each platoon has its own barracks where twenty men share ten bunk beds. We also have a recreation room, shower room and a john—that's what the bathroom is called. Sergeant Hood has his own room as does his assistant, Corporal Wade. We are a Horse Cavalry training troop, and we're troopers—not to be confused with soldiers, according to Sergeant Potter. Regardless of what we're called, we all need to be trained as soldiers first, and for the inexperienced men, trained with horses.

Our training is scheduled to last three months, into the

coldest part of the year.

❀❀❀

1 January, 1943:

This place is freezing and windy and flat. I'm miserable. I miss Baltimore and The Block and my old life. And there are no buildings crowding in on me, and believe it or not, I miss the crowding of the buildings.

There's barely any trees and only a few structures—barracks mostly. I've been at Fort Riley at the Cavalry Replacement Training Center for over two months training how to be a soldier and a cavalry trooper simultaneously. We march a lot, do physical training—which is easy for me—and in our spare time, we ride and care for our mounts. That's what we call our horses, our mounts. Our training will last another month. After that, none of us trainees know what will happen to us.

I can't wait for this to end, for something important to happen. We continue to hear rumors about the disbanding of the Horse Cavalry.

❀❀❀

15 February, 1943:

Winter doesn't seem to want to ever end, but our training is finally complete. We are now officially cavalry troopers of C Troop, 1st Squadron. All of us privates, the new recruits, receive our first promotion; we are now Privates First Class. With our new rank, we get one chevron on our uniforms and get a pay raise. We also have a lot of free time on our hands.

Since it's too cold to do much outside, we play cards in the barracks or our rec-room. I start out losing at poker more times than I win, but that's only because I don't want anyone to know how well I play. Losing only lasts a few days as once the stakes get raised, I start to win. None of the other card-playing troopers wants to admit that I'm better than they are at cards; consequently, I have no trouble finding a game and no problem taking their money. I've always been good at making money.

When we are outside training, we're with our mounts. I'm getting good with a rifle while on horseback. The more I think about it, I'm not sure joining the Horse Cavalry was such a good idea. There is no expectation among us that we will be deployed overseas as a combat unit. I've heard a rumor that we may end up patrolling the southern border of the United States. The last time a Horse Cavalry unit went into combat was in the Philippines after the Japs invaded—that was in December of 1941.

❋❋❋

3 April, 1943:

My birthday has arrived. I'm nineteen years old. I had wanted, but was made to wait, to get into the service when I was seventeen. Time was rushing by back then. I seemed to be racing toward some sort of destiny. Now, time stands still. I've been at Fort Riley at the Cavalry Replacement Training Center for over six months. Yet we have heard nothing regarding what will become of us. The United States has been at war for sixteen months and I've done nothing but train for the last six.

I'm a cavalry trooper in C Troop, riding a horse named Suzy

Two on the prairies of Kansas. How could this be my destiny? The days have gotten longer and the weather has improved so the troopers of 1st Platoon get to ride for many miles away from our home in the barracks. Now we get to camp outside in tents. I get to pretend I'm a soldier.

Meanwhile, I see thousands of other soldiers coming and going, training in armored vehicles. They are learning how to be Mechanized Cavalry troopers.

❊❊❊

1 May, 1943:

"Listen up, boys," First Sergeant Potter says. "Orders have been received by Captain Long that 1st Squadron is finally going to be broken up. And that includes C Troop." The entire troop is assembled on the parade ground, on our mounts. It would make quite a picture. All of us together on horseback look spectacular.

"You're all going to be given a choice as to where you go," Sergeant Potter continues, "As long as it's into a combat unit."

"I'm joining the paratroopers, Siggy," PFC Cook, my closest friend in the platoon, says.

"No, not me, Cookie," I answer. "Jumping out of a plane isn't for me."

"What then? Don't tell me infantry. I'll shoot ya myself."

"I'm gonna stay with the cavalry."

"Mechanized Cavalry, Siggy? You're gonna stay with reconnaissance?"

"Yeah, I think I am."

Only twelve men from C Troop elect to stay in the cavalry. The rest scatter throughout the combat branches of the United States Army and leave Fort Riley within the week. I join a Mechanized Cavalry training unit, still on the base. Unfortunately, I say goodbye to Suzy Two. But I do promise her that I'll see her as often as I can to take her out for a ride.

It turned out that one of the most important aspects of the Horse Cavalry was taking care of your horse. We always made sure our mounts had food and water before we did.

※ ※ ※

"How many of you men know how to drive?" First Sergeant Cobb, my new troop's top sergeant, asks a group of recruits who have just arrived at Fort Riley.

They are all newly drafted into the Army except for the twelve of us old horse troopers from C Troop. I raise my hand as do about fifteen or so other young men. Most of these guys look like kids. I'm still a kid myself, but I look older than these guys. And I've got a stripe on my uniform. That alone makes me older.

"Step forward to the front," the sergeant orders. "You men will drive our jeeps and armored cars, but don't get me wrong, you'll also carry a rifle and fight."

I move to the front and assemble with the others. I've seen the jeeps and armored cars on base and have watched some of the training. If given the choice, I'm going to pick the armored car to drive.

"What's your story?" Sergeant Cobb asks me.

"I was in the Horse Cavalry, Sergeant. Here at Riley."

"Welcome to the Mechanized Cavalry, son. How long you

been here?"

"Seven months."

"How long you been driving?"

"Since I was twelve," I answer.

"You a good trooper? A good soldier?"

I answer immediately, "Yes, Sergeant, I think I am."

"Good. Well, it looks like you'll be trading your horse in for something with wheels and a motor."

The Mechanized Cavalry is just that—trading horses for vehicles. No longer will I be riding around on horseback. Instead, I'll be driving a truck. But our mission remains the same—scouting ahead for a larger body of soldiers, trying to find the enemy and determining his strength and position.

"The cavalry, or reconnaissance, primarily utilizes two types of trucks; the mainstay is the M8 armored car," Sergeant Cobb explains. "The armored car is a six-wheeled vehicle with armor plating. On top of the chassis sits a gun turret. The M8 has a 38mm main gun; this is essentially a small-barreled cannon that fires a 38mm shell. Any questions so far?"

He pauses as we follow him to the vehicles. We stop in front of a parked armored car. "Also in the turret is a .30 caliber machine gun that is fired from inside the turret." Sergeant Cobb points at the barrel of the machine gun that's sticking out of the turret. "That's a .50 caliber machine gun up there, mounted on top of the turret. The armored car has plenty of firepower, boys, and she's fast, reaching speeds up to sixty miles an hour. Four men crew the M8's—a car commander, a driver, a gunner, and a radioman. Once y'all learn how to handle her, you'll be the driver."

We follow the sergeant to the next parked vehicle. He stops and waits for all of us to gather around the truck.

"Some of you boys will drive this one here. She's a quarter-ton truck known as a jeep," Sergeant Cobb tells us. But I've already made my mind up; I'm choosing the armored car.

"Our jeeps come ready for battle," Cobb continues, "Either with a .50 caliber machine gun like this one, or an M2 60mm mortar mounted in its back like that one over there. In case you don't already know, a mortar lobs shells into the air, falling on the enemy up to 2,000 yards away. But it's more effective when the enemy is close at hand. The jeep has a crew of three men, with each having a primary role. The jeep's commander is the driver. One of the other crewmen fires the machine gun while the last member of the crew is called a scout. The scout is responsible, when required, for finding the enemy on foot."

Our new sergeant really knows his stuff.

❀ ❀ ❀

I start training all over again. The last seven months had been nothing short of a complete waste of time. Since I was given the choice, I'm learning how to drive the M8. It's not all that different from driving a regular truck. There's a steering wheel, which turns the front two wheels of the six-wheeled vehicle. The transmission has four gears forward and one in reverse. The clutch is hydraulic and foot-operated, and the gear shifter is to my right. I sit on the left side of the armored car in an uncomfortable metal seat. I can drive with my head out of the M8 through an open hatch, or if the hatch is closed, look through a six-inch viewing slit under a visor. Driving with your head out an open hatch is exhilarating. Conversely, driving while straining to see out of a six-inch-by-three-inch slit is nerve-wracking and will take some time to get used to. And it's magnified, which further distorts your view. You can only see what's directly in front of you. Our instructor tells us that we better learn how to drive with the hatch closed. Otherwise, your head sticking out in the open has a bulls-eye on it.

The instrument panel is sorely lacking—it only has an oil gauge, fuel gauge, engine heat gauge, and a speedometer. There's no tachometer on the instrument panel. The inside of the M8 is too loud to hear the engine rev, and with no tachometer gauge to see the RPMs, I must figure out when to shift by feel. This is giving most of the men learning how to drive the M8 fits. But after only a few hours the first day of driving, I have the shifting figured out. Much like with horses and riding, I quickly establish myself as the best driver in the training troop.

The inside of the armored car is small, and with a four-man crew, very cramped. I sit on the left and the radioman sits on the right. The turret is an open-air design and the car commander stands with part of his body and his head out of the turret. The gunner, also in the turret, can sit in a seat while he operates the main gun. His only job is to fire the 38mm main gun and the .30 caliber machine gun, but sometimes the gunner can be used as a scout and leaves the armored car. Because of the limited space, our extra equipment is stored in storage bins attached to the fenders of the M8, or attached by straps to the outside armor. We look like a traveling moving van. I've been placed in 1st Platoon and the Platoon's lieutenant is my car's commander, making our armored car the command car when the platoon trains together.

Now that I'm training for combat, the sense of purpose has returned and days once again have meaning. Although our training schedule is not overly demanding, I get much accomplished in a day. I rise at sunrise with the rest of the men in 1st Platoon's barracks, and after a run or some physical training, eat breakfast. By mid-morning, I'm training in the M8 with the other members of the platoon. We practice maneuvers, formations, and with weapons—all the while preparing for our eventual deployment overseas. But that also seems to be a problem—we are a training troop, not an individual unit. Meaning, we may not be assigned together as a reconnaissance troop or as part of a cavalry squadron.

❈ ❈ ❈

18 May, 1943:

"What in tarnation is *that*?" Sergeant Ward, my platoon's staff sergeant, yells.

The barracks is shaking so violently I think the roof is about to collapse. My body is covered with soap; the hot shower water has yet to rinse me. Four other men are showering besides me, including Sergeant Ward. I quickly rinse off and grab a towel, wrapping it around my waist. The noise from outside is deafening, and the building is buckling and swaying. Other men are running for cover. The sky outside is black and ominous.

I ram one leg into my pants, and while hopping toward the barracks door, I manage to get my other leg in. I'm racing toward the door—the safest place has got to be outside. Still wet, bare-chested, and without boots, I push the barracks door open. Men are yelling and scrambling all around me, crowding out the door. Rain is now pounding down from above; the sky is blacker than I've ever seen. An hour ago, it looked like a storm was coming. The platoon finished the day's training early, but nothing like this was expected.

The sight of it is both awe-inspiring and terrifying. This is nature at its most furious. The funnel, reaching down from the black clouds, spinning with relentless force, is churning up the ground and trees and everything else in its path. It is massive and breathtaking. I can't help but stare at it. The path seems to be running almost parallel to where I'm standing, less than a half-mile away, but it could change course in a moment's notice. It must be over 200 yards wide—300 maybe. I see the tornado tear a building apart. A truck vanishes right before my eyes. This monster is really moving!

Trucks are speeding out of its path, and soldiers are racing for cover. I see men from my platoon running in the opposite direction. I take several more steps toward the massive funnel as its direction has now put our barracks out of harm's way. In the distance I hear the siren blasting out a warning. It's a little late for that. The destruction wrought upon the Cavalry Replacement Training Center at Fort Riley is already extensive, and the storm is still raging.

Two weeks after the tornado, we're still cleaning up the mess and helping to re-build the destroyed buildings. Over 200 men were injured during the storm. I also received a promotion to corporal—I've now got two stripes on my uniform. Besides my duties as an M8 armored car driver, I've been assigned to the cavalry squadron's supply depot. I requisition supplies for the squadron from the base supply. But I only drive the truck when we need to make pick-ups and check off the items as they're loaded. I'm also introduced to the commanding officer of the squadron, Major Boyd.

"Who's your best driver, Sergeant?" Boyd asks the supply sergeant.

"Siggy is, sir."

"Corporal Signori? Good. Have him meet me with a jeep in front of my office in twenty minutes."

I pull up in front of the major's office and wait. Major Boyd casually strolls up to the jeep and hops in. He's maybe thirty-five, has a mustache, and a perfectly tailored, clean uniform. He's wearing his major's garrison cap slightly off to one side. He looks impressive, tall, and straight-backed.

"We'll be gone for a few hours, Corporal. I cleared your schedule," Major Boyd says.

I don't know what to say, so I say, "Thank you."

"Do you know your way around here? Can you get out to old highway 40?"

"Yes, sir," I answer.

"Good. We're heading up to Manhattan. I'm meeting someone. Should take about an hour to get there."

"Yes, sir."

"They call you Siggy, right?"

"Yes, sir."

"You don't need to keep calling me sir, Siggy, now that we're away from the base."

We're quiet for a few minutes as I drive us off the Fort Riley grounds. Major Boyd acknowledges the salutes from the men standing guard duty at the gate. The road is two lanes and flat, like everything else, and there's very little traffic.

"How do like being in the Mechanized Cavalry, Siggy?"

"So far, I like it, sir," I say after a few seconds.

"M8 driver, right?"

"Yes, sir."

I'm watching the road, but I can tell he's trying to find something for us to talk about.

"Where you from?" he decides on.

"I'm from Baltimore."

"I grew up in Indiana but have been in the Army for the last ten years," he tells me. "You started out in the Horse Cavalry, right?"

"Yes, sir. I enlisted in the cavalry and chose horses."

"Seems odd. A city boy wanting to ride horses."

I don't want to explain, so I just say, "Yes, sir, it is odd."

"But now you drive an M8," he says it like he's stating a fact, which he is. We ride on in silence for a while until he says, "Are you curious about what we're doing?"

I don't want to be rude, but I'm not curious. I assume he's running an errand and wanted someone to drive him.

"A little, I guess, sir."

"I'm making a booze run, Corporal. But it's a secret."

I glance over at him. He's looking at me. "Your secret is safe with me, sir."

"I don't want you to tell anyone what we're doing, understand?"

"Yes, sir, I understand."

"That's good, Siggy. Very good."

We drive on in silence. Eventually, we pull off the highway and head into town. We stop at a warehouse and are met by a gray-haired man in a suit. The major shakes his hand, then turns to me and waves me over.

"Siggy, Mr. Smith will show you where the merchandise is. Carry it on out to the jeep."

I follow Mr. Smith into the warehouse; he stops at a stack of boxes. "This here is the major's order. I'd help ya, but I got a bad back," Mr. Smith says as he's turning away.

I make five trips into the warehouse retrieving the cases of booze. After I stack the cases in the back of the jeep, I cover them with a canvas tarp. I don't see any money changing hands, but I have the impression that the major sells the booze to the officer's club under the table, so-to-speak, and the transaction is not Army-authorized. Major Boyd is in a jovial, talkative mood for the hour-long drive back to Fort Riley. I listen to his version of his life story. College playboy who never marries decides to join the Army is the gist of it. When we get back to camp, he has me park behind the officer's club and carry the cases in through the back door.

When I'm done he says, "Remember, Siggy, mum's the word. We'll probably make another run in a couple of weeks."

Exactly two weeks later, we make another run. And again, two weeks after that, but this time, he sends me alone with a list. As I'm driving to the warehouse, I get an idea. Why not buy a few bottles for the barracks? I have enough money on me to get about a case. Do I buy the booze behind Major Boyd's back or do I ask for his permission first? Liquor in the enlisted men's barracks is forbidden, but Sergeant Ward goes out on the town with us when we have leave. I don't think he'll care. He'll probably buy some.

"Mr. Smith, Major Boyd sent me alone today. Here's his list," I say to warehouse owner.

"I've already got his stuff boxed up. Go on now, you can check it," he says with a slow Kansas drawl.

The list I have matches the contents of the boxes—two cases of scotch whiskey, one of bourbon, one of vodka, and one of gin. Once the shipment is loaded and covered, I head back into the warehouse to find Mr. Smith.

"Sir, I was wondering if you'd sell me a case?" I ask with as much confidence as I can muster.

"Your money is as good as anyone's. What do you want?"

"How about four bottles of scotch, four bourbon, and two each of vodka and gin?"

"You got enough for all that?"

"Will sixty bucks cover it?"

Mr. Smith—if that's even his real name—does some math in his head. I figure five bucks a bottle is more than Major Boyd is paying, but I can sell a bottle in the barracks for more, maybe get ten bucks.

"You got a deal," he says.

I load the sixth case under the tarp and start back to Fort Riley. How do I get the extra case into the barracks without anyone seeing? And then, where do I hide it? Well, I've got an hour to figure the answers out. It's just like being a kid in Little Italy again, sneaking around behind the adult's backs, trying to pull one over on 'em. And I've always had a knack for making money.

I drop off the major's merchandise at the officer's club before going to my barracks. During the drive back to Fort Riley, I decide I need to include Sergeant Ward, because without him, this scheme would never work. I pull up to the back of our barracks, out of sight from the main pathway and where the front of the barracks is located. The jeep is out of view and the extra case of booze remains hidden under the tarp. I find our platoon sergeant in his room, reclining on his cot reading a magazine.

"Sergeant Ward, a minute of your time," I say.

"No need to be so formal with me, Siggy," he says. "What's on your mind?"

I have a speech worked out in my head, but I freeze. He's older than me in not only age. Sergeant Ward is an old-school sergeant from long before the war. He's seen it all, done it all, and been all over the world. He's probably dealt with thousands of soldiers just like me. For the most part I do my job, do it well, and don't cause the platoon any trouble. He knows I'm a card shark and only laughs when he's asked to join a game. He always says the same thing, "Not if Siggy is playing." He likes to hang out with the enlisted troopers but in an older, wiser brotherly way, looking out for us if we celebrate our freedom from the base with a little too much enthusiasm while in town. I think I know him—or rather, the type of person he is—well enough to trust him.

"I've got something to show you," I say.

"Lead the way," he says as he hops off his cot.

We make our way out of the barracks and around back to where I stashed the jeep.

"You have a jeep to show me?" he asks.

"No, Sergeant Ward, not the jeep, but what's under the tarp."

I pull back the tarp revealing the case of booze. I undo the tucked-in flaps of the lid to expose the contents. I watch as the sergeant stares at the tops of the bottles. His gaze shifts from the case of booze to me and back to the booze.

"Where'd you get the liquor, Corporal?" Now he's being formal.

"I bought it up in Manhattan."

At this point I have two choices—lie about how I'm able to buy booze in a town an hour away or tell the truth. The truth would mean breaking a promise I made to my highest ranking superior officer.

"Sergeant Ward, I made a promise to someone that I wouldn't reveal the details about how I can get liquor," I finally say.

"It's a secret, huh?" he asks.

"Yes, it's a secret."

"You have five seconds to tell me, Corporal!" he yells.

I can't believe the mistake I've made! "I drive Major Boyd to a warehouse where he buys cases of booze for the officer's club!" I shout back.

"Now that wasn't so hard was it, Siggy?" he says with a grin on his face. He reaches in and pulls out a bottle of scotch. He puts the scotch back and pulls out a bottle of bourbon. "A man after my own heart," he says. "What are you planning on doing?"

"I was thinking we could sell to the enlisted men in the troop."

"Nope. Can't leave 1st Platoon. If word gets out that our barracks has booze, the whole camp will find out. No, we gotta keep this under wraps."

"Whatever you say, Sarge."

A nice little profitable enterprise is born. I sell off the bottles in portions, filling innocent-looking containers to the troopers in 1st Platoon. Most of the men are overjoyed with the addition of booze in our barracks, and the protection of Sergeant Ward keeps those who are opposed in check. No one will go behind the sergeant's back and rat me out.

My next dilemma—should I ask Major Boyd for permission or continue to conduct my business behind his back? My supply runs out at about the same time as the next booze run.

"Major Boyd, sir, can I ask you something?"

"Sure, Siggy,"

"I was wondering, sir," I start out saying. I seem to diverge back to calling him "sir" whenever I need something. "If, um, you would be okay with me buying a few bottles for myself?"

167

I'm trying not to look at him. I know this must be a difficult decision for him; one that would normally require much deliberation. But to my shock he answers almost right away.

"If I know nothing about it, I don't see why not," he says.

He's giving me permission to buy booze without giving me permission—so typical of an officer. If he doesn't know about it, I can do whatever I want, but if my endeavor is exposed, he will not come to my rescue.

"Thank you, sir," I say, and immediately after loading his five cases, I procure a mixed case for myself.

During my stay at Fort Riley as a member of 1st Platoon, C Troop, Mechanized Cavalry, my booze running enterprise remains concealed. I don't make a lot of money doing it—nowhere near enough to justify the risk I take—if I'm found out, I'll be court-marshalled—but it sure makes barracks life in flat and boring Kansas a heck of a lot more agreeable.

❀ ❀ ❀

"Siggy."

"Yes, Sergeant Ward?" I know by the way he's approaching me that he has something unpleasant for me to do.

"I need you on KP duty."

"What? KP duty?" I ask, incredulously.

"That's right, Siggy, KP duty. It's your turn, so get to the kitchen by 0500 tomorrow morning," Sergeant Ward says as he turns and walks away. I hear him chuckling.

No one wants kitchen patrol, or KP. Many times, it's a form of punishment, but we also rotate the personnel from our unit, and I guess it's my turn. This means I need to start getting breakfast ready at five in the morning for the first group of troopers who'll arrive by 0700.

Me—I'm in charge—and three other men from the platoon have scrambled eggs made, bacon fried, and potatoes peeled, cut, and frying by 0600. The coffee has long since been brewed.

"You guys ready to eat?" I say. It's about an hour before the rush of hungry men arrives.

"Sure are, Siggy," they all answer.

We fill our trays with food and are about to dig into our bacon and eggs when three men walk into the mess hall. "Mind if we eat?" one of them says.

They're dressed in uniforms, but they don't look like Army personnel.

"Go ahead and grab some chow," I say. "Coffee, too."

I'm curious, so I watch. Two fill canteens with coffee and scoop up some bacon. They shake hands with the third man and leave. Then he piles a load of eggs and at least eight pieces of bacon on his plate. He turns and surveys his surroundings. All four of us are staring at him. Now that he has turned, I instantly recognize him, as do the three troopers with me. All of them have their mouths hanging open.

He starts to walk toward us. "Mind if I join you? I hate to eat alone."

"By all means," I say. "What are you doing here at Fort Riley, Mr. Reagan?"

"Here shooting a film for the Army," Ronald Reagan says. "Oh, and call me Ron. What's your name?"

"Paul Signori, but everyone calls me Siggy," I say. "Welcome, sir. I mean Ron. It's an honor to have you eat with us." As we shake hands, I add, "Ain't that right, boys?"

All three are still speechless, star-struck, but manage, "An honor, sir." And they shake Ron's hand.

Ronald Reagan, Hollywood movie star, starts laughing his behind off. "Thanks for the reception, but you guys have it wrong, I'm the one who's honored to be sharing breakfast with you," he says. "You know, before the war, I was in the Army reserve, in the Horse Cavalry. I was a major. Now they've got me making training movies. What I'd give to be in your place," Reagan says as his voice tails off.

"We're Mechanized Cavalry," I say. "1st Platoon, C Troop. Before I was transferred into my unit, I was in the Horse Cavalry like you were."

"Darned if I don't miss those days," Ronald Reagan says.

We spend the next forty minutes listening to him tell us stories about Hollywood, making movies, and the pretty actresses he knows.

# Chapter 12

# FORT BENNING

In the early spring of 1944, orders come transferring me to Fort Benning, Georgia. Me and eleven other members from my cavalry platoon are joining a newly formed reconnaissance troop attached to a division that's training in Colorado. The division, the 71st Infantry Division, has been considered a light division—fewer men than a standard division—but is in the process of re-fitting to adhere to the new divisional format of three regiments. During this process, special units, such as the reconnaissance troop, must be formed and integrated into the division. Over the next month, recon troopers arrive at Fort Benning and the 71st Reconnaissance Troop is officially created and manned by four officers and about ninety enlisted men.

Once we start training as a unit, the three platoons of the troop train together. I'm placed in 1st Platoon and receive my third stripe—I'm now a sergeant. Because of the training I've had, I'm considered a Technician, Fourth Grade and a "T" is under the three chevrons on my shoulder.

I was considered the best M8 driver in the Mechanized Cavalry squadron I had been a part of; establishing myself as the best in the new recon troop does not pose much of a problem. No one handles the M8 as well as I do, and because of this, I become the armored car driver and assistant car commander for the troop's commanding officer, Captain Johnson. The training I've received up to this point includes Horse Cavalry and Mechanized Cavalry. I'm now about to embark on reconnaissance troop training. Our focus is how to work with the infantry units our troop is assigned to. Once again, our ultimate mission remains the same—to scout ahead of a larger body of soldiers, find the enemy, and determine his strength and position.

❊❊❊

By this time, the United States Army has seventy-four infantry divisions and sixteen armored divisions. I know this because everyone talks about when we will deploy, and when divisions are sent overseas for combat, we cross their number off the list. No one knows when the 71st's number will come up. What we do know is that only two armored and eighteen infantry divisions are in combat, fighting in either the Pacific Theater or the European Theater. The remaining divisions have yet to be committed to battle.

One of the most difficult decisions that lay ahead for the U.S. Army war planners is when and how to deploy the massive army that has been produced. The building of this behemoth started during the Mobilization of 1940 when, for the first time during peace-time, a draft was put in place. The mobilization also included the National Guard. Millions of fighting men are now in uniform. Many soldiers, like me, have been training for up to two years or longer. Logistically, the Army can only support and maintain a limited number of divisions in combat. When a division deploys for combat may come down to a coin toss, or a number pulled out of a hat.

Established units from the 71st Infantry Division start arriving at Fort Benning the middle of May. By this time, my unit has been together for two months. A month later, the D-Day invasion of France takes place and the U.S. Army begins its battle with Nazi Germany on French soil. A dozen more divisions are committed to battle—but not the 71st. Paris is liberated on August 19th. In the meantime, the 71st Infantry Division and its recon troop continue to train. No matter how much training a soldier receives, he can always receive more. The movements of soldiers in combat must become second nature. Situations on the field of battle must be routine, and the combatants need to know exactly what to do and how to do it in all circumstances, and in any weather or on any terrain. And all the while, with the enemy fighting back.

❀ ❀ ❀

"Captain Johnson, this is a bad idea," I hear Lieutenant Gibb saying. "If we stay here, we'll be surrounded."

"Are you questioning my orders, Lieutenant?" Johnson responds.

"I'm just pointing out the obvious," Gibb says.

"Do you know who runs this recon troop, Lieutenant Gibb? Well, I do. I'm the captain and you're a lieutenant," Captain Johnson says. "That means I do."

Lieutenant Gibb is 2nd Platoon's commanding officer. We're in the middle of the last live action maneuver we'll participate in before we deploy. This mock battle is as close to real combat as I've experienced—live munitions are being used. Artillery explosions start to reverberate from the other side of the hill we are behind. All three platoons of the recon troop are together, waiting behind the hill for the artillery to let up. Captain Johnson is ordering everyone to stay put. Lieutenant Gibb thinks—and I agree with him—that two platoons should break off and scout in opposite directions to the other side of the hill.

I've been training for combat since I first arrived at Fort Riley in October 1942. It's now more than two years later. I've been through dozens of this type of maneuver and have seen just about everything a recon trooper could see, and I've experienced everything, too. I have also been lucky—I've been the driver and assistant car commander for the officer in charge of every platoon I've been in. Now I'm the M8 driver for the troop's commander, Captain Johnson, and have been for over six months. And he's wrong.

"Lieutenant Gibb, return to your platoon and await further

orders," Johnson says. "Dismissed."

I hear Gibb say under his breath, "He'll get us all killed."

Ten minutes later, we are surrounded by a superior force and surrender. I exchange a glance with our troop's top sergeant, First Sergeant Wall. He shakes his head and looks away. This is an embarrassment to the entire troop, although the blame lies solely on our captain.

Sergeant Wall and I spend much time together. He's never far from Captain Johnson, which means he's never far from me. I've come to respect him immensely; he is the best soldier I've met in my two years in the Army. He's responsible for all the enlisted men in the troop, and every one of us looks to him. Without him, I have no idea how the 71st Recon Troop could exist—he's that important.

"I've called you officers and a few non-coms together to discuss today's events," Captain Johnson says after we return to our area. I'm a sergeant, and one of the lucky ones who are present. "Despite being forced into surrender, I believe we garnered much useful experience. Next time, a flanking maneuver will be in order."

"Sir, I suggested a flanking maneuver in the first place," Gibb can't hold his tongue. "And you ordered me back to my platoon."

"Lieutenant Gibb, regardless of what was discussed on the battlefield, now is not the time to bring it up."

I see our other two junior officers, the lieutenants in charge of 1st Platoon and 3rd Platoon, lower their eyes. It's never a good idea to question your superior officer in front of others, but I respect Lieutenant Gibb for speaking his mind and not backing down. I know just about every member of the troop and have friends in 2nd Platoon. I hear nothing but good things about Lieutenant Gibb.

The meeting breaks up and everyone heads in different directions. I can't get what has happened today out of my head. Likewise, I can't forget what Lieutenant Gibb said, either. "He'll get us all killed."

If Captain Johnson is the first to get killed, how far behind am I? I come to the realization that I don't want to be his armored car driver. I don't want to go into battle with him. I find First Sergeant Wall; he always knows what to say and always has the right advice.

"Sergeant Wall, I've got a dilemma," I say. "Can you help get me a transfer?"

"A transfer, Siggy? I don't follow. You want out of the troop?"

"Not out of the troop—out of Captain Johnson's M8."

"Siggy, don't let what happened today bother you. It could happen to anyone," he says, but I know he's not happy, either. "He just got a little carried away with the live rounds going off."

"If it happens over there, we're gonna get killed," I say.

"If it happens over there, it won't matter whose car you're in. Just do your job and do it the best you can," he says. "Anything else?"

"No, Sergeant Wall, nothing else."

❈ ❈ ❈

"Siggy, come on in," Captain Johnson announces after I knock on his door. "Good to see you."

I don't take Wall's advice. Johnson is all smiles when I enter. We're very informal around our barracks and office.

We've spent so much time together over the last six months that it's impossible not to establish personal relationships with everyone and I know Captain Johnson is fond of me.

"What's on your mind?" he asks.

At first, I struggle with what I want to say. I respect him and genuinely like him, too. I really don't want to hurt his feelings. And I have certainly not considered all the possibilities that may come from my act of disrespect. I'm thinking he will understand and ask where I want to go, but I also realize that this is the best possible outcome.

"Captain, it's like this," I say, but pause.

"Go on, Siggy, you can tell me."

"Captain, could you please transfer me out of your armored car and into another platoon?"

The expression on his face instantly changes. I can see that he is hurt, and his eyes turn to anger. There is a long pause before he says, "Sergeant Wall, please show Private Signori out," he says. "You can have your transfer, Private. I'm sure you'll be perfectly happy in 2nd Platoon."

Sergeant Wall is standing at the door to the office when I turn away from Captain Johnson.

"I told you it was a bad idea," Wall says.

"I don't mind losing the rank, Sergeant Wall."

Later that day, I report to Lieutenant Gibb and 2nd Platoon. He's already heard the news, as has everyone else. Like I said, we're a close-knit group. The troopers of 2nd Platoon are waiting for me—I'm greeted with back-slaps and handshakes. Apparently, I said what everyone else was thinking.

"Welcome aboard Siggy, glad to have you," Gibb says as he's shaking my hand. "Oh, and don't worry too much about the rank, I'll slip a promotion to corporal through without
178

anyone noticing. I'm sure Sergeant Wall will sign off on it."

"Thanks, Lieutenant Gibb," I say. "After today and what you said, I needed to get away from the captain."

"That he'll get us all killed?" he states. "I was just spouting off. I don't really think he will. But like I said, we're glad to have you. As a matter of fact, I'd like to put you in my M8, but Captain Johnson has black-balled you—says you ain't driving an M8. You're gonna be driving one of the mortar jeeps."

He's black-balling me because I don't want to be his driver! Now I'm stuck driving a jeep.

"Welcome aboard, Siggy," Staff Sergeant Finn, 2nd Platoon's top sergeant says after Gibb leaves me.

Finn was with me at Fort Riley. He was the first of the Mechanized Cavalry troopers from Riley to get promoted to staff sergeant. He was originally a recon scout, now he's a platoon sergeant. We're friends, but not especially close. He lost a lot of money in poker games to me, but he did partake in the drinking of the booze I brought into our barracks.

"Glad to be aboard, Finn. It's like old times getting back with some of the boys from our 1st Platoon days at Riley," I say. "Me an' Halby will be raising hell together again."

A trooper named Halby is my best friend from Riley that was assigned to the 71st Recon.

"Not too much raising hell, Siggy," Finn says.

"Of course. Not too much," I agree.

After my exchange with Finn, I watch Lieutenant Gibb walking away. I instantly know I've made the right decision to join 2nd Platoon. Somehow, and I don't know how or why I feel this, but I know I've been put in Lieutenant Gibb's platoon for a reason. Maybe to look after him or something like that. I feel a sudden exhilaration and goosebumps spread across my body. Maybe I'm a watcher again, a protector. Do all those years on The Block looking out for other people finally have meaning? The life I left behind on The Block of Baltimore working for the Mob really did amount to something.

I think about Mrs. Russell. After a letter from her over a year ago, I've not heard from her since. But I remember how she took care of the girls, and I think about Beans and how he looked after me and Naughty and Thrill. It's been a long time since I thought about any of the people that have suddenly popped into my head. The face of Sarah Gilbert, innocent and beautiful, appears. In my heart, I know I was doing the right thing when I protected all of the girls. I am now doing the right thing again. Although I won't be driving his M8 armored car, I can still try and keep my new lieutenant out of harm's way.

❊❊❊

I'm boarding a train—our destination is Camp Kilmer, New Jersey. It's the New Year, 1945. The recon troop is part of the advanced group, leaving nine days before the bulk of our division. This is it. We are deploying overseas for combat.

Before I have a chance to rest my head, let alone think about what lay ahead, I'm walking up a plank onto a transport ship. It's January 10, 1945, and I'm on my way—two years, two months, and ten days after stepping foot on Fort Riley's parade grounds as a Horse Cavalry trooper.

# Chapter 13

# THE WAR

6 February, 1945:

I have spent the last two weeks in England training as part of a small detachment of soldiers—recon troopers, combat engineers and artillery spotters. Most of the soldiers in my division have been at sea, on a transport ship for eleven days. The night before, I boarded a transport barge loaded with our vehicles—M8 armored cars, the mainstay of the recon troop, and jeeps. I spend the night in a harbor in England; there's too much fog for the ship to cross the English Channel.

But tonight, I'll cross the channel. Tomorrow, I enter the war.

I'm not sure what has prepared me more for what lies ahead —growing up on the streets of Baltimore working for the Mob or the almost two and half years I've been in the Army. It's hard to believe that I've been a soldier for that long. I find myself wondering why it took so long to be sent overseas. Does this make me one of the lucky ones? What would have happened to me if the 71st Division had landed in France in June of last year during the invasion? I would probably be dead. GIs have been fighting and dying for nine months in France, Belgium, Holland, and now Germany. I'm here now—at least the transport ship is, as I have yet to touch the ground. The ship is docking at Le Havre, France just past midnight.

Finally, I'm walking down the gangplank. The city of Le Havre and its harbor are in ruins. The results of numerous bombings have left the once modern and pristine harbor ninety percent destroyed. Engineers from the Army have been rebuilding the harbor since September when the Germans were finally driven out, but this long after the invasion, everything is still a mess.

Everyone around me is quiet, just walking—a combination of exhaustion and apprehension. No one knows what we're supposed to do; we simply follow the man in front of us. No one knows what to expect or what is expected of us. I have spent the many months leading up to this point wanting nothing more than to get here. Get here, fight the Germans, win the war, and then go home.

My unit, the 2nd Platoon of the 71st Recon Troop, is small—only thirty men. The platoon is broken up into three equal sections, each with ten men and three vehicles. My section of two jeeps and one armored car is the command section. Our platoon lieutenant, Lieutenant Gibb, commands the armored car, and I drive our section's mortar jeep. There are three platoons and less than a hundred men in the troop.

We've all been together for about a year, training and waiting to get overseas and into combat. I think I'm ready for this.

On the first night ashore, I'm in a tent city. I'm exhausted but can't sleep, silently waiting for the sun to rise. Many of the men around me are awake, too. I can sense it. It'll only be about another hour. At first light, I'm finally leaving the harbor. I'm being herded along with the rest of the men to a staging area, waiting for trucks.

It doesn't take long. My platoon is being ordered to move out. All of us fit onto two 2.5-ton trucks. We call the them "deuce-and-a-half's." Our vehicles are still being unloaded from the transport and will catch up to us once we're in camp. I can't help but notice two men from another unit already on the truck as I get on. I nod at them and they nod back.

"You guys on the right deuce-and-a-half?" I finally ask.

"Just trying to hitch a ride back to our unit," one of them says, a staff sergeant.

"2nd Armored?" I ask, noticing the division insignia patch on his shoulder.

"Yeah, that's right, 2nd Armored, 82nd Armored Recon. Name's Grady. This is McKenna. He's with the 41st Armored
184

Infantry."

"We're the 71st Recon Troop, 2rd Platoon," I say. "Name's Siggy."

I can tell he's thinking, but he says nothing. He probably looks at us as fresh meat just arrived for the slaughter. He's right, that's exactly what we are. He pulls a drag on the cigarette he's smoking and slowly exhales.

"You guys aren't supposed to be here, right?" I ask. I can tell that something isn't right.

"Nope," says the other sergeant, the guy named McKenna. "Just hitchin' a ride."

"Where you from?" I ask McKenna. "Baltimore accent, right?"

"That's right, Baltimore," McKenna says. "You too?"

"Yeah, sure am. Little Italy."

"Looks like we're neighbors."

"We probably crossed paths," I say. I want to ask if he's been down to The Block, but don't. The three of us shake hands.

"How'd you get on a transport from England?" I ask. I can't help but be curious about these two strangers. Obviously combat veterans.

"We were in an English hospital. Went AWOL to get back here," Grady said.

Absent without leave, AWOL. These guys wanted to get back here? Get back into the war? "I know I shouldn't ask, but why come back?"

They look at each other and start laughing.

"Been asking ourselves that very question these past few days. But on the level, neither of us could leave. We couldn't leave the guys we've been fighting with," McKenna says.

185

"Grady had a ticket home, even."

I stare at the man named Grady. Tough-looking guy. Someone I wouldn't want to mess with—someone whose eyes tell you that he's seen and done things.

"Tell me what's it like?" I ask Grady.

"Not what you think it's gonna be like. It's a lot harder than that," Grady answered.

Grady and McKenna leave at our first stop. I watch them as they hitch another ride heading closer to the front and back into the war. I'm heading to a camp called Old Gold. I have no idea how long I'm supposed to stay or what I'm supposed to do at Camp Old Gold. I know I can speak for the men with me when I say we want to get to the front—to the action. I've been on the sidelines, waiting, while men like Grady and McKenna have been doing the fighting.

Now it's my turn.

❀❀❀

I watch as our jeeps and armored cars are delivered. I've had just enough time to claim a bunk in a tent and get a cup of coffee. First Sergeant Wall is calling the troop to assemble. I see a chaplain walking between our M8's and jeeps, blessing them I think.

"Lord our Father, watch over these trucks as they carry your servants forward into battle. Protect them and the men that travel within them," he says loud enough for me to hear.

He's walking toward us, the assembled men of the 71st Recon Troop. He stops every few feet and quietly prays in front of a group of soldiers. I watch men with their heads bowed and eyes closed, some silently praying. I haven't prayed since St.
186

Leo's School when I was kid a long time ago. Maybe I'll start praying again.

❈ ❈ ❈

I've spent the last two weeks at Camp Old Gold. The recon troop has been segregated from the rest of the division, training in long-range reconnaissance, calling in artillery attacks and spotting the rounds, and learning new radio procedures. We also receive our platoon's new radio operator, an American Indian. They call him a Code Talker. I've never heard of such a thing before, but he'll travel in Lieutenant Gibb's armored car. Our Indian Code Talker goes by the name Daniel. Just like we trained, we'll act as the eyes and ears of the division once we get into combat, and Daniel will relay information back to the division using his native language, communicating with other Code Talkers.

Camp Old Gold is like seeing a million tents, field after field covered by canvas. The camps are named after cigarettes—Cigarette Camps—and are staging and assembly areas for incoming troops. We were told that Camp Old Gold has a capacity of 35,000 soldiers at a time, but we're the only division that's here. All the units, down to company size have their own main streets—two rows of tents with a path between them. We get to live in our tents along the main street for the foreseeable future, which means as long as the Army decides to keep us here.

Since I've been away in the Army, I've only received a handful of letters from home. Mrs. Russell wrote one, but no one else from The Block has sent me any—not Beans, not Thrill, not Naughty—no one. Not even my mother, but that's to be expected since she can't read or write. And my father only reads Italian, but I didn't expect much out of him. It's been my

187

brother Nicky whose kept me informed as to the goings on back home.

"Siggy, I've got a letter for you," Corporal Cody, the troop's clerk shouts. Every few days since we've been at Old Gold he does mail call. This is my first letter from home in over a month.

"Thanks, Wild Bill," I say as I grab my letter. I'm used to not getting many, so when one does show up, I'm excited to read it.

*February 15, 1945*

*Dear Paulie,*

*I hope this letter finds you in good health and spirits. How was the ocean voyage? Did you get seasick? I know it must be an exciting time for you, as you've finally been deployed. Exciting for you, but we are all worried about your safety. Momma keeps pictures of you everywhere so we can remember what you look like! I must admit, it's been so long since I've seen you that the pictures really do help. I even see Poppa stop and look at your pictures. I think he misses you, too. No one misses you more that Norma, though. I hear her at night sometimes talking to you like you're in her room.*

*Not much has changed around here, honest, since the last time I wrote you. Momma is still the same, always struggling to keep the younger kids fed. Your friends still help her out. As for me, I'm working with Uncle Marco, but I'm bored with the job, and I'm taking some college classes. I wonder how you handled the job so well. Unfortunately, Poppa hasn't changed much, either. Still drinking his paycheck away and doing the bad stuff we know all too well. Frankie, Glory, and Norma are still in school. I don't think they're going to be pulled out*

188

*like you and me were. They all send their love. Everyone sends their love.*

*Well, little brother, that's it for now, but I promise to write again soon. Stay safe and write when you can.*

*Nicky*

❄❄❄

After finally getting our deployment alert back in the States, and given twenty-four hours to get our gear in order, and rushing to the train depot, then racing to Camp Kilmer, only to hurry onto a transport boat, and finally arriving in France, I've done nothing but wait since arriving. Rush, rush, rush only to spend the next several weeks waiting. It doesn't make much sense, but I'm only a sergeant. What am I supposed to know? Lieutenant Gibb is a man of his word—he promoted me twice since I've been in his platoon, and I'm a sergeant again, but unfortunately, I'm still driving a mortar jeep, not an M8 armored car.

"Men, I've called us all together to announce our new orders," Captain Johnson starts the meeting. All ninety men of the recon troop are gathered together. "We move into the line tomorrow. We'll be relieving a unit that has been in combat for over four months. We'll be facing elements of the 16th Division. Reports are they're retreating back toward Germany."

After we leave Camp Old Gold, we move about 200 miles by truck through France and into the Alsace-Lorraine region of eastern France, close to the German border, where we are now.

"Sergeant Wall, give the men the general low-down on our mission," Captain Johnson says.

"Listen up, everyone. We're finally gettin' into the fight. Every man in this outfit has been preparing for this moment for a long, long time," Sergeant Wall pauses, then yells, "Men, are you ready?"

Most of the men around me cheer. I cheer. I am ready. I think I'm ready.

"Yes! We're ready!" we all yell.

"The Nazis have been retreating back to Germany since the beginning of the year, but they'll have some surprises for us, I'm sure of that. The first will be their 88mm artillery. They shell our forward positions most nights. There is very little to prepare you for this. We've been through live round maneuvers, but nothing—and I mean nothing—can prepare you for the real thing. When the shelling starts, dive in your hole and cover your head. And pray," he says. "If you get hit, there's nothing you can do about it anyway."

All of us have been prepped for the eventuality of German artillery attacks, so this is nothing new. After a few times, they say, it's not so bad. Just don't get caught out of your hole when it starts.

"Our mission will be to make contact with retreating enemy units. They'll be fighting delaying actions, so expect to be in combat in a couple of days. And we, of course, will be heading out alone, so don't expect much support."

❈ ❈ ❈

I pass columns of somber men—dirty, exhausted men from the 100th Infantry Division, the unit we're replacing. They've been in combat chasing the Nazi Army across France since November of last year. It's now mid-March. By the look of them, they need a break. What was it like? What was the combat they have seen like? How many of their friends are no longer walking away with them?

"2nd Platoon, find a hole or dig a fresh one!" First Sergeant Wall yells. "I want you dug-in covering this sector in twenty minutes. 1st Platoon will be to your right and 3rd to the left."

I'm still amazed by Sergeant Wall. He never stops. He always knows exactly what to do and what orders to give, and no one questions him. Once we relieve the 100th Division, we'll assume their spot on the front lines. But it's not what you would think—it's not two armies facing each other across a no-man's land. We're in a wooded area. The enemy could be ten miles away, a mile away, or he could be in the next group of trees, no one knows for sure. It'll be our job to find him. Tomorrow we'll leave the safety— if there's such a thing— of our patch of woods and set out to find the remains of the German 16th Infantry Division.

I grab Halby, my friend from Fort Riley and 2nd Platoon mate, and push him into a shallow hole in the ground. We call these holes-in-the-ground foxholes.

"You stay put Halby. I'll get the rest of our gear," I tell him.

He nods his approval. I start to retrieve our gear from our jeeps parked behind the line of foxholes. All our platoon's vehicles are parked behind us in a semi-circle and Lieutenant Gibb has set up the platoon's headquarters inside the semi-circle. The sun is setting behind us; darkness is only a few minutes away.

"Incoming!" I hear men yelling.

The sounds of artillery rounds screaming toward their targets are unmistakable. No one needs to yell what is obvious. I start to panic as Sergeants Wall's words echo through my head, "Don't get caught in the open."

I sprint to the shallow hole in the ground that protects me

and Halby and dive in, landing on top of him. I pull myself up as the first of the rounds start to impact into the ground around me. The explosions are deafening, mud and splinters of tree branches flying in every direction. I desperately try to get deeper into the hole. It seems like the explosions go on forever. It's like being caught in the middle of a tornado, but worse. And they are right—nothing can prepare you for this. Just stay as deep in your hole as you can get and wait it out.

After a minute or so has passed, I can't help myself. I raise my head and peer out of the top of the hole. I need to see what is happening. I see Sergeant Wall running toward a wounded man, explosions all around him.

I yell, "Don't get caught out in the open…!"

Before I get the last word out, I witness an artillery shell impacting almost directly on him. His mangled body flies through the air. Parts of our First Sergeant land near me, his boot still attached to the lower portion of his leg. I have a sensation that for a moment time stands still. Noise ceases. The sun drops below the horizon, smoke fills the air, and a darkness ensues.

Then suddenly, explosions reverberate again and events continue.

I pull my head back down into my foxhole and close my eyes. I remember back to when I was a kid. I remember the day a large man nicknamed Beans called me over for a talk. I was a numbers runner, a bag boy, I'm eight years old. I think about riding a horse named Brown Eyed Suzy. Now, look at where I am—with my head buried in the mud, wishing I was eight again or riding a horse without a care in the world.

❋❋❋

22 March, 1945:

I don't know how we'll survive as a unit without Sergeant Wall to guide us, but I feel lucky to be in Lieutenant Gibb's platoon. He's a competent, dependable, and courageous leader. This place is different, I come to realize, from the place I left so long ago. This place, this war, is nothing like surviving on The Block and protecting the young ladies of the clubs. Any one of us can get killed in a moment's notice and there is nothing—absolutely nothing—you can do to change that outcome. You can be the most careful, conscientious soldier around and get killed by a random artillery shell or a bullet fired from a hundred yards away.

In a strange way, though, I don't feel fear. I remember my last night at the Two O'Clock Club and telling Bones Sullivan that I'm not afraid of going into combat. Now I'm here, in combat, and I'm not afraid. I probably should be.

My platoon attacks into the Siegfried Line on the German-French border today. Most of the enemy positions have been abandoned as we encounter little opposition crossing this barrier. The landscape is dotted with concrete bunkers, pill boxes and anti-tank structures. The Germans have placed concrete barriers every few feet to slow the advance of our tanks. I weave my way through the maze. By mid-day, I reach a clearing and leave the German-fortified area known as the Siegfried Line behind. My platoon makes camp in the woods near the German town of Eppenbrunn, a mile from the border. The enemy is retreating toward the Rhine River.

24 March, 1945:

I reach the Rhine River, traveling fifty miles in two days. We are in the lead, ahead of the infantry. The 71st Recon Troop is the first unit from the 71st Division to reach the famous river. In all my life, I have never seen anything quite like it. I pass through a wooded area into an open field and the river suddenly appears. The Rhine River is magnificent, massive and blue. I drive my mortar jeep, third vehicle in our small column, across the river near the town of Germersheim on Highway Bridge 35, re-fitted by combat engineers the day before. The platoon makes camp for the night on the enemy side of the river in the woods. I'm surprised the German Army isn't fighting harder.

We don't travel at night, electing to camp in the concealment of woods—or if we're lucky—in a house. We pass through small towns and bypass farms. At night after making camp, Lieutenant Gibb sends out scouts looking for prisoners and to secure our perimeter. I sleep as close to one of the armored cars as possible, sometimes under it or under the canvas tarp we attach to the back. The rain falls almost non-stop, but the tarp helps. I'm sick of being wet all the time.

"Siggy, you got guard duty tonight, second watch," Sergeant Finn tells me. "You better grab some shut-eye."

Second watch is 0100 to sun-up. There are always three men on guard duty on the perimeter of our makeshift camp. We are in enemy territory—anything can happen—so we must stay awake and alert. Silence isn't mandatory, but no one talks. Our voices carry in the noiseless night air for miles. Another trooper from the platoon has decided I need company, and he won't shut his mouth.

"Springy, if you don't shut your pie-hole, I'm gonna shoot you," I say after a trooper nicknamed Springy finally stops talking.

The guy always walks on his toes, bouncing like a spring, so we call him Springy. He also never shuts up. I have no idea why he's bothering me tonight. He's not on guard duty and I didn't invite him. I don't want the company; I just want to walk my portion of the perimeter in silence.

"I can't sleep, Siggy," he says. "You ever get home sick, Siggy?"

"Shut up, Springy, I mean it."

"Seriously, do you miss back home?"

"Another word and I'm gonna shoot you."

I pull my rifle up to my waist and point it at him. I haven't loaded a round, or at least I think I haven't. I'm just trying to scare the guy.

"Come on, Siggy, you won't shoot me."

I pull the trigger, thinking I haven't loaded a round. My gun goes off. Luckily, I didn't aim at him and the bullet misses. I play it off as if I meant to shoot him.

"How did I miss you at this range?" I say.

"You tried to shoot me!" Springy yells.

"I told you I would if you didn't shut up."

Gunshots at night from the perimeter are common, and when no other shots are fired and if no alarm is sounded, the few men who wake up go back to sleep. As did Springy—he retreated to his tent for the remainder of the night. He never bothered me again—not on guard duty or any other time.

28 March, 1945:

The three platoons of the 71st Recon Troop are ordered to find crossing points for the rest of the 71st Division. We are traveling in our usual format—1st Platoon on the right, 2nd Platoon in the middle, and 3rd Platoon on the left. Why do we always have to cover the middle?

Up ahead is a small town with a smattering of buildings just east of the Rhine River. Several houses appear to our left. Our column of 2nd Platoon vehicles moves onto the main street of the town. I've lost sight of the other two platoons as they are covering a different route, but we're in radio contact. I see movement up ahead—several people running behind buildings. I can't tell if they're soldiers and if they're armed. Five of them run into the street armed with machine guns. They look like kids, but they have uniforms on. They open fire and bullets start flying.

We return fire from the mounted .50 caliber machine guns in the M8s and the machine gun jeeps. I stand up in my jeep and start firing. In less than a minute, five dead bodies lay in the street.

"They're just kids," I hear Halby say.

"They fired at us first, Halby," Sergeant Dorn answers.

I'm staring down at the bodies of five kids killed by me and my platoon mates. Clouds cover the sun and light retreats. I look to the sky and at the black clouds. My gaze returns to the ground and I see our shadows as they cover the bodies of the boys we killed. I see what appears to be five shadows, but there are only three men with me. I blink my eyes and only four shadows remain. I shake my head several times, trying to clear my sudden vertigo, and close my eyes. I'm brought back to reality when an explosion goes off a couple of streets to my right. What did I just see? But I have no time to ponder this.

"That's 1st Platoon's sector!" Lieutenant Gibb yells from behind me. "Sergeant Kane, Sergeant Signori, Sergeant Dorn, get your jeeps over there and find out what's going on."

I jump into my jeep and speed away with the other two jeeps. I see smoke coming from the bottom of an M8 armored car. It looks like my old armored car, Captain Johnson's armored car.

"What happened?" I ask the first trooper I reach.

"Some kid jumped out of a doorway with a Panzerfaust and fired at the captain's M8."

A Panzerfaust is a rocket launcher, like a bazooka.

"Captain get killed?" I ask.

"No, but he got knocked out of the turret," he says with a snicker. "The shell must have hit right below the front armor and bounced off, went under the M8, and exploded. His driver got wounded. He must have whacked his head or something. Knocked him out, bleeding from his head and both ears, too."

"Now ain't that something," I say.

"Hey, wait a minute. You used to be his driver and that was your M8, right Siggy?"

30 March, 1945:

The rest of the 71st Division crosses the Rhine River on pontoon boats. My platoon moves ahead of the division and into the town of Heusenstamm.

"Siggy, is that what I think it is?" Hog Jaw says. His name is Hogg, and he has a big jaw, so we call him Hog Jaw. He's a recon scout and the machine gunner in Halby's jeep in my section.

"It looks like a distillery," I answer, rather deadpan. The old wooden building stands two stories tall with its entrance blocked by a massive double door. Above the door is a large placard, displaying carved barrels and the figure of a man holding a glass over his head, examining its contents.

"What are we waiting for?" Halby says.

My friend Halby, also in my section, drives the jeep that Hog Jaw is in. The three of us tend to get into trouble together and are exploring the town looking for trouble. The German Army is long gone, still retreating, so we feel relatively safe. Plus, other American units have caught up. Lieutenant Gibb has given us leave—in other words, we have no orders until tomorrow morning.

Hog Jaw kicks open the wooden double doors of the distillery. They make vodka. Kegs of the stuff are stacked in long rows.

"My God, Siggy, I'm in heaven," Halby says.

Hog Jaw pulls out his .45 pistol and fires six rounds into the nearest stack of kegs. Clear liquid starts spilling out of the holes.

"What are we waiting for?" I yell as I run to the nearest keg. At first, I drink straight from the flow, eventually switching to filling my helmet.

❊ ❊ ❊

My head is pounding. I struggle to open my eyes. I'm hot and feel like I'm surrounded, the walls around me are closing in. My sight comes into focus.

"What are you doing here?" I ask.

"Question is, what are you doing here?" a black soldier answers.

"I'm in an M8 from my platoon. I'm supposed to be here," I say.

"No, Sergeant, you ain't in no M8 armored car. No, sir," he says. "You're in my tank. And I knows for sure that you ain't supposed to be in my tank."

"How'd I end up in your tank?"

"Good question, Sergeant."

I can't piece together the specifics of my night drinking vodka out of my helmet, but luckily, I'm able to find my way back to my platoon, about a mile away. Somehow, I ended up with a tank unit from the 761st Tank Battalion. The 761st is made up of black servicemen and has been part of our spearhead, attached to the 71st Division. I have no idea whatever happened to Halby and Hog Jaw last night, but the three of us nurse the worst hangovers of our lives for the next three days.

I'm still on Captain Johnson's punishment list. He manages to find ways to make my life miserable. Maybe he found out about my drinking excursion last night, who knows? But he sends his new first sergeant to order me on guard duty again tonight. I've spent the better part of the day puking my guts out from the passenger seat of my jeep. I couldn't drive. The first sergeant finds me sitting on a toilet in the latrine; it's coming out of both ends.

"Siggy, you got duty tonight."

"Come on, Sarge, I can't handle duty tonight. Look at me."

"Don't care. It's coming straight from the Captain."

"Let me switch with someone. I'll do double when I'm better."

"Can't do, Siggy."

"We got shoot-on-sight orders for tonight?" I ask. Shoot-on-sight means I can shoot someone and ask questions later.

"You know we do. We always do."

"Who's doing the rounds?"

Doing the rounds means someone goes from guard to guard throughout the night making sure none of the men on guard duty is sleeping at his post.

"I am, why?" First Sergeant Cole answers.

"Because if it's you, and I got shoot-on-sight orders, I'll shoot you," I say.

"Haha, Siggy, real funny," he says as he walks away.

I finish in the latrine, knowing I'll be back in there in a matter of minutes. Something must have been in that vodka. I've never been this sick from booze before.

"Hey Siggy, got a minute?" Sergeant Finn, my platoon sergeant, asks a few minutes later.

"Yeah, sure, but probably only a minute," I say. Who knows when nature will call again?

"I just had an interesting conversation with First Sergeant Cole. He asked if I thought you were crazy enough to shoot him."

"Okay, what'd ya say?" I ask with a grin on my face.

"I said yes. Yes, Siggy is crazy enough to shoot anyone," Finn says. "By the way, you're off guard duty tonight."

❋❋❋

1 April, 1945:

My platoon is ordered to leave the Heusenstamm area and advance to the outskirts of the German town of Budingen, about thirty-five miles away. We are the farthest east of any unit in our division, we're behind enemy lines, and everyone is on edge. There is nothing in front of us but our enemy. Before we broke camp this morning, we were told that the German's 6th SS Mountain Division is out there somewhere.

Our mission is to find them.

Although I'm still nursing my hangover from the other night, the puking has finally stopped. I'm doing my best to stay sharp and alert. It's hard for me to believe that I've been on German soil for over two weeks and I'm across the Rhine River and into the heart of Germany. To this point the Nazis have not put up much of a fight, but I have a feeling that the German Army, especially the SS troops, their most loyal Nazis, will start to fight for every mile.

It's just past one in the afternoon with overcast dark skies, and it's cold, about forty-five degrees. The rain has finally stopped, but I know it'll start up again. It always does. My mortar jeep is third in the column, behind the lieutenant's M8 and the machine-gun jeep Halby drives. That's how the lieutenant likes to travel—machine gun jeep, M8, and followed by the mortar jeep. Behind us are the other two sections of the platoon, each with two jeeps and one M8. The lieutenant orders two of the machine gun jeeps forward and one man from each, our scouts, to proceed on foot. The rest of the platoon stays hidden in the woods. Up ahead is a farmhouse and barn—we can barely see the buildings through the thick forest.

Not a sound can be heard except the low rumbling of our engines. We all hear the crack of a gunshot. A second later, the bullet smashes through Lieutenant Gibb's face. He falls backwards. I'm next to the armored car he's in. I jump out of my jeep and scramble onto the M8 and up into the gun turret and grab him, standing him back up. I hold the front of his uniform coat with one hand and the back of his head with the other. I'm trying to keep his brains inside of his head. I know it will do no good, he's already dead. I stare at his face, at the small hole in his cheek, under his eye. His eyes are open. Lieutenant Gibb is my friend, but I feel nothing. Not sadness, not pity, nothing. Maybe anger—I'm angry at my enemy for killing him—not so much that he's dead.

I've learned to keep my emotions in check, the same way I did on The Block. I feel a darkness setting in on me. I feel my heart hardening with every passing day. I have seen plenty of death and horrible, unimaginable sights over the last month and I know that at any time, any of us can get killed. This is what we live with. We live with death. Now that we have again made contact with the enemy, I am certain that Lieutenant Gibb will not be our last casualty. I wonder if my number will eventually come up.

But I'm not afraid. I still don't feel fear.

❊❊❊

2 April, 1945:

It's a day before my twenty-first birthday. Until a replacement arrives for Lieutenant Gibb, Staff Sergeant Finn is leading the platoon. I know him well—he's been the platoon sergeant since my first day with 2nd Platoon and we trained together at Fort Riley, but I don't consider him a close friend. He's a decent enough guy, from Boston.

Finn is now in the command armored car standing in the

turret, just like Gibb the day before. It's just past dawn and we'll be on the road soon. Another day of moving forward, moving closer to contact with the enemy.

Yesterday's ambush weighs heavy on all of us. Lieutenant Gibb was liked by every man in the platoon. I thought I had been watching his back since we arrived in France; I feel as though maybe I let him down. But what could I have done? Regardless of what I did or said, he would still have been standing in the gun turret of his armored car. Now that a day has passed, I can form clearer thoughts about what has happened. I guess I've changed a lot since the first time we were shelled by German artillery in France.

❀ ❀ ❀

Yesterday, moments after the lieutenant's death, the Germans hiding in ambush in the barn and farmhouse attacked our group in force. The armored car was the target. I barely had enough time to pull Lieutenant Gibb out of the turret before I would get my own head blown off.

Once on the ground, Gibb was loaded into my jeep and the platoon pulled deeper into the woods. The men of the platoon gathered around him. No one talked; we stood over him in silence.

"What should we do with him?" The silence was broken.

"Get him back to the aid station," Staff Sergeant Finn said. "I guess until they send a replacement, you guys are stuck with me."

"What are we going to do about the Nazis who did this?" Hog Jaw asks.

"We can lob some mortar rounds from Siggy's mortar jeep

and then move in on foot," Finn answered, already taking control of the platoon.

My mortar jeep has a mortar tube bolted in its back bed, which is why it's called a mortar jeep. We lobbed a few rounds into the house and barn. Following the explosions, a bunch of us moved back into the clearing on foot. I'm prepared to kill any German that survived our mortar attack—all the men with me are. Both buildings are on fire, the result of direct hits by mortar rounds. The German soldiers answerable for the ambush have stopped firing their weapons. I moved across the clearing toward the barn at a fast jog. Four men were with me. The fire had spread across the roof and smoke filled the ground level as we pushed open the barn door. We couldn't see much, but you could hear the animals screaming.

"No one alive in here except a few horses," Sergeant Dorn said. Dorn is the next highest-ranking sergeant in the platoon after Finn. He commands one of the armored cars.

"Right," I agreed. But I couldn't leave the horses. Despite the fire and admonishment from the soldiers with me, I raced into the barn, opening the horses' stalls as I went.

"Now we can move on to the house," I said after I emerged from the burning barn behind the freed horses.

"Real smart, Siggy. You could have been killed," Dorn said.

I didn't respond. I had nothing to say. In my heart, I knew I couldn't let them die. I knew if I had, I would never be able to forget their screams.

"Move on me," our scout sergeant, Sergeant Kane said. We all follow.

In combat, conversations are limited. We communicate more with hand signals and gestures. My group of five men moved on to the house. Another group of soldiers approached from the other side of the clearing. Still no weapons had fired at us. I wondered if we were moving into a trap, another ambush.

The house was burning when we entered, but we saw movement. I opened fire with my rifle; the rest of the men with me did likewise. We went only as far as the flames allowed, then backed out and waited. Two German soldiers ran out of the inferno, and we promptly cut them down with gun fire. The entire platoon, over twenty-five men, had entered the courtyard in front of the house. We watched as the house burned to the ground. It took all of ten minutes. None of the enemy survived.

We made camp less than a mile away. Daniel, our Indian radioman, contacted his fellow radiomen in 1st Platoon and 3rd Platoon. Each platoon has their own Indian as a radioman. I don't know what tribe they're from or what language they speak, but neither do the Germans, that's for sure. We don't need to use secure lines because no one knows what they're saying, except each other.

"We are to make camp and wait for the rest of the troop," Daniel told us after speaking to the captain's radioman from 1st Platoon. "Captain Johnson said Sergeant Finn is in charge."

We already knew Finn was in charge, but this confirmation made it official. Gibb's body was sent back to the 71st Recon Troop's aid station, somewhere many miles behind us.

❊ ❊ ❊

The platoon's commander is always in the command M8— that's why Finn has taken over the number one armored car. He can communicate with the platoon using Daniel's radio and also with the other platoons in the recon troop. I'm still driving the mortar jeep in the first section, with Finn's armored car in front of my jeep.

Our mission is to continue to scout toward the town of Budingen and report back enemy strengths and positions, and if possible, to call in artillery strikes. This is our primary mission—scout the enemy, report our findings, call in artillery strikes, and then act as spotters. Artillery is the big cannons that fire shells at enemy positions from miles away. They need eyes on the target so their accuracy can be adjusted and controlled. Our platoon acts as the eyes and ears for the artillery, and for the infantry—the foot soldiers who engage the enemy. We've been assigned to the 14th Infantry Regiment, one of the 71st Division's three regiments.

The American Indian radioman in the recon troop relays the information as given to him by the platoon's commander. Since I'm with the command armored car in the first section, I'm part of the spotter team. All of us are used to the way Lieutenant Gibb ran the platoon. I'm not sure how Finn will do, but I'm glad he's doing the right thing in calling us all together for a talk.

Before we pull out of camp he jumps off the armored car. "You guys all know me," he starts, "We've been together for a long time. The lieutenant was a good man, I'm sure you'll all miss him. I know I will, but we've got to move on, you know, the war's not going to take a break just because someone gets killed."

Not the greatest speech, but it needed to be said.

"Everyone, let's mount up and move out," Finn orders after an appropriate period of silence. "We're scouting ahead to the outskirts of Budingen."

Our column of nine vehicles pulls onto the road. My mortar jeep is in its usual spot—third in line. The road is two lanes and paved with forest on either side. Our visibility is limited. As far as we know, we're the first GIs in this part of Germany, and the enemy could be around the next turn. We've been told to expect heavy enemy activity—the entire 6th SS Mountain Division is defending this area.

Our speed is slow, our moves deliberate; we're taking no chances after yesterday's ambush. The lead jeep stops about fifty yards from the end of the forest. There's a field up ahead past the trees, not long ago planted with crops. Now it resembles a wasteland. We have reached the outskirts of Budingen. We move into our standard operating procedure, by this time perfected. The three sections of the platoon separate, moving to different locations near the clearing.

Next, the scouts are sent out to reconnoiter. One trooper in each of the section's two jeeps is a recon scout, plus the recon scout's sergeant, who travels with my section in the lead jeep. A total of seven scouts spread out into the forest moving toward the open field. They have the job of spotting the enemy before the enemy spots us. Within minutes, the scouts are back and the three sections regroup at the command M8.

"Town is loaded with activity, soldiers, trucks, artillery," recon scout Sergeant Kane reports.

Staff Sergeant Finn thinks for a few moments before he says, "Did they spot you?"

I'm next to Finn's M8, looking up at him in the turret. Finn seems to know what he's doing. He should, he's been Lieutenant Gibb's right-hand man.

"Don't know, but they've got an observation post across the field," the scout sergeant says.

Finn pulls out his map and finds the coordinates for Budingen.

"I'm calling in artillery," he says. "Second section and third section, head back to the rally point."

We always have a pre-arranged spot for the platoon to meet, called the rally point. Since we often split up, this is crucial.

When artillery coordinates are called in, only the platoon's radioman and the spotters are needed. Daniel and our spotter—usually the scout sergeant from our section—plus the rest of the section must stay. Consequently, we're the last ones to head for safety.

We move up to the clearing for a better vantage point to radio the map grid coordinates to the recon troop's headquarters. The coordinates are then relayed back to division artillery. This only takes minutes. Division artillery is always ready and waiting; they need almost no preparation time to start firing rounds.

Now we wait. This is the hardest part. This is the time we are most vulnerable. Once the incoming rounds—you can hear them coming overhead—start exploding to our front and into the enemy, we are needed as spotters. It's our job to radio back any adjustments to the incoming artillery.

Once the rounds are hitting their targets, Daniel radios, "Fire for effect!" This is our cue to high-tail it to safety as fast as we can as now the artillery continues to fire for as long as they deem is necessary.

Gunfire erupts to our front minutes after the coordinates have been relayed. Tracer rounds start screaming past my jeep and the armored car, the little red streaks representing a single bullet, giving the shooter his targeting. Once the rounds start bouncing off the armored car, the last place you want to be is in the gun turret. Sergeant Finn is in the gun turret firing his rifle. I'm standing in my jeep next to him firing my rifle, and the .50-caliber machine gun from the other jeep is blasting away. The armored car gunner, Private Shaw, is firing the 38mm main gun, and Daniel has division artillery on the radio. We all want nothing more than to leave the clearing, racing away from danger. Every second longer we stay is one second closer to death. Any minute now, German artillery rounds will start falling on us. It's what usually happens once we've been seen.

But we don't leave. We stay because we need to see where the first rounds, fired from miles behind us, land so we can adjust.

I hear two sounds almost layered on top of each other, as if occurring as close to simultaneously as possible. The first reminds me of a splintering sound, like what I remember hearing while working at the lumber yard. The second is a heinous scream. Sergeant Finn's face is gone. He's slumped back in the turret. I'm staring up at bloody pulp that used to be his face. His hands are still holding his rifle, but the entire wooden stock is gone. A bullet hit the stock of the rifle and disintegrated it, spraying a mass of wood splinters into his face.

I'm sure he died instantly. I cannot imagine anything else.

# Chapter 14

# THE NEW LIEUTENANT

8 April, 1945:

After we found the German 6th SS Mountain Division in Budingen and called in the artillery attack, the infantry regiments of our 71st Division annihilated the remnants of the German division. The battle resulted in the complete destruction of the 6th SS. After the battle, we received our first installment of replacement soldiers, but not a new lieutenant. We have had three men killed and three wounded since joining the fight over a month ago. All the replacements we received came straight from the States with no combat experience, and all were privates.

This by no means meant we got a break. Instead, we were ordered to move onto the town of Meiningen, a day's journey away. The town surrendered without a fight and we had the privilege of spending the night in houses. It was my first bath in over a month. I even shaved. The prospect of clean sheets and a pillow was overwhelming, the first since leaving America. Me, Halby, and Hog Jaw found a nice little cottage at the edge of town owned by an old German woman. We also found a few bottles of booze. She made us fried eggs and sausage. I slept like a baby.

It has been six days since we lost Staff Sergeant Finn. Sergeant Dorn has been running the platoon while we wait for a new lieutenant to show up and take over. We expect him today. After my night's sleep, me and the rest of the platoon are assembling around our vehicles. I'm watching as a jeep pulls up and a lieutenant jumps out—our new platoon commander. He looks like a kid.

"Who's in charge?" he asks the group of men in front of him.

"I am until I'm replaced," Sergeant Dorn answers.

"Looks like you're being replaced, Sergeant. I'm Lieutenant Case."

Dorn spends a minute or so introducing the lieutenant to the non-coms, the sergeants and corporals in the platoon. Next, we review our mission for the day. Daniel had received orders from Captain Johnson and relayed them to Dorn. Next on our list is the city of Coburg, southeast of Meiningen. After several minutes of discussion, it's agreed that Sergeant Dorn will remain in the command armored car and Lieutenant Case will ride in a machine gun jeep in third section, the back of the column.

"Meaning no disrespect, sir, but until you get your feet wet, it's probably best if you let the sergeants—Me, Siggy and Kane—run the platoon," Dorn says. "We know what we're doing."

We are the sergeants who are in the first section; this wins the argument for the time being. We're traveling through woods on a single-lane road, our visibility is limited, and our pace is slow. The machine gun jeep ahead of me abruptly stops and our scout sergeant, Sergeant Kane hops out. He's kneeling in the road looking ahead. He suddenly jumps up and starts signaling with his hand for us to back-track down the road.

Gunfire erupts to our front. German troops and vehicles emerge from around a bend in the road a hundred yards to our front. Hog Jaw cuts loose with the .50 caliber machine gun in the lead jeep as Halby throws it in reverse. Sergeant Kane is barely able to jump in. The M8 armored car in front of me with Sergeant Dorn in the turret likewise starts firing while driving in reverse. I'm next in line and begin to make a U-turn when I see Dorn get hit in the chest. He's knocked out of the turret, bouncing on the ground. He stops rolling at the edge of the woods. Machine gun rounds from the enemy are bouncing off the armored car.

Daniel, the American Indian radioman in the lead M8, is yelling into the radio as the M8 abruptly stops, "The driver has been killed! "He's been killed!"

This makes no sense as he's inside the car and his hatch is closed, but Daniel keeps yelling. I hear someone get on the radio, Sergeant Kane I think, telling Daniel he needs to drive the armored car. Seconds later, we're moving again, but the body of Sergeant Dorn is left behind.

After back-tracking about five miles, the column of 2nd Platoon vehicles stops in a clearing. The sun is low on the horizon, about an hour before sunset. We are a somber group as we dig in for the night. We have now lost our third platoon leader in eight days, plus the M8's driver, Corporal Mann. He was killed in the most bizarre way. One of the many bullets that was hitting, and bouncing off, the armored car, somehow ricocheted through the open turret and hit him in the back, just below his neck. The bullet went straight down his spine.

"Tomorrow morning, just before sun-up, we'll go back and find Sergeant Dorn's body," Lieutenant Case says. "Who's volunteering?"

I immediately jump up, raising my hand. "I'm in. I'll drive the M8," I say.

"Good. Who else?"

Halby, Hog Jaw, and Kane all volunteer to take their jeep. Most of the men in the platoon volunteer, but Lieutenant Case cuts them off.

"Thanks, but we've got enough with the M8 and machine gun jeep. I'll clear it with the captain," Case says.

❀ ❀ ❀

"Siggy, I got bad news. Captain Johnson says you're not driving the M8," Case says to me later that night. "What the heck did you do to the guy?"

"I told him back in the States before we went overseas that I didn't want to be his driver anymore. He's held it against me ever since," I reply.

"You used to be his M8 driver?" he asks.

"From the beginning, when we first got to Fort Benning until we just before we deployed."

"Why did you want out his M8?"

"I guess I didn't like the way he treated the lieutenants under him," I say. "It was his way, or else. I guess I stopped trusting him."

"I heard from some of the guys back at headquarters that you were the best driver in the troop." He pauses for a few seconds. "Do you still want to come tomorrow morning?"

"I'll take the mortar jeep, if it's all right with you."

"It is. I'll see you at 0430."

Our three vehicles leave a few minutes before 0500 and about an hour before sun-up. It takes almost a half-hour to get to the spot of the ambush from the day before. We find Sergeant Dorn's body still on the side of the road with two bullet holes in his chest. My best guess is he died right away and didn't suffer. His body was on the leaves and dirt at the wood's edge beside a one-lane German road in the middle of nowhere.

❈ ❈ ❈

"Siggy, I've been on the radio for the last hour with Captain Johnson," Lieutenant Case tells me. "I insisted that you drive the M8 and he finally relented. You're in my armored car. Congratulations, you're an M8 driver again."

I shake his hand and thank him. I really am the best armored car driver in the troop. It's only right that I'm back where I belong.

"Look," he says, "I'm from the infantry, I know nothing about recon. I'm gonna have a lot of questions."

He is a kid, probably my age, and is as green as they get. He came straight out of the replacement pool, just arrived from the States. If ever there would be an opportunity for me to watch someone's back, this is it. I thought maybe I was watching out for Lieutenant Gibb, but I wasn't even in his armored car. I am in the new lieutenant's armored car and I will watch his back.

"Just listen to me and the other sergeants and you'll do fine," I tell him. "And don't worry about asking questions. That's what I'm here for." I pause for a few seconds as I gaze at my new lieutenant. "Don't worry, Lieutenant Case. I've got your back."

"What's it like? Combat, I mean?" he asks. "I know we were in combat yesterday, but I was at the back of the column and didn't see anything."

I think back to when I landed at Le Havre and asked this very same question to two combat vets who were hitching a ride back to the front. I wonder whatever became of Grady and McKenna. I decide not to answer the same way they did.

"It's not that bad," I say. "Just do what I tell you."

"That's it, Sergeant—that's all you got?"

I think about the three men I've seen killed in the turret of the lead armored car. Combat and death go together, and we are a reconnaissance platoon; our life expectancy is not very long. There is nothing I can say that will make it any easier for him.

"Lieutenant, three men have been killed standing up in the

turret of this armored car. Remember that the next time we see combat," I say.

After Sergeant Dorn's body is sent back to the aid station at the troop's headquarters, we start out on the road again, reclaiming the ground we lost the day before. And I'm back to driving the command M8.

Blood from Dorn and Corporal Mann is splattered around me; it is impossible to clean it all up. Daniel nods to me when I take my seat next to him. Private Shaw, the gunner, slaps me on the back. I hear Lieutenant Case give the order to move out; he has assumed the command position and no one argues about it. Slowly, 2nd Platoon gets back on the road.

We have no contact with the enemy as we approach the outskirts of Coburg. The villages we passed through today all had white sheets hanging from the windows. I saw no soldiers or civilians. It was a good day. I'm glad we had no enemy contact as it took the better part of the day for me to get used to driving the M8 again while viewing the world outside the armored car through a six-inch magnified viewing slit. After digging in for the night and securing our perimeter, most troopers of the platoon try to get some sleep.

I'm standing by my armored car when I see Lieutenant Case approaching. I can see by the light of the moon that he has something in his hand.

"Share a drink with me, Siggy?"

The last time I shared a drink with an officer was with Major Boyd back at Fort Riley after a booze run.

"Sure, Lieutenant Case," I answer.

"A lot of people call me Casey," he says.

I take the bottle he's offering me and take a chug; it's vodka. This is my first taste of vodka since my night of drinking the stuff out of my helmet. I gag.

"Problem with the booze?"

"Bringing back a bad memory."

"I still don't really know what it is we're supposed to do, you know," he says. "I know we scout out in front of the infantry, but what do we do?"

"What we did today. We were out in front, scouting the roadway. If we see the enemy, and have the time, we call in artillery. But like what happened yesterday, we had to clear the ambush first, then after we made camp, we called in the German's strength and position."

"That simple?"

"Yup. We try not to fight it out, but we will if we have to," I say. "And we're always alone, Lieutenant, we're the expendable ones. We've only got the other two platoons of the troop with us, but they're usually at best a radio call away."

Eventually, after more questions, I explain to Lieutenant Case how we chase the enemy; make contact, and then call in artillery attacks. We stay long enough to make sure the rounds are hitting their targets before heading for safety. I tell him that this is our hardest time—the waiting—exposed to enemy counter-attacks.

We pass the bottle again. This time the booze goes down easy. I think Lieutenant Case just needs a friend. No one in our platoon wants to get close to this man, and I think he knows it. He's an outsider, so no one knows him or trusts his judgment. Plus, he's the only officer amongst a bunch of enlisted men. We spend another hour together talking and drinking his vodka. It turns out that our new lieutenant is a regular guy who just wants to fit in. He tells me that he has an older brother serving in an infantry unit nearby. Maybe I'll meet him someday.

Eventually, I reluctantly tell him about our First Sergeant getting killed in the very first artillery attack we endured, re-living the horror of the night. 'Don't get caught out of your hole when the shelling starts' is probably the most useful piece of advice I give him—that and 'don't stand up in the gun turret of the armored car.' Which, of course, led to me telling my new lieutenant how the three men who lead our platoon before him were killed.

"Siggy, what did I get myself into?"

❀ ❀ ❀

24, April 1945, on the banks of the Regen River in Austria:

Before we reach the Regen River, we are ordered to advance to the city of Coburg. The platoon heads south, south-east seventy kilometers. This is when we first start seeing white sheets hanging from the windows in the small towns we pass through. The townspeople are surrendering the towns without a fight, but we see no people. This is both disquieting and nerve-wracking, like going through a ghost town, expecting to be bounced upon by ghouls. I know we are being watched, but no ghost—or any attacker—materializes. This is when we start to think the war may be coming to an end soon.

Then, we reach Coburg and resistance stiffens. We are the first to reach the city and quickly advance past an elaborate trench-works that has been abandoned by the enemy. By the time the infantry arrives, the city has no stomach for a fight, and surrender is negotiated before a battle breaks out. By April 13th, we've reached the outskirts of Bayreuth, north of the Main River. The Germans are determined to put up a fight. It takes two days of fighting to secure the town. Next, the town of Schonfeld falls after a short battle and the recon platoons
220

are sent out once again to maintain contact with the retreating enemy. Our mission for the last several days, after leaving Schonfeld, is to scout toward the Danube River.

Meanwhile, we must find bridges still standing—the ones the Germans have not destroyed—over the many smaller rivers in the area. Yesterday we found a railway bridge, partially damaged, but we crossed the Naab River without enemy opposition. Today, the 24th, we need to find a bridge across the Regen River, a tributary of the Danube.

※ ※ ※

"We need to move into position," Lieutenant Case says.

Up ahead is a roadblock manned by German troops, maybe twenty, with machine guns and anti-tank guns. Just past the roadblock is a bridge, standing but damaged, and we need to take the bridge before the Germans bring it down. I'm with a group of sergeants at Sergeant Kane's jeep discussing our plan.

Although Lieutenant Case has been our leader for two weeks, he's wisely still allowing us non-coms, the sergeants—the men who have been here from the beginning—call the shots. Although, he has grown immensely as a combat commander since he first arrived and most of the troopers of 2nd Platoon have warmed to him.

"We need to take the bridge intact, so we can't storm the roadblock," Sergeant Kane says. "I can scout ahead with a few guys."

"They've got too much firepower," I add. "We need the M8s and the .50s. Maybe even the mortars."

Our platoon may be small, but we pack a lot of firepower— easily enough to take out the roadblock. But we need the bridge, and surprise is our best weapon.

"We can send the scouts ahead on foot. They can flank the roadblock and take the bridge intact. The rest of us hit the roadblock with everything we've got at the same time," Case says. It's a sound plan.

No one says a word; we're all deep in thought. We've run into many roadblocks along the way and have fought our way over a bridge before. But every time we're going into battle, it's like the first time. The good thing is I trust the men with me with my life.

"Unless anyone can come up with a better plan, I say we move out," Kane says, "The sooner the better."

"Let's mount up and prepare to attack," Lieutenant Case agrees. "I'm taking the point with Siggy's M8. We need the firepower up front."

"Once the roadblock is in range, we'll let 'em have it," I say. "Kane, we'll give you a fifteen-minute head start. If you're spotted, start shooting and we'll be there in less than a minute."

"Roger that," Kane says.

The seven scouts led by Sergeant Kane leave our gathering and head toward the bridge using the thick woods we're in as cover. The rest of us move back to our vehicles, passing the attack plan to the rest of the platoon.

"I hope I made the right decision putting us first in line," Lieutenant Case says.

"You did, Lieutenant. Just remember, when we're charging the roadblock, you need to be in the armored car, don't stick your head out."

"How can I fire the .50 if I'm in the car?" he asks.

"We'll have plenty of other .50s firing, we won't need ours. Private Shaw will be firing the main gun. That'll be enough."

222

We're all using the open mic, allowing us to talk to each other over our radios. After several minutes, Lieutenant Case gives the order to move out. I slowly pull my armored car to the lead position.

"Okay, Siggy, take us in. Slow and steady at first, then gun it. Once we're in range, we'll open fire," Case says.

Behind me, the road fills with armored cars and jeeps. We're using both lanes. At a half-mile away, I gun the engine and the race toward the roadblock is on. Shaw fires the first round; the deafening sound fills the M8. As if a dam has broken, the rest of the platoon opens fire. I'm watching the road ahead of me and the roadblock defended by my enemy through my six-inch Plexiglas viewing slit. Smoke, fire, and explosions fill my sight as well as German tracer rounds. I hear bullets pinging off the M8 and an explosion nearby rains debris on my passing armored car. I look back at Lieutenant Case. His eyes are wide, but he seems in control. He looks at me and we make eye contact. I give him a reassuring nod; he smiles back. I'm glad to see that he took my advice and isn't standing in the turret.

It is very difficult to put a battle into perspective when you're viewing it through a small six-inch by three-inch magnified viewing slit. I'm forced to have tunnel vision, but the alternative—my head sticking out of the open hatch—is out of the question. I'm able to see the bridge ahead of me and just past the roadblock. I can see that Sergeant Kane and his troopers have gained the bridge entrance under heavy fire from the opposite river bank. We need to neutralize the roadblock and get on the bridge to support the recon scouts or they'll never make it across.

I've almost reached the roadblock when I hear an explosion just to my left. One of our jeeps is hit, and the men inside are tumbling on the ground. I realize that it's Halby's jeep, but I can't stop, I'm too close to the enemy. At least Hog Jaw is not in the jeep—he's up ahead fighting for his life with the rest of the recon scouts on the bridge. I hope my friend Halby makes it. One last round from the 38mm cannon is fired by our gunner before I slam into what's left of the roadblock.

"Hang on!" I yell.

I hit the center, smashing through the crossing gate. I barely have enough time to see dead enemy soldiers strewn across sandbagged bunkers on either side of the road. Fire and thick smoke is all around me. I've made the bridge entrance and I'm forced to slow down. Sergeant Kane and his men are at the halfway point of the bridge, still taking enemy fire, but we've made it. The bridge is still standing. I race past my platoon mates and gain the other side. Another armored car is next to me. Three of our jeeps are now in sight. I pop open the hatch and stick my head out for a better view. I see the enemy rapidly retreating into the town of Regenstauf. This part of the battle is waning and the first phase of our mission is complete. We've taken the bridge intact. Now we need to hold it until the infantry catches up with us. This is the second part of the mission—holding the bridge.

This may prove to be the harder of the two.

Two companies from the 14th Infantry Regiment, about 400 men, are less than a day behind us. They can't get here soon enough. The Germans look to be itching for a fight and it's going to be for the town of Regenstauf; our platoon can't win. We quickly dig in and secure our perimeter on the southern bank of the Regen River. We'll defend the bridge at all costs—to the last man if necessary. That seems rather odd to think, or worse, say out loud.

"We've been order to defend the bridge to the last man," Lieutenant Case tells us as the platoon gathers around my M8 armored car. "We should be relieved in a few hours, so let's prepare defensive positions."

No one argues with the orders. None of the recon troopers in my platoon seems particularly surprised or upset by what we are being ordered to do. There can be no surrender, and going back across the bridge is out of the question, so we dig our foxholes in the ground and position our vehicles in the best defensive format we can. We have about 100 yards of open field to our front before the town of Regenstauf. A handful of abandoned houses are between us and the town.

Now we sit and wait. The waiting has always been the hardest part.

❊ ❊ ❊

We load our M8s and jeeps onto flatbed rail cars commandeered from the Germans at the rail yard in Regenstauf two days after crossing—and holding—the bridge. Two days before, though, we were counter-attacked three times before the infantry arrived.

During the last of the attacks, the Germans had pushed us back to the river, forcing the infantry to fight their way across the bridge. We gladly relinquished our position on the front lines and welcomed the break from action. The one-day break was our first in over a month as we watched the soldiers from the 14th Regiment take the town of Regenstauf.

After the vehicles are loaded onto rail cars, I grab a seat in a passenger car. Halby—he barely got a scratch when his jeep was hit—is sitting next to me. We're both hung over from drinking with Casey—I mean, Lieutenant Case—the night before. He always seems to have booze, but I don't know from where. He couldn't have brought that much with him.

Our next stop will be on the other side of the Danube River.

Now that we are on the bridge crossing the river, some of the guys start singing the old song, *Blue Danube*. I don't know the words, so I watch the river below as we cross. The Danube doesn't look very blue to me. It's green. And we're across in a matter of seconds—fifteen at most. After another ten miles on the railroad, the train stops and we drive our vehicles off the flatbeds and start for the city of Linz, 250 kilometers away.

We'll cross into Austria in a couple of days.

# Chapter 15

# WHAT YOU SEE

4 May, 1945:

You cannot un-see the things you see. We have seen plenty—enough of war to last a lifetime. But nothing can prepare us for what lies ahead.

I think we crossed into Austria two or three days ago. It seems like forever since we fought our last battle. That's how slow time is moving. We have been in combat for three months. Non-stop moving—moving deeper and deeper into the country we invaded. Most of our tough fighting was in April after we crossed the Rhine and were still in Germany. That's where we lost the most men.

Our enemy is a defeated enemy; we see signs of their defeat every day now. Abandoned tanks, trucks, and equipment litter the fields, and soldiers without weapons walk aimlessly toward us. We let them pass, elated that we don't have to kill them. Why haven't they all surrendered? We are mostly concerned with meeting our allies, the Russians, and not fighting the Germans.

The roadways have also been crowded with refugees for days; some are calling them displaced people. Most of them are nothing more than skin-and-bones, walking skeletons—scared, tired, hungry people aimlessly trekking down the road. Fleeing west from an enemy they have only heard about, towards an enemy they are seeking help from. The Americans are the better option as opposed to the Russians. The people are a combination of civilians and slave laborers. By now, we have all heard about what the Nazis have done. Other American units have seen it firsthand and it's impossible to stop the rumors. At first, none of us believed it. Now, we would believe anything.

We've reached the town of Lambach, fifty miles inside the Austrian border. From Lambach, we'll push forward another five kilometers to Gunskirchen. We're the farthest east of any

American unit. My 2nd Platoon has joined with 3rd Platoon; Lieutenant Burns of 3rd Platoon is in command. We're advancing into the town in two columns; my M8 is first in line of our column. My head is out of the open hatch on the front of the armored car. I prefer it this way when driving in a crowd. Daniel, next to me in the armored car, is also watching the road from his open hatch.

Daniel says something in his native language. He sounds shocked.

I can't look away, as much as I want to, I can't. I continue to move forward, barely making five miles an hour. The rest of our column of M8s and jeeps slowly follows. We stop in the town's central square. They crowd around us, hands outstretched, begging for food, water, or any type of comfort. Most have clothes that are torn, filthy rags on their frail emaciated bodies. Some have nothing, no clothing at all, their exposed skin stretched tightly over their bones. Most can walk, many are holding others upright. Some are pulled in carts by the strongest of them. There seems to be no end to the stream, hopelessly wandering into the town square.

One of them yells in heavily accented English. "We are coming from just up the road!"

Then another, "You must go to them! Go now!"

Lieutenant Burns orders our platoon to continue. He is staying to administer help to the hundreds who have wandered into town. We only drive another couple of kilometers. At first, I can't see the camp. The Nazis have carefully concealed it in the woods. I know I'm going in the right direction because the road is littered with bodies, lying where they fell; many of them are dead, the others too weak to continue. I start to smell the foulest smell imaginable; I know I'm close to something horrible. The smell is the only reason I find it. We have found the Gunskirchen Concentration Camp.

❋ ❋ ❋

The bodies, nothing more than skeletons, are stacked in rows or simply dumped into piles, all dead. Virtually nothing is left alive in this horrible place. The smell of death and dying is everywhere. I know it is fog that is covering the ground, but it seems that the smell itself has morphed into a vapor. I cover my mouth and nose with whatever piece of cloth I have, but still the smell permeates through the shield.

Me and the soldiers with me walk in silence amongst the dead. There must be thousands. The ones left alive are on the verge of death; the survivors strong enough to walk have already left. There is nothing we can do for them.

The ground is dirt and mud mixing with excrement. The buildings are gray. There are no trees within the barbed wire fences. There is no color here, like a black and white picture. I see the blackness all around me. I cannot explain what it is.

"Get on the radio and report what we've found," Lieutenant Case orders Daniel.

What we've found. How do you explain what we've found?

"We've been ordered to clear the main building," Case tells us.

I enter what we're describing as the main building. It's a large structure, built of brick with barred windows evenly spaced around its walls. Large chimneys are sticking out of its roof. The man ahead of me kicks in the door. Even with a towel wrapped around my mouth and nose, the smell is overwhelming. It is easily the most atrocious smell I have ever experienced.

What my eyes are seeing cannot be explained. If the smell is

231

horrible, the sight of the atrocities I am witnessing is ten times worse. The bodies of the dead are stacked from the floor to the ceiling. Stacks and piles of the dead are everywhere, dead people that are nothing more than skin and bones.

I see the ovens, filled with bones and ash, along the back wall. In another room, I see the gas chambers.

How will I ever forget what I am seeing?

There is an evil in this place that cannot be explained, a darkness, a blackness. I feel as though those of us who have seen this will be haunted by it for the rest of our lives. Somehow, I need to purge this blackness.

# Chapter 16

# SURRENDER

6 May, 1945:

I don't think our mission for today could be stated in more vague terms. We have been ordered to find the Russians, our allies. We do not know where they are, how far west they have advanced, or what to do when we find them.

Most of us are still in shock from what we saw at the concentration camp. We spent part of yesterday clearing the bodies from the buildings and doing whatever we could to help, but once the news of what we had found reached our division, other units arrived and replaced us. I could not have been happier, grateful to be leaving that place. I don't think I will ever be able to put what I saw behind me. How could the world we live in do such things? The stink is still attached to me and every other man in the platoon, making it difficult to forget. It's in my hair, coming out of my clothes, it's everywhere. We need to find a town to commandeer some houses and take baths—maybe that'll get the stench out of us.

We traveled about fifty kilometers yesterday, arriving at the Austrian town of Steyr on the western side of the Enns River. We found bathtubs. The roads are mostly clear, but the presence of German soldiers is still nerve-wracking. They're mostly in small groups and not armed, seemingly wandering towards what they believe is the safety of the American lines. Despite not having a clear mission, all of us troopers are glad to be doing something. The war is close to ending, and the German soldiers on the road not fighting are all the proof we need.

\*\*\*

The demarcation line between U.S. forces and the Soviet Red Army is the Enns River, across from the town of Steyr. We are not allowed to cross. But that's exactly what we are being ordered to do. We cross the river on a bridge an hour after sun-up and start heading east. No other units are traveling with us. We are alone, just three recon platoons. We have no extra supplies or extra gasoline, just what's in our gas tanks. The troop's headquarters stays behind in Steyr.

Once again, 2nd Platoon is combined with 3rd Platoon and Lieutenant Burns is in charge, and Lieutenant Case, riding in my armored car is second in command. We cross just north of Steyr. 1st Platoon under the command of Lieutenant Samuel crosses to the south. My guess is the recon troop's commander, Captain Johnson, doesn't want a new lieutenant leading a recon mission this late in the war and across the demarcation point; that's why he has my platoon under the command of Lieutenant Burns.

The roadway is narrow and the scenery is lush and green. Forests and open fields surround me. This far east, the road is now clogged with German Soldiers heading west, but they move out of our way and watch us move past, defeat in their eyes. I'm driving with my head out of the hatch; the German soldiers' stares, when they make eye contact, are unnerving. These men are supposed to be our enemy. I've spent the last few months trying to kill them, and them me. And how can any of us forget that this is the enemy responsible for what we saw at the concentration camp?

After only a couple of kilometers, 1st Platoon joins us in the town of Kleinraming. Our column of vehicles is nine armored cars and sixteen jeeps strong, with about eighty men. We stay together for another fourteen kilometers. I'm second in line behind a scout jeep as we approach the town of Neustift. I emerge out of a wooded area where the road bends southward; I see a group of German soldiers along the road and in a field adjacent to the road. There must be 400-500 men, most of them with rifles slung on their shoulder. If a battle breaks out, we don't stand a chance. The column slows down but doesn't stop.

Every recon trooper is at the ready; we'll fight if we must. The German soldiers are all standing, watching us. My armored car has passed the last of them, another twenty-two more vehicles in our column to go.

"Steady Siggy, keep us moving, steady," I hear Lieutenant Case saying.

There is very little radio communication. We know the standing order—don't start a fight if you don't have to, and don't fire first—there's no reason to communicate the order again. Instead, we simply drive past.

Then over the radio, I hear an armored car driver in the rear of the column say he has skidded off the road. Next, I hear that German soldiers are coming forward to help push the M8 back onto the road. The column stops and waits. Lieutenant Burns tells the Germans to keep moving west toward Steyr and to surrender to American authorities.

Once we reach Neustift, Burns orders Samuel and 1st Platoon to travel parallel and north of 2nd and 3rd Platoons toward the town of Waidhofen, another sixteen kilometers away. Our goal is to reach the Ypps River. Our mission remains to find the Russians. My group reaches the river by early afternoon. I start to wonder about gasoline. If we push farther across the Ypps, we may not be able to get back on the gas we'll have left.

Up ahead is a bridge over the Ypps River, but soldiers are on the bridge blocking the path. There's much congestion on the other side, also blocked by German SS troops. Hundreds of German soldiers are trying to cross, heading in our direction. We guardedly approach the SS roadblock. An officer dressed in camouflaged battle gear and with a StG 44 assault rifle at the ready comes to meet us. I've just started seeing this new weapon carried by German soldiers.

"There is no crossing the Ypps River," the SS captain says loud enough for me to hear. "We are under orders to stop all traffic. No German soldier will fire on you."

"We've been ordered to find the Soviets. Do you know where they might be?" Lieutenant Burns asks.

"They haven't reached the Ypps yet."

Lieutenant Burns has a few more words with the German officer before returning to his armored car.

The two platoons under his command pull off the road and re-group, gathering around the lieutenant.

"Looks like this is the end of the road," Burns says. "I'll contact 1st Platoon to hook up with them and start back toward Steyr. Doesn't sound like the Russians are close."

Daniel is in my armored car monitoring radio traffic from all three platoons. He intercepts radio communications coming from 1st Platoon after they reached the river just after we did but a couple of kilometers to our north. While stopped before a bridge over the Ypps, they are approached by several German soldiers who ask if they need help. Lieutenant Samuel asks if they have gas. The Germans agree to show them their gas dump if 1st Platoon doesn't report its whereabouts.

While gas is being retrieved, a German messenger riding a motorcycle approaches. Samuel calls Technician 5 Staudinger, a corporal, to act as an interpreter. Staudinger was born in this region of Austria and speaks perfect German. The messenger says he can show the Americans where gas is, but more importantly, he was sent to make contact. Samuel orders Staudinger to leave with the messenger and find out what he's talking about.

Over the course of the next couple of hours, Staudinger is brought to the Schloss Rothschild, a picturesque castle on the Ypps in the town of Waidhofen. Blindfolded, Staudinger is brought inside. He overhears a loud conversation, and when he hears that he should be shot and killed, he storms into the room.

238

Several high-ranking officers are present. Staudinger slams the table with both fists and in German demands the surrender of all forces in the area. The Generals are shocked by his perfect German, and his arrogance. Eventually, he is brought to the office of Lieutenant General Heinz Von Gyldenfeldt, Chief of Staff of German Army Group South.

Once convinced to surrender, Gyldenfeldt brings Colonel General Lother Von Rendulic, Commander of the Army Group, the largest German field command still in existence, into the conversation. The Army Group includes four field armies, each with 200,000 men, fully equipped and with thousands of tanks and vehicles. This massive group was feared to have retreated into the Austrian mountains where it could wage war for many more months and inflict a tremendous number of casualties on American soldiers trying to defeat them.

After a brief negotiation, it is agreed that General Rendulic and General Gyldenfeldt would be brought to 71st Division headquarters in Steyr where they would officially surrender the entire Army Group South to the division's generals. The tiny 71st Recon Troop—through the work of one man—had secured the surrender of over 800,000 men without a shot fired. Rendulic signed the Articles of Unconditional Surrender at 1800 hours, 7 May, 1945.

Meanwhile, Lieutenant Samuel brought his platoon north and re-connected with Lieutenant Burns in the town of Waidhofen. Once the recon troop was assembled, we proceeded to the castle where Corporal Staudinger had negotiated the surrender.

I spend the night at a castle in Austria. In the middle of warming up my C-Ration on a gas-flame heater, much to the amazement of our new German friends, soldier-waiters start bringing us beef and potato stew from the castle's kitchen. I reluctantly accept the gesture but feel bad eating in front of German soldiers. They were not so lucky, they received no such treatment from their officers.

❀ ❀ ❀

7 May, 1945:

Events of the last couple of days have been a whirlwind. Yesterday we reached the Ypps River in Austria, but German SS troops wouldn't allow passage across the bridge. We reluctantly yielded to them. It was an easy decision, as we were outnumbered at least a hundred to one. There are literally thousands of German soldiers on the roads. Some are armed, some look ready to fight, but many others are weaponless and just wandering in large groups.

The end of the war is here; it may not yet be official, but there is little fight left in the enemy. But still we are on edge, in a constant state of stress. The war may be ending, or even over, but all it would take for the shooting to start would be the first shot fired. One of the only things I remember about American history from school was the start of the Revolutionary War. A single shot was fired in the village commons in the town of Lexington, Massachusetts; a war erupted as the result.

Today, we are able the cross the same bridge we tried to cross yesterday. The SS have left the area, probably abandoning their positions during the night. The flow of German soldiers has also been reduced to a trickle. They are still on the roads, just not as numerous. Our mission is the same as yesterday—find the advance elements of the Soviet Red Army. My platoon crosses the Ypps and speeds through the old streets of Waidhofen, Austria. This is the second day in a row that the recon troop is advancing alone without any support. We are the farthest east of any American forces, and it is a stretch to call us much of a force. My platoon has all of thirty men and nine vehicles. By

240

now, after over three months, we are used to the feelings of isolation. I know I am.

I'm driving my M8 south, southeast on a two-lane road, second in the line of vehicles. On my right are thick woods, to the left are fields and farmland. An occasional farmhouse dots the landscape. I'm driving with my head out of the hatch, as is our radioman, Daniel. There is a tension in the air that I can't explain, as if the troopers know something is going to happen today. My eyes are constantly scanning the road and terrain ahead, my head acting as if on a swivel. We are about five miles out of Waidhofen before we pass through a small village. Townspeople are going about their business, barely acknowledging our passing. They know the long, hard war is finally over.

Five more miles deeper into the Austrian countryside, another village appears on the horizon. The scenery is magnificent; snowcapped mountains surround us as we press on through a valley. Our column slows to a stop just before the village. The lead scout jeep has spotted vehicle movement. The platoon continues toward the town at a snail's pace, and then as if dropped out of the sky in front of the lead jeep, a motorcycle appears. The soldier does not appear to be German. He has a red star on his cap. He is wearing an oversized, muted, green trench coat. He is filthy and looks exhausted, but he's smiling ear to ear. I have never seen the type of submachine gun he has across his back. I cannot understand the words he is shouting, but he doesn't sound angry. On the contrary, he seems overjoyed.

After a few minutes of deliberation, we follow this strange man into the village. A small force of men and machines is hastily assembling to our front. I see the hammer and sickle of the Soviet flag. We have stumbled upon our Russian allies. The vehicles of 2nd Platoon, 71st Recon Troop fan out in the village square facing the spread-out vehicles of the Red Army.

We are at an impasse. Neither side knows what to do, unsure how to react. A man in what appears to be an officer's uniform jumps off the turret of a Russian armored car. His arms are spread wide, and his head is nodding up and down as if to tell us everything is all right.

"Comrades!" he yells. "We are Soviet Red Army," he continues in broken English.

He is joined by several more men. I look around at the American fighting machines and the warriors I have lived with side by side for the last year, and almost as one, we start whooping and hollering. Men all around me are jumping off gun turrets and out of jeeps. I climb up and through the turret of my armored car and join the celebration. We are hugging each other; some of the Russians are kissing both sides of our faces. I find myself in the embrace of a Russian soldier. I offer him a cigarette. I speak no Russian and his English is limited, but he manages, "Thank you." I light his cigarette and one for myself. I pull out a Hersey's chocolate bar and give it to him. He pulls out a bottle of vodka.

"Vodka, my friend," he says. "We toast."

He drains several ounces and passes me the bottle. I do likewise. I pull out my C-Ration container and open a can of prepared meat. I offer my new friend the can. His eyes go wide. He grabs the can and practically drinks its contents, he is gobbling the food so fast.

"Fish, fish, fish," he says, "All we eat is fish, fish, fish. Every day, fish."

An impromptu feast is prepared. Tables and chairs from the surrounding homes are brought out to the town square. The Americans contribute whatever rations we have, including our stashes of special treats, like eggs, sausages, or fresh meat. The Russians supply fish. And plenty of vodka. It seems I'm forever getting the taste of vodka. I'm willing to admit that the

Russian vodka is the best I've ever had.

We are ordered to stay the night in the Austrian town, with our new friends and await orders for the next day.

❊ ❊ ❊

8 May, 1945:

The announcement of Germany's surrender is made, effective at just before midnight. Although the war is officially over, I'll wait until tonight to celebrate. Of course, I'm yelling and whooping it up with the soldiers near me, and even hugging a few, but it doesn't seem like the war has ended.

Once things quiet down, my platoon is ordered to re-cross the Ypps River and head west, back to the Enns River and the city of Steyr. We're still armed to the teeth and ready for anything, and we're in enemy territory as far as we are concerned. It's ludicrous to think every German soldier has surrendered, especially the SS.

I have gone from Fort Riley to the surrender of Germany in two and a half years—from a cocky, confident eighteen-year-old who thought of himself as a man to a twenty-one-year-old who is someone I'm not sure I know. I don't know what I am besides a soldier who has seen unspeakable things, a soldier who has survived. And I'm only twenty-one. I do not know where I'll be or what I'll be doing in a year, or two years, or five years. Somehow, I'll have to put this behind me.

Luckily, Lieutenant Case has asked me to join him in finding his brother, an officer in the 80th Infantry Division. We had been advancing with the 80th on our flank for the last two weeks; our sectors of control border each other.

"Siggy, you wanna take a ride with me?" Lieutenant Case asks. "My brother, I told you about him, he's only ten or so miles away. I just got hold of him on the radio."

"You want me to find us a jeep?"

"You get the jeep, I'll bring the booze."

I still don't know how he always has booze. For our trip to meet his brother, Casey brings a single malt scotch and a bottle of bourbon.

"How do you get the booze, Casey?" I ask as we pull out of our troop's area. The roads are jammed with partying soldiers.

"Traded a guy in supply some war souvenirs I had. A German Luger got us the scotch and a Nazi flag I grabbed yesterday got the bourbon. My brother's a bourbon man."

❖ ❖ ❖

The tears in my eyes at one minute before midnight must be because I'm drunk. The war is over. I look over at my friend Casey. He's hugging his brother, rocking back and forth. I miss my brothers. I miss my little sisters. I wish I could hug them, celebrate with them.

Lieutenant Case walks to me with his arms extended. "Siggy, thank you," he says. "Thank you for taking care of me."

"We took care of each other," I say.

"No, Siggy, when I showed up, I didn't know a thing. You kept me alive. I'll never forget that."

He hugs me and we clink our bottles together in a toast. I can't explain the emotions I feel—elation, but also a feeling of satisfaction. I've survived and I helped keep another man alive. When I think back at the dangers Lieutenant Case faced

244

when he arrived, knowing as I did, that the three men who led our platoon before him were killed, I do feel justified in my effort to keep him alive. I'm not sure what intervention put us together, but I'm glad it did. I'm glad Casey fought to get me in his armored car, glad he fought to get me my old job back. Yes, I feel satisfied, and very happy. And now, I'm going to get drunk with my friend and his brother.

# Chapter 17

# HOME

It's early February 1946. It's cold and windy, and I find myself standing on a street corner on Baltimore Avenue in the middle of The Block. My war has been officially over since May of last year, but that doesn't mean these past months have been easy; in many ways, I'm still fighting the war. I wake up screaming from nightmares often enough. Although I've been gone for three and a half years, nothing seems to have changed; all around me people are hustling from one place to another on the crowded streets.

I have changed. When I left for the war in 1942, I was a cocky eighteen-year-old kid who was far from innocent. At least I thought I was far from innocent. Now, as I stand on the all-too-familiar streets of Baltimore, I'm almost twenty-two. I'm not so cocky anymore. I can't help but feel lucky—lucky to have survived—but also old and a bit used-up. I have no idea what I want to do today, or tomorrow, or for the rest of my life for that matter.

Right now, I'm content to just stand here and watch. I'm not watching anything or anyone. I'm just watching the people going about their business. I've been gone for so long I doubt anyone even notices or recognizes me. There are lots of guys wearing their uniforms. I'm just one of many. One of the thousands of returning GIs and sailors wondering what they're going to do next. I could always go back to work for my uncle, if he has my old job available. And I'm sure Beans will take me back, but do I want to work for the Mob after all this time? When I became part of the Mob family when I was fourteen, was it really for life?

I arrived back in the States three days ago after spending many months of occupation duty in Austria and Germany. Two destroyed countries inhabited by ruined people. So much destruction and suffering, I can't imagine the amount of time it will take to fix all that is broken, if there is enough time. The most exciting thing that happened to me during the occupation was guarding some of the vast treasures the Nazis had stolen from its neighbors during their reign of terror. Me and the men from my platoon were ordered to guard crates full of priceless works of art—everything from paintings to sculptures to precious metals to millions of dollars in currency. For a while, I guarded the prisoner pens: fenced-in holding areas for German soldiers. They begged constantly to be released, to be allowed to go home to their families. I was powerless to help.

I spent a lot of time drinking in the bars.

All of us in the platoon were relieved when Japan surrendered in August of '45. There was a good chance we'd get reassigned and shipped to the Pacific to fight. My pals, Halby and Hog Jaw, got discharged and sent home a couple of months before me. We all promised to look each other up once we got settled back home. It probably won't happen. It's funny to think about how much time we spent together, and went through so much, only to shake hands and say goodbye, claiming, "Look me up when you get home." It was like the last two years with them never happened.

Three days ago, I was walking down a gangplank off a giant transport ship full of returning GIs. Tens of thousands of servicemen returning home. Most of the men I was with have no clue what they're going to do. Spend some time recovering from our experiences during the war, no doubt.

I returned to America at Fort Meade, just outside of Baltimore, where I spent a couple of days processing out of the Army. A friendly sergeant, upon giving me my discharge papers, suggested I take a few days to decide if I wanted to re-up in the Army. He said lots of the returning GIs were doing it. I'm done with the Army; I don't need three days to decide.

Standing on this street corner on The Block, dressed in my Army uniform full of ribbons after more than three years of service, I'm contemplating what to do and where to go. The reality is I have nothing to do, and no one is ordering me to do anything. Likewise, I have nowhere in particular to go. I'm about to make my move to destinations unknown when I hear a shout from across the busy, crowded street. I think I hear the word funeral. I scan the faces of strangers. I see the face of a large man. I instantly recognize him as it comes into focus.

"Funeral," he yells again. "Over here!" He's smiling from ear to ear and waving his arms over his head. "As I live and breathe!" he shouts. "It's Funeral—it's my boy, Funeral, back home from the war!"

I could easily turn and walk away. I could ignore him, acting like he had the wrong guy, but I wave back and fake a smile. I'm not exactly overjoyed to see Beans waving to me. I had hoped for a couple of days of peace before deciding what to do next with my life. Now, I'll have to decide much quicker—or has a decision already been made about my future without my consent?

"Hi Beans," I say, "Good to see you."

He bear-hugs me and slaps my back a few times.

"Good to see me!" he bellows, "Is that all you've got to say? I'll make a few calls and get all of the boys together at the Two O'Clock for a celebration."

I'm now a reluctant passenger on the run-away train that is Beans Galbo. "Sounds great, Beans."

"How long you been home, kid?" he asks as we walk toward the Two O'Clock Club, his big arm around my shoulder.

"Just pulled into town."

"And you didn't call to tell us you were coming?"

"I haven't called anyone, not even my family."

"Wanted to surprise everyone, that's just like you, Funeral. Always with the surprises."

The biggest surprise for me is that my family moved out of Little Italy, out of the house I grew up in. They sold the house to a family named Monaco when I was overseas, and they are now living on Collington Avenue about five miles away. I'll head to the new home after seeing the old gang.

Twenty minutes later, there's a crowd of people around me shaking my hand, asking questions and handing me drinks. Seeing my friends for the first time in so long has me a little apprehensive. Will they be the same? I wonder how they've changed. My apprehension and nervousness disappears the second I lay eyes on Tony Mazzotti, my friend we call Naughty. He pulls me out of the crowd and shakes my hand. We haven't seen each other since 1943 when I was still in the Horse Cavalry and spent a few days home while on leave.

"You haven't changed a bit," he says. "Except for the fancy uniform."

"Neither have you. Except for a few extra pounds," I say as I fake a punch to the gut and then pull him into a hug.

"Where's Thrill?" I ask.

"He'll be here any minute," Naughty says. His demeanor then turns serious. "Tell me what it was like, Funeral."

"What do you mean, Naughty, the war?" I ask, knowing full well that's exactly what he means, but I have no idea how to answer. I'm stalling for time.

"Yes, the war, Funeral. What was the war like?"

"It wasn't too bad," I say. "I was lucky, I got over there when it was almost over."

"You must have done something," he says.

I have no idea how to answer him. "I'll tell you over some beers sometime. Come on, I see Thrill coming in. I wanna surprise him."

252

I've tried to forget some of the things I saw, but I can't stop the nightmares. I don't think I'll be able to tell my friends the things we did and what I saw. Of course, Thrill asks the same questions. Neither of my friends went to war; I understand their curiosity, but I don't think I can tell them the truth.

"This one time," I finally answer, "Me and Halby and Hog Jaw—they're a couple of the guys—liberated a vodka distillery. I drank vodka out of my helmet all night and ended up passed out in some guy's tank. Was sick for days afterwards."

"Great story, Funeral, but what about combat? Tell us what combat was like. Were you afraid?"

"Oh, it wasn't too bad and I never was afraid, honest. It was only bad when the bullets started pinging off my armored car. That's what I did, I drove an armored car. Or when the artillery started falling on you," I say. "But we usually ran from trouble."

I can't get the images out of my head, but I can't bring myself to tell them about the men I saw get killed. Or the men we killed. And certainly, not about the concentration camp we liberated. I'm starting to sweat despite the cool temperature just as Beans pulls me back to the bar and into the crowd, saving me from more questions I'd rather not answer.

"Funeral, how about you, Thrill, and Naughty start up as a team again? Say tomorrow night?" Beans asks.

But he's really telling me, not asking.

"Can I have at least a few days back home before I decide what I'm gonna do?" I answer.

"Come on, Funeral, you don't need a few days. Of course, you're gonna start up where you left off," he says. "How long were you gone, anyway? It seems like yesterday we were throwing you a going-away party."

"I was gone for three and half years." I still can't believe it myself. I left for Fort Riley in October 1942. It's now February 1946.

He ignores my answer and starts introducing me to some of the new guys in his crew. There are many new faces, tough-looking guys. He tells me that he's got someone who runs the enforcers—the watchers—working for him. A guy named Jimmy, that's who I'll be answering to. My future already decided. Turns out that Beans, Fish, and Bats are now made men. They have lots of guys answering to them.

"As much as I like the uniform and all the decorations, you'll have to dress better tomorrow night. Get a new suit with all the money the Army paid you," Beans says.

I want to tell him that I've not decided if I'll be coming back.

※ ※ ※

The walk up to North Collington and my parents' new house is long and cold. But it's exactly what I need after Beans and the guys showered me with questions and drinks. I knew it would be hard for me to talk about the war, especially with people who were not there. Other vets, no problem; we all saw pretty much the same thing. All the bodies, some dead, some dying, some wishing they were dead, but somehow hanging on. And the friends you saw die right in front of you. I think it's best to keep this stuff inside.

I was surprised to find out that Mrs. Russell had moved away. I was disappointed that all she left me was a letter. She reminded me about a talk we had one night a long time ago about not ending up spending the rest of my life in a place like The Block. *I'm too good for that type of life*, she wrote. But what else do I have? I have a bunch of people I've known all my life welcoming me back. Not only back home after having been away for a long time, but welcoming me back into the life I left as if no time had passed at all. How do I know Mrs. Russell is right about me? Why am I too good for The Block? She also mentioned in her letter that I need to find myself a good girl to take care of me, not one of the girls who works on The Block.

Up ahead, I see the house my parents moved to while I was gone. It's not all that different from the house they left. It's bigger, and the street is wider, and it's a lot busier, but it's still just another row-house in another part of town. As I get closer, I hear a commotion coming from inside.

I burst through the front door of the house on Collington and there he is, beating my mother. He hasn't changed. After all this time away, I come home to this? I grab him by the collar of his shirt with both hands and fling him across the room. I take two steps and stand over him. I grab the front of his shirt and pull him to his feet and throw him into a nearby wall. He bounces off the wall and staggers towards me, bent over. I stand him up with my left hand, and while holding him upright, I punch him a couple of times in the face. There's blood dripping on the floor. I'm in a rage; my vision goes black for a split second. I've seen and done too much while in the Army. I won't stand for this any longer.

I remember all those times as a kid, my father throwing me across a room, hitting me. Now, the roles have been reversed; I'm the one with the power.

I hear my mother screaming at me to leave him alone, not to kill him. She's pulling on my back as I'm leaning over him, bent at the waist, punching him. I drop him to the floor. I run my fingers through my hair and start to regain my composure. I walk past my mother, into the kitchen, and pull a knife out of a drawer. I yank my father back to his feet and prop him against a wall. I put the knife to his throat.

"If you ever lay a hand on my mother again, I'll kill you."

I nick his neck and a small bead of blood appears. I will not hesitate to kill him the next time.

My mother is behind me wailing and crying. "He doesn't mean it, Paul!" she's howling. "Leave him alone!"

I don't care if he does or doesn't mean what he's doing, he's been warned; there will be no next time. But I can't figure out why she's defending him. I drop him and the knife and leave.

What a homecoming.

Maybe I should have told them to expect me today. I'm heading back to The Block to tell Beans that I don't need a day or two to decide. I want my old job back. And I want to start right away.

❖ ❖ ❖

"Tell me about this new guy, Jimmy," I ask Thrill.

"Jimmy Cagliano? He's been around for about a year. Came down from New York."

"Tell me about him. What do I need to know?"

"He's not Beans, that's for sure."

"Come on Thrill, what's that supposed to mean?"

"He comes on a little strong, if you know what I mean," Thrill says. "Out to prove he's a tough guy."

"We don't answer to Beans anymore?" I ask. "Just because he's a made man now?"

"Oh no, Beans still calls the shots. Jimmy is like the floor manager."

I don't think I'm gonna like working for Jimmy Cagliano. His philosophy is to hit first and ask questions later. This is the opposite of how we handled our business before I left. We tried to talk the guy down first, only resorting to violence if we had to. My job will be the same as before—watch out for the girls, especially when they take their tricks upstairs to the private rooms. The dreaded red light all over again.

I find it rather fascinating that the three of us are picking up right where we left off. No matter the amount of time apart, we are like brothers, naturally fitting back together like no time has passed at all.

Our relationship may not have changed, but I have come to realize that The Block certainly has. It's rowdier, seedier, and different in ways I can see right away—even the people here seem different. Thrill warns me before we start our shift to be on my toes always, he also gives me an iron rod coated with a thin layer of rubber to carry. The handle has a leather strap attached.

"Let me show you. You put your hand through the strap and let the pipe hang from your wrist," he tells me. "You'll learn how to spin it soon enough."

"Never needed something like this before," I say.

"You'll be glad you have it."

"It's changed a lot down here in four years."

"It has, Funeral, it sure has."

America is no longer the innocent, isolated place it was before the war. The war seems to have brought out many things in people, and much is not good. An entire generation of men is coming home after going to war. We saw a lot of friends get killed, and we did our share of killing, too. It will be impossible to forget. Most are leaving the Army, or the Marines, or the Navy, and are now back home looking for work. Many are

257

competing for jobs they left to go fight, thinking they would return home to the same job—only to find it occupied. There is certainly an abundance of tough men on The Block. And it's a heck of a lot more crowded here, too.

On my first night back on the job at the Two O'Clock Club, I use my pipe—that's what I call my rubber-encased iron rod—three times on men who wouldn't leave the girls alone. The Block may have become rougher and raunchier, but I've also become angrier and quicker to fight. I no longer have the soft side I had before the war. That's what I've become, what the war has made me. I guess I've become exactly what The Block needs. While I was away in the Army, I never had a fist fight with another man because of anger. It's as if I put my fists away for four years in a box and locked it. Now, back on The Block, I've unlocked the box.

"Where's Bones Sullivan? I expected him to get promoted," I say.

"You must not have heard," Thrill answers. "He got drafted after you left in late '43 I think. Got sent over to fight the Japs. Was killed on Okinawa."

"I would have thought he was too old. Or could have gotten himself out somehow," I say. "Too bad he wasn't one of the lucky ones who made it alive."

I know it's not much, but that's how I feel; he wasn't one of the lucky ones. Knowing one more person who was killed in the war has very little effect on me. I didn't agonize over the people I saw get killed right in front of me. I guess I'll miss Bones Sullivan, he was the best head-basher I ever saw.

❋ ❋ ❋

"So, you're *the* Funeral," Jimmy Cagliano says to me my first night, even though he met me the day before at Beans' impromptu party. "I'm not much for nicknames," he adds.

"Yes," I reply. "I'm called Funeral. Remember, we met yesterday?" I don't bother to add that I've had the nickname since I was eight.

"Yeah, yeah, right. Yesterday," he says. "Just back from the Army, right."

I know what he's doing. He's putting himself in the position of power, like he's in charge and I'm inconsequential, not important to him.

"That's right, just back from the Army. You can call me Paul, Paulie, or Funeral."

"What'd ya do in the Army?"

"Stay alive," I say and walk away.

No, I'm not going to like working for this Goomba. That's a Mob word, usually used as an adjective for respect, but not always. In this case, not so much. He's one of the reasons I'm forced to use my pipe. The clientele have become accustomed to aggressive repercussions.

❖❖❖

*I'm crawling on my hands and knees away, but the bodies are everywhere, all around me. They're moaning, their expressionless eyes are staring at me. They're clawing at me with fingers of bone. I try to push them away, but they keep coming, surrounding me. I'm piling the bodies on top of each other. The stack is getting taller and taller. I'm floating in the air. The dead bodies are floating with me. Clawing at me. Scratching me. I'm on the ground, running, but I'm not moving. The bodies are all around me. They're covering me. I can't breathe. I'm screaming.*

I wake up screaming and panting, covered in sweat. The same damned nightmare.

❋ ❋ ❋

I can't believe the boys kept the Funeralmobile running. She drives perfect, although I think I'll be in the market for a new car. An old hearse may have been a great car for a teenager nicknamed Funeral, but it doesn't suit a man. Nevertheless, I need a way to get to the stables. I have a couple of old friends I need to see.

It's been over three weeks since my return. I feel bad that I haven't made this trip sooner. I'm watching a frail old man slowly, methodically, going about his business, things he's done thousands of times. He abruptly stops in his tracks. He turns around. We stare at each other for a few seconds as the recognition sets in for him. I walk toward the man I met twelve years before, and a smile appears on my face. Upon reaching him, I throw my arms around his narrow shoulders and pull him into a hug.

"Jack," I say.

"Paulie," he replies.

And we hug again. I hear him sobbing. I have a tear in my eye.

"It's good to see you."

"How long have you been back?"

"Just got in town," I say, not wanting him to know I waited this long to see him.

"Let me look at you," he says as he pushes away from me, but still holding my elbows. "You look good, Paulie. You look all grown up."

"How are you doing, Jack?" I can't help but notice how much he's aged. Right on cue, he coughs a phlegmy cough.

"Oh, not so bad for an old man," he says. "Sorry I never wrote you."

"It's all right, Jack. I didn't expect many letters," I reply. The men with girls back home were the ones who got all the mail.

"Well, sorry anyway."

"You're still tending to the horses? Taking care of Suzy?" This is my way of finding out if Suzy is still alive. It's been about four years since I've seen her, and she was old when I left. "I don't see her around."

"Suzy?" He says. "She's doing fine. Stays in the stables most of the time now, though. Where I should be," he adds.

"Can I see her?"

"Sure, of course you can. Come on, follow me."

We walk the fifty or so yards to the stable where my favorite horse lives. "You got an apple for her?" Jack asks as we enter.

"Sure do," I reply.

When Suzy recognizes me, she brays and whinnies and bounces on her front hooves. It reminds me of being ten.

"Can I take her for a ride?"

"I'm sure she'll love it."

Together we saddle her and walk her to the fenced pasture. I hop onto her back and gently nudge her. She responds with a gallop. I hear old Jack O'Donovan let out a hoot and a howl. I'm once again propelled back in time.

"I've missed you, my beautiful girl," I say as I rub her muzzle.

❀ ❀ ❀

"Do you want a beer?" Jack asks after my ride.

"You bet I do. We've got some catching up to do."

"Not much catching up as far as I'm concerned. All I've done since you left was get old."

"You look great, Jack, haven't changed a bit," I say.

"Ha," he snorts. "You never could lie, Paulie."

"Well, maybe a little older."

"Enough about me. You're the interesting subject around here. You've been all over the country, the world, fought in a war," Jack says. "You're the one who needs to do the filling-in."

"Yeah, I guess so," I say, but pause. I'm thinking about what to tell him.

"I'm sorry, Paulie, I didn't mean to pry. You don't have to tell me anything."

"But I want to, Jack. I need to talk to someone. I guess that's why I came here today."

We are silent again, sipping our beers. Not being able to talk to the people on The Block, with my friends, or with my family has left me feeling anxious and uneasy, like I'm carrying a burden.

"I guess I was lucky, I didn't get over there until it was almost over," I tell my friend. "Did you know I trained for over two years to fight for less than four months? I got to France last February. Saw my first real combat in March."

"I bet that four months was plenty."

"It was, Jack. It was."

"Like I said, you don't need to talk about it."

But I cut him short with a wave of my hand. "I saw one of their concentration camps, Jack. We were the first ones there. I don't even know how to describe the place or the smell, what it smelled like. I'll never forget it as long as I live. Then there's what we saw."

"I've seen the pictures. Awful enough seeing the pictures. I can't imagine firsthand, up close like you did."

"Bodies everywhere. Starved to death, and just left on the ground. And the ovens." A cold shiver goes through my body.

We're both silent again. This is the first time I've spoken about Gunskirchen. I couldn't bring myself to tell him the most horrific details. There is no vantage point for someone who has not seen the horror I saw to relate. I eventually tell Jack about my time as a mortar jeep driver and an M8 driver. I tell him about Lieutenant Gibb getting shot under the eye and me holding his head, and what he meant to me, but that I didn't feel anything after he died. I leave out the gory details of the deaths of the other men I served with. The hardest part of my story, as hard as Gunskirchen, is telling my friend about the people I killed, or was a part of killing. I still see the faces of the five young German soldiers we killed on the street after crossing the Rhine.

"But I was never afraid, Jack. That's probably the strangest thing of all. I was never afraid of dying."

"You probably were but didn't realize it," Jack says.

Maybe he's right, I don't know. Then I couldn't help myself, I had to share my vodka-out-of-the-helmet escapade. That made both of us laugh. I'm glad I could talk to someone about the concentration camp. He'll never be able to fully understand what we saw, but it's a start for me, getting it off my chest.

❋ ❋ ❋

"I'm sorry, Paulie, but I don't have your old job for you," Uncle Marco tells me.

I wait almost a month before I approach my uncle about my old job. He's had the position filled for years and can't let the person go. Plus, he'd have to create an entirely new and different job if he were to hire me. I didn't expect him to do that.

"But I can get you in at Motor Vehicles," he adds.

"Do you really think you can, Uncle Marco?" I ask.

"I know everyone there, Paulie. And most owe me a favor. I'll put out the word that my nephew just back from the war needs a job. They're always looking for vets."

"Thanks, Uncle Marco, I knew I could count on you."

"When it's time for me to retire, we'll talk about you taking over the business," Uncle Marco adds. "I wouldn't trust it to anyone else."

Two days later I'm being interviewed to be a driving instructor. And I'm hired on the spot.

# Chapter 18

# MARY

"**Y**ou work at Motor Vehicles, right? I've seen you there."

I know she does. I've been watching her for the past couple of weeks. And I see her out dancing most weekends. I know that she's noticed me, too. We've caught each other's eye more than once.

"Yes, I work there," she answers.

"Me, too. I'm a driving instructor," I say.

"Oh, really?"

"What about you? What do you do?"

"I work at the registration counter."

"Are you here with someone? Do you want to dance?" I ask.

"I'm here with my date."

I know the guy she's with. He's from the neighborhood, named Eddie. I don't think they're serious.

"Well," I say, "do you want to dance?"

"I probably shouldn't."

"Okay. I'll see you at work, then. Maybe Monday?"

I walk away from her without telling her my name, but I suspect she knows it. I know hers—it's Mary Stefano. I also know that someday soon she'll say yes when I ask her to dance.

❄❄❄

"Hi Mary," I say the following Monday. I've been waiting for her by the break room. I know her schedule; I know when she takes her lunch break. "You wanna eat lunch together?"

She blushes and looks around. I wait for her answer in silence. Finally, she says, "Okay, I guess so."

"Great," I say. "Come on, I'll get us a table. Oh, and my name's Paul Signori."

She packs her lunch; I buy mine at the counter. She sits at the table and waits for me to return before she starts eating. This young lady is exactly who Mrs. Russell was telling me about all those years ago. She's a nice girl—doesn't curse, is pretty, sweet, from a good family...perfect. She is exactly what I'm looking for. Forget about saying yes to dancing, I'm going to marry her someday.

❊❊❊

*Of course, I know who Paulie Signori is. Everyone knows him. He's a guy from around the neighborhood and the dance halls, and he's always fighting. But I think he's nice, and he's very handsome. I didn't always think that, though. I remember seeing a picture of him when I was in the eighth grade. It was hanging in a photography shop next to Minnie's Soda Fountain. Me and my friend Jackie would go to the soda shop practically every day. He was in his Army uniform. Jackie thought he was handsome. I liked the guy in the photo next to Paul. And now, all these years later, he's asking me to dance. I don't think he has a girlfriend. My boyfriend, if you can call him that, is Eddie Mazzilli. We're not that serious. At least I don't consider us serious. He's more like a friend I like to go dancing with. I hope Paul asks me to dance again next time I see him out. I'll say yes.*

❊❊❊

"I don't like the look of those guys, Funeral," Naughty says.

"Me neither," I agree.

268

This is our dance hall, our turf. Keith's Roof, the roof-top above Keith's Theater, has been our hang-out since before the war. Whenever we had a night off from the clubs, we'd go. It's in downtown Baltimore, but we consider it ours. We know pretty much everyone who comes here and a couple new faces isn't a problem. But when six or seven guys we don't know show up, there's always a problem, and usually a fight. I guess we don't like the competition.

"How many of 'em?" Thrill asks.

"I count seven," I answer. "What do ya wanna do?"

"Finish my beer first," he says.

We nod our agreement and chug our beers.

"Finished?" I ask.

But before anyone answers, I watch as one of them approaches Mary. He says something; Mary blushes and shakes her head no. Her boyfriend Eddie looks away. He's not much of a tough guy. Two of his friends join him, and now all three of them are laughing. One of them puts his hand on Mary's shoulder.

"I think she told you get lost," I say to the one who's touching her after I make a bee-line to Mary's side.

"I think you got it wrong. You're the one who needs to get lost."

My words-to-punch ratio is extremely low. I clobber the guy in the jaw. I hear it crack. He drops to the floor. The rest of his gang rushes over; we miscounted, there's nine of them. Minus the guy knocked-out on the floor. Thrill and Naughty are by my side, but we're surrounded by eight foes. We assume our back-to-back-to-back fighting stance, like Killer Marino taught us all those years ago and perfected by many times of use.

"Let's get this done," Naughty says as he grabs the nearest guy.

A free-for-all fight has begun. I'm grabbing and punching like a crazy man; so are my friends. We soon narrow the odds down to five against three. Brawls like this usually go in one of two directions. The most common is after me and my two friends have taken a few combatants out, the others back away and want nothing else to do with us. This is the preferable outcome. The other direction is unfortunately the way this fight is going. The remaining five are not giving up. On the contrary, they're coming at us full force. I see two guys pouncing on Naughty as he gets separated from me and Thrill.

"Thrill, get to Naughty!" I shout.

I grab a guy who's punching it out with Thrill and slam his face into the floor. Another one jumps on my back, as does another. But this frees up Thrill. He can now get to Naughty. I struggle to get to my feet. No one wants to be on the floor in the middle of a fight. Just as I regain my stance, a chair comes flying at me. I'm hit in the forearm and instantly can't close my hand. A wave of pain shoots up my arm all the way to my shoulder. Luckily, by this time, the fight has finally gone out of the ones who are still on their feet. They gather their friends off the floor and head for the exit. Naughty shouts something sarcastic at them as they file out the door.

"Thanks for coming!" he yells.

The national anthem starts playing. This signifies that the fight is over.

"I think I broke my arm," I say to Thrill.

"Let me see," he says as he takes hold of my wrist. I howl in pain.

"Yeah, I'd say it's broken. You need to get to the hospital," Thrill says in a matter-of-fact way.

"Thanks, Thrill, I never would have figured it out on my own."

270

"Paulie, are you all right?" Mary says as she walks up to me. She dabs at the blood on my face with a cloth.

"Mary, do you think you could get Eddie to drive me to the hospital? My arm's broke."

Shortly after the fight at Keith's Roof, me and Mary start dating.

❋ ❋ ❋

"Why doesn't your father like me?"

"He doesn't know you, Paul. Give him a chance to get to know you and I'm sure he'll like you," Mary says.

"Every time I come over, he turns his back on me," I say. "He won't even acknowledge I'm there."

"Give it time," Mary says.

*My father doesn't like him because he thinks he's no good. He thinks he's a bad influence. I know he's got a reputation, but once you get to know him, Paul Signori is a good man. My father likes Eddie because he's safe. Eddie is always nice and polite, never does or says anything wrong. But he's not what I'm looking for. He might be perfect for my father, but not for me.*

"Why don't you come over tonight before we go out? My father will be home. You two can talk."

I show up a half-hour early to pick Mary up. Her father is sitting at the kitchen table. He ignores me as I walk into the kitchen, like usual. He's reading the horse betting sheets, making notes on the racing forms. Here's my in. Something I know about—horse racing. Mary's father is a gambler; I didn't know that.

"Mr. Stefano," I say, "I've got a tip from the bookmakers on The Block about a race in California. You interested?"

He puts down his paper and takes off his glasses. He stares at me without saying a word.

"First race at Santa Anita. Lucky Stars to win."

He puts his glasses back on and scans his sheet.

"Lucky Stars is a ten-to-one underdog," he says.

"He's gonna win by five lengths." I say it with such confidence and without breaking his stare, that he should know it's going to happen—or better yet, has already happened.

Every once in while, a sure thing comes into the bookies. Santa Anita is in Los Angeles, three hours behind us. The first race has already gone off, and finished, but the results have not been posted—yet. They'll be posted in about twenty minutes. I got the tip just before I left the Two O'Clock Club, ten minutes ago. This is the only race that gets delayed in posting. No reason why, it just happens, occasionally, like I said. I check my watch.

"But you have less than twenty minutes to get your bet in," I add.

I can practically see the wheels spinning in his head. He continues to stare at me, finally putting his glasses back on as he goes back to studying the sheets.

"You ready to go, Paul?" Mary says as she comes into the kitchen. "Bye, Daddy."

Mr. Stefano grunts something and waves.

"What did you and my dad talk about?"

"Horse racing," I say.

***

"I like that new boyfriend of yours, Mary," my dad says. "When's he coming by again?"

"Really? Suddenly you like him?"

"He's grown on me."

"Well, he'll be here any minute."

"It's Paul, right?" Mr. Stefano asks when I walk into the kitchen.

"Yes, sir, Paul Signori."

"You were in the Army, right?"

"Yes, sir."

"Saw action in Europe?"

"Yes, sir," I say again. He did some research on me?

"Good, good, good. Well, I'm all right with you dating my daughter," he says, and promptly goes back to his newspaper.

"Thank you, sir," I say, looking at Mary. She shrugs her shoulders.

"Bye, Daddy. Me and Paul are going dancing."

Mr. Stefano grunts something.

"What was that all about?" I ask Mary as we're driving away.

"He's been in a great mood ever since he won a big bet on a horse the other day. Lucky Stars, I think its name is. He says he got a hot tip on it."

❋❋❋

It's been four months since me and Mary started dating. I've waited long enough. I'm asking her today. I see her in the hallway, walking in the other direction. I run, catching up to her. I put my hands on her shoulders and turn her around. She smiles up at me. She is beautiful. I go down on one knee and pull a small jewelry box out of my pocket. It's empty, but she doesn't know that. We can pick our rings together after she says yes.

"Mary, I want to marry you. I love you."

❀ ❀ ❀

*I'm a little shocked by his proposal. I didn't even know he loves me. I guess I love him, too. But I'm not even eighteen, yet. I won't be for another couple of months.*

"Paul, I don't know what to say."

"Say yes, Mary," he says. "Say yes."

*I'm speechless. I don't know what to think, let alone say. I think I want to marry him, but what about Eddie? He may still think we're dating. He's in the Merchant Marines and out to sea right now. And I don't know what my heart is telling me.*

"I need to understand the feelings in my heart," I say. "And Eddie, he'll be back in a few weeks."

"Feelings in your heart? And Eddie?" Paul asks. "You mean you don't have feelings for me?"

"I do, but I want to be sure."

*He stands up and is now looking down at me; I can't read what his blank expression means.*

"I mean, I think I do," I finally say.

"Well, forget about it then," he says and turns and walks away.

*I immediately start to cry.*

❋❋❋

She needs to understand her feelings? I don't know if I should be hurt or offended. But I do love her, I want her to say yes. I want to spend the rest of my life with her. I'm deep in thought and don't see the woman coming, but I sure feel the slap to my face.

"What did you say to Mary, Paul Signori?" she shouts. "She's bawling her eyes out."

It's Mary's friend, Jane. They work in the same department.

"I asked her to marry me and she said no. She needs to understand her feelings about me, or something like that," I say.

"Oh. I see," Jane says. "I guess you took her by surprise."

"It would seem."

"I know she wants to marry you. You're all she ever talks about. Paul this, Paul that, it's driving me crazy," Jane says. "Wait here, I'll go talk to her."

❋❋❋

Eddie, the old boyfriend, has been back in town for a few days, but this is the first time I see him. He's probably been avoiding me. I'm sure he's heard that me and Mary are engaged, but I could care less what he thinks. He can't help himself, it seems, as he shouts from across the street when he sees me.

"I used to know Mary when she was a good girl!" he shouts. "Now look at her. She's gonna marry a no-good troublemaker like you."

He can call me whatever he wants, but he ain't insulting Mary and getting away with it. I flick the cigarette I'm smoking into the gutter. I don't bother to respond; instead I charge across the street. Eddie takes off running. He's fast. I chase him up, down, and across the streets of Little Italy for twenty minutes. I finally catch him on the corner of Lombard and Broadway.

"Mary's not a good girl anymore because me, huh?" I say.

I grab him by the shirt collar and hold him up. I punch him in the jaw, not too hard, but hard enough for him to land on his rear end. I pull him back up to his feet and smack him around a little.

"Don't ever say anything about Mary again, Eddie. She's still a good girl and I'm gonna marry her and I'm gonna treat her good, you hear?"

Mary isn't happy when she finds out I beat up Eddie. I know I shouldn't smile when she's confronting me about it, but I can't help myself. What Mary doesn't understand about me is that I like to fight. She has no idea that I've spent most of my life having three or four fights a month. Sometimes in a week.

❊ ❊ ❊

*We didn't mean to have such a huge wedding. It's just Paul knows so many people and I've got a big family—Italian father and Polish mother. There must be 800 people here! I'm not kidding, 800. I need a break, I'm overwhelmed. I'm in tears. Tears of joy. Everyone from Paul's side of the family came up to us while we were sitting at the head table, after the greeting line. They kissed our cheeks, they shook our hands, and they handed us envelopes full of money. Thousands of dollars are now stuffed into a bag that is sitting on the table. Paul says we have nothing to worry about—no one would ever dream* *of taking the bag. After the Italians from Paul's side and from my father's side paid their respects and left the envelopes in an oversized bag, I performed the traditional Polish money dance. I think I danced with 400 people. They all stuffed money into my money purse. It's overflowing—there must be over $1,000 filling the purse! We're rich and we didn't do anything to deserve the riches except get married.*

*But the best part of our wedding, after the ceremony at St. Leo's, is dancing with my husband at the reception. We've had so much practice dancing together these past months that we move perfectly together. Now, I love watching him walk from table to table. Everyone likes him; he's always laughing and joking. People around him are always laughing. I even like his friends, Phil and Tony, the guys he calls Thrill and Naughty. I don't like the nickname they have for Paul—Funeral. Paul says it's because when they were kids, he worked at a funeral parlor. I watch as my Paul stops in front of a table. He has a most peculiar look on his face. He's now hugging three men I have never seen.*

❊ ❊ ❊

Before I make my way around to the tables, mingling with the guests, I grab Beans out of the crowd and bring him to my family's table.

"Everyone, Dad, this is Beans Galbo. He's an old friend of mine."

"Pleased to meet all of you," Beans says. My mother and both sisters wave and shift in their seats and my brothers mumble hello.

Beans turns to my father and says, "Mr. Signori, I don't know you, but I want to compliment you on your son. You raised a fine man."

He bends down and shakes my father's hand. My father stares up at Beans and doesn't say a word. The two most influential men in my life: my father figures, staring at each other with my own father speechless.

I also bring Jack O'Donovan over to say hello. He shakes my father's hand and kisses my mom's. They reminisce about the night on the town they spent together. I quietly sneak away and start making my rounds.

I had no idea they would show up. The hundreds of other people—sure, I knew they all would. When one of the boys, or girls, from the neighborhood gets married, everyone is invited. Same with the Mob guys from The Block. They're all invited and they all show up. And they all give envelopes stuffed with cash. It's our tradition, giving lots of money. I bet me and Mary walk away from this with ten-grand. But the three men at this table I never expected.

"Lieutenant Case. Casey," I say as I grab him by the arms. "Halby. Hog Jaw. I can't believe you guys are here."

Halby and Hog Jaw come around the table and join in on the hug.

"We wouldn't miss this for the world," they all say.

"How long has it been?" I ask.

"Two years, Siggy. Two long years since we've seen each other," Casey says.

❋ ❋ ❋

"Who are those men Paul is hugging?" I ask Tony.

"Beats me, Mary. Never seen 'em before," Tony answers.

278

"Are they crying?"

"Sure looks like it."

❋❋❋

"Mary, I want you to meet these guys," I say. "This is my lieutenant from the war. Mary, meet Lieutenant Case. We call him Casey. We were in the same armored car."

"Very nice to meet you, Lieutenant."

"The pleasure is all mine, Mrs. Signori," Casey says. "Siggy, your husband, he's the reason I'm alive today."

"We all kept each other alive," I interject. "These other two are Halby and Hog Jaw. We were all in the same unit."

I realize at this moment that I have never told Mary anything about the war or the men I served with. This must come as a shock to her.

"I'm pleased to meet all of you," Mary says. "I'm sorry I don't know anything about you, Paul hasn't told me much about the war."

"I haven't told my wife very much, either," Casey says. "I suspect most of the guys keep much of it inside."

"Come on, the bar awaits. We need to do a toast," I say.

Turning back to Mary, I say, "I need to spend some time with these guys, but I won't be too long." I kiss her and walk away with my arms around my friends.

Casey is right—it's been hard for us to talk about the war, except with other veterans. I tell them about the nightmares I have. They share their nightmares; we all have that in common. Eventually, I introduce my three wartime friends around, but I end up spending most of the reception drinking with them. I don't know when we'll see each other again, if ever. Maybe at some reunion twenty-five years down the road.

❋❋❋

*I'm crawling on my hands and knees away, but the bodies are everywhere, all around me. They're moaning, their expressionless eyes are staring at me. They're clawing at me with fingers of bone. I try to push them away, but they keep coming, surrounding me. I'm piling the bodies on top of each other. The stack is getting taller and taller. I'm floating in the air. The dead bodies are floating with me. Clawing at me. Scratching me. I'm on the ground, running, but I'm not moving. The bodies are all around me. They're covering me. I can't breathe. I'm screaming.*

"Paul, honey, wake up," Mary says while shaking me.

"The nightmare again," I say.

"This is the third time this week, Paul."

"It's usually not this bad, Mary, I promise. I guess it was seeing Casey and Halby and Hog Jaw that's got me thinking about the war."

"Tell me about the nightmare. What is it you're doing or seeing?"

"I can't, Mary. Not yet, anyway."

❋❋❋

It takes five years after the wedding before Mary gives birth to our first child, Phyllis. Over the next four years, we have three more girls: Judith, Jeana, and Vicky. Our fifth daughter,

280

Lori, surprises us nine years later. I call my girls "Paul's Fillies."

I love them more than anything in the world—and not a day goes by without me telling them so.

# Chapter 19

# I MUST BE CRAZY

"**I** must be crazy to still be doing this," I say out loud.

I've spent the last seven or so years—ever since I got home from the war—working down on The Block as an enforcer, keeping the ladies safe. The past five, I've been married. Now I'm a husband and a father. I must be crazy to still be doing this.

Besides, I'm working full-time at Motor Vehicles. I've mellowed considerably since my first year back on the job. I no longer look for a fight and almost never need to pull out my iron pipe. There are no more dance hall fights either, and far fewer fights at the clubs for me. I only work the busiest nights now, but I'm always on call. That's how it works—I get a call in the afternoon from Jimmy Cagliano, my boss. He calls me at my office or at a pre-arranged time on a pay phone, almost never at home.

I hardly ever see Beans anymore now that he's moved up the ladder and is a made man not working the clubs. I work two or three nights a week only—sometimes Thursdays, but mostly Fridays and Saturdays. It's been hard keeping my alternative life secret from Mary. I tell her I'm playing poker or out bowling. I even tell her I'm helping tend bar for a friend. One time I told her I was playing poker and that her dad was playing. I had no idea she would check up on me. She called her dad. He wasn't playing poker with me. I had some explaining to do. But for the most part, Mary doesn't know about The Block, and rarely questions me. It's just the way things are—the man can do most anything he wants, and the wife stays home and takes care of the kids.

Then there's the money. I make a lot of money working for the Mob. I hide the considerable amount of cash I make—I'm always paid in cash by the Mob—from Mary. But she's good at finding stuff.

"Paul, please explain why you have almost $1,000 in your

jacket pocket," Mary confronts me.

"I was about to tell you. I got lucky yesterday, Mary. You're not going to believe this, but my number hit. I hit the number!" I may not be a bag boy anymore, but I play the numbers like everyone else.

She stares at me. She knows I play the numbers. I think she believes me. "I guess it's congratulations, then."

"You go ahead and keep it, Mary," I say.

"What do I need $1,000 for?" she asks.

I've got thousands of dollars saved from working on The Block hidden from Mary in my secret stash. It's hard to believe that my number hits as often as it does—so often, Mary's sister wants to know my system!

❖❖❖

"Jimmy, you got a minute?"

"Sure, Paulie. What's on your mind?" Jimmy says.

He's grown on me, what can I say? Jimmy Cagliano isn't that bad after all, and after many years of working with the guy, I must admit I like him. "I don't think I can do this anymore."

"Do what, Paulie?"

"Work down here, Jimmy. Work on The Block for the Mob."

"I don't understand," he says. "You can't quit."

"I can't quit?"

"Paulie," he says with a laugh, "There's no quitting the Mob. Besides, you know too much."

I am in it for life after all. I guess I knew it all along, but I had to ask. I'm about to walk away from Jimmy when she walks into the Two O'Clock Club with the owner, Mr. Goodman. I stop and watch her as she struts by. I've never seen a woman quite like her. Beautiful, exotic, classy, all rolled up in one person.

"Wow," I say. "Who's *that*, Jimmy?"

"She's Blaze Starr—that's what Mr. Goodman calls her, anyway. He discovered her waiting tables in Washington," Jimmy says. "She's been doing shows for a few weeks up in DC, but now she'll be headlining here at the Two O'Clock."

I look around the club and every eye is on her. She's going to be a star, just like her name says, there is no doubt about it.

"She's gonna be a star, so the name fits," I say.

"Mr. Goodman wants his best man watching out for her, Paulie. I'm making you her personal bodyguard whenever she performs," Jimmy tells me. "You'll only be working here at the Two O'Clock Club from now on."

"Still on call?"

"Yeah, still on call, but only the nights she works."

That's good for me. As the headliner, she'll only work a few nights a week. Her first night on stage she sets the place on fire, literally—she has a flaming couch routine. Blaze has smoke rise from behind the couch she's sprawled out on, and then wind blows red streamers into the air from the couch's cushions. The effect is magnificent—it looks like the couch is on fire. The sold-out crowd leaps to their feet, the ovation lasting for five minutes. I have never seen anything like it. Eventually, she adds a baby black panther to her show.

Her act is a combination of showmanship, strip-tease, and humor with props. No other Burlesque dancer on The Block is quite like her. She strips, but always leaves at least her feathery boa wrapped around her so as not to reveal everything, always leaving them wanting more.

❀❀❀

"Hi, boys," she says to me and Jimmy after her show. "Like the show?"

"It was wonderful, Miss Starr," Jimmy says, gushing. "Simply wonderful."

"What about you?"

"Yes ma'am, I certainly did."

"Oh, I like the way that sounds," Blaze says with a giggle. "What's your name?"

"Paul Signori, ma'am."

"So, you're gonna be my bodyguard?"

"Yes ma'am," I say.

"You can guard my body anytime," she says with a wink.

I blush a little.

"Any nickname?" she asks. "You boys always have the cleverest nicknames."

I think about whether I should tell her Funeral. I decide against it. "When I was in the Army, the guys called me Siggy."

"What unit were you in, Siggy?" she asks.

"71st Recon Troop, 71st Division. Served in Europe."

"I bet you saw a lot of action," she says. "I love the vets, Siggy. Like I said, I'd be proud to have you watch my back anytime."

Show after show, she gets more popular. Within a month
288

Blaze Starr is the biggest attraction on The Block with every show sold out. Everyone wants to be next to her, and she's so personable, loving the attention, that she walks the crowd before and after every show, sometimes for hours. I watch Blaze Starr's back for the next couple of years. No one that she didn't want to get close to her ever got near enough to hurt her—I wouldn't let it happen. Always discreet, me and my partners, Thrill and Naughty, never let Blaze see us hurt anyone. She wouldn't have stood for it. We would clear the problem, get her to safety, and then deal with whoever caused the situation. It was usually just a drunk guy wanting to touch her.

In 1954, she is the feature of an Esquire Magazine article titled, *B-Belles of Burlesque—You Get Strip-Tease with your Beer in Baltimore*. She gets so famous that she takes her show on the road, but Blaze Starr considers Baltimore, and The Block, home and the Two O'Clock Club her home base. She always returns to the club, and eventually, she buys the Two O'Clock Club from Mr. Goodman in 1970.

I guess I should consider myself lucky that someone tracked me down. Jack O'Donovan dying is not much of a surprise, I'm just mad at myself for not visiting him more these last couple years. After Brown Eyed Suzy passed away at the ripe old age of thirty-three, I've only visited Jack three or four times. My life has become chaotic and time-consuming; I have very little free time. I wish I would have found the time to bring the girls out to the stable. I promise myself, when Phyllis and Judith are old enough, I'm getting them riding lessons.

Jack's funeral is not widely attended, only the folks from the stable and a few other people. I bring Mary along. She always enjoyed listening to Jack's stories when we visited. I should probably shed a tear for my old friend, but I don't. I'm honored that he left me all his horse racing memorabilia and his most prized possession, his racing saddle. It's hard for me to put into words what this man meant to me. I feel as though he was put into my life to have a calming effect on me. A wise old man capable of putting perspective into my actions, almost like a guide. I was very close to him, maybe closer than any other adult during my youth. Perhaps more than Beans or my father. I think about Mrs. Russell. Whatever became of her? Why did she abandon me, leaving without so much as a forwarding address? Why were both Jack and Mrs. Russell put into my life? Two normal people to help guide me, I guess.

❋ ❋ ❋

Next, it's my Uncle Marco.

"Paul, your Uncle Marco has died," my mother says over the phone. "Everyone is coming to the house. When can you make it?"

Uncle Marco had been sick, but we all thought it wasn't serious. Now he's dead? How?

"What happened, Mom?"

"He died in his sleep, Paul. Maybe a heart attack, who knows? I know Aunt Betty wants to talk to you about the company."

"Uncle Marco's title company? I haven't been a part of that since before the war."

"You're the only one she trusts to run it now that Marco is gone."

"He did tell me when he retired, he wanted me to run the company," I say, thinking back to before the war. Working with
290

my uncle were some of the best times of my life, and I would love to get away from Motor Vehicles and be my own boss. After hashing out a deal with Aunt Betty, I end up buying part of the automobile title company from her, only the route I want. Once the sale is final—I use some of my hidden cash from The Block—I quit my job with the MVA and start running the title company full-time. I have ten or so dealerships I work with, all within a five-mile radius. I can work as hard as I want, or I can take as much time off as I want. But I'm too hard a worker, trained by my father, to take time off.

Running the title company is like riding a bike. It only takes me a few days and I'm back at it like I never stopped. The neighborhood has changed over the years, and people have become more sophisticated, but most still need help with the paperwork of getting the title for their car. I have more work than I know what to do with. It helps that all the dealerships liked and respected Uncle Marco, and most already know me. I also have the best connections at the MVA. I've worked there for over twelve years and know everyone at the registration desk. My old friends send me more business that I can handle—well, almost more than I can handle.

After my first year, I've doubled the business. Mary helps in the office and I've hired two other employees. Somehow, I still manage to balance my regular job, being a husband, raising four girls, and working two or three nights a week at the clubs on The Block. It's getting harder to find excuses to get away on Friday and Saturday nights. And hiding the money I make. How many times can I tell Mary that I hit the number and have her still believe me? I'm already up to five times—the odds of that happening are astronomical.

Mary and the girls go to church on Sunday, have been for a long time. She asks me to join them, but I always have an excuse. "Sunday morning is for paperwork," I tell her. To myself, I say, why would God want anything to do with me?

And I've never had the time for him, either.

I think about my litany of transgressions. The list is long, dating back to when I was young and always scheming to make money, taking advantage of anyone who was in my way. Old Mr. Joe pops into my head. I think about my card playing and taking advantage of lesser players. What about the selling of booze in the Army barracks? Does that make me a bad person? I think about the war. I stop thinking about this subject when I ponder all the people I've fought, all the heads I've bashed.

❀ ❀ ❀

"Paul, I want you to know that I never hit your mother again. Not once after you got home from the war and set me straight," my father tells me from his deathbed in the hospital. His excessive drinking has finally caught up with him.

I don't know what to say to him. He made my mother's life miserable for so many years. I guess I should be thankful that he stopped beating her in 1946. If it's true, at least for the last fourteen years of her life, she didn't have to endure his wrath.

"Thank you," I say. "Mom deserved to live her life in peace."

"If I had beat her again, and you found out, I would have welcomed you killing me."

I wonder if I would have killed him. The thought still bothers me.

"I am sorry, Paul, for the way I treated you growing up," he says. "I did love you and your brothers and sisters. I'm sorry I couldn't show it."

I stay silent. The influence he has had on my life is profound. I remember when I shook his hand before leaving for the Army, the look in his eye, the squeeze of my hand. I knew he loved me. He just couldn't say it. Or show it, for that matter. He's crying now, on his deathbed with so many regrets.

"Don't be like me," he adds through his tears. "Love your family, Paul. Tell them you love them. Every day."

"I already do, Dad," I answer. "I tell them every day that I love them."

He died the next day. He was blessed to see four grandchildren born. He was always the model grandparent. He loved the girls and spoiled them—nothing like the way he was with his own children.

Until his last day, he struggled to show his love for us, his kids.

"Paul, I want you to know he wasn't always like the way he was. When we were first married, he loved me. And when Frank and you and the kids were born, he loved you all, too. Loved you very much. He used to roll around on the floor playing with you."

"Why did he change, Mom? What happened to him?"

"You wouldn't remember, would you? You were too little."

"What happened?" I ask. "Tell me."

"He was working two jobs. Always tired. He never told me how it happened. Maybe he fell asleep on the truck. Anyway, he fell off a truck when it was moving. Landed on his shoulder and broke his collarbone. He spent a week in the hospital. They gave him morphine, Paul, for the pain. His shoulder never set right and always hurt him. He was always in pain. He started drinking when he stopped getting the morphine."

"So that's why he always drank," I say. "Why didn't you tell me this before? Why did you let me go on thinking he was just a lousy drunk?"

"He wouldn't let me."

Sometimes things are not always the way they seem. He probably had the most profound influence on my life. I hated him for so many years, but I tried so hard to make him respect me—no, love me. My entire childhood was spent this way, embroiled in a love-hate relationship. I spent as much time away from him and our home as possible, but on the other hand, I worked side-by-side with him for years. We worked the same job sites and we worked side jobs together—yet we never connected outside of a few words.

When I returned home from the war, I moved into his house. After Mary and I were married, we lived the first year of our marriage under his roof. We ate meals at the same table, but we hardly said more than a few words to each other. As much as I thought I knew him, we were strangers. But I never did see him hit my mother again after I threatened his life.

❄❄❄

*I'm crawling on my hands and knees away, but the are everywhere, all around me. They're moaning, their expressionless eyes are staring at me. They're clawing at me with fingers of bone. I try to push them away, but they keep coming, surrounding me. I'm piling the bodies on top of each other. The stack is getting taller and taller. I'm floating in the air. The dead bodies are floating with me. Clawing at me. Scratching me. I'm on the ground, running, but I'm not moving. The bodies are all around me. They're covering me. I can't breathe. I'm screaming.*

"Paul, wake up," Mary says while shaking me awake. "You're having the nightmare. Everything is going to be all right."

I'm in a cold sweat, panting. Mary is hugging me to calm

me down.

"When will it end, Mary?" I ask. "When will the nightmares end?"

Maybe my father's death triggered the nightmare. It had been months, maybe longer, since the last one. But it rears its ugly head whenever it feels the need to encroach on my life, to remind me of what I saw all those years ago. It's already hard enough—not a day goes by that I don't think about the war. Why does it have to invade my sleep?

❀ ❀ ❀

"Come on girls, I've got a surprise," I say. "We're going for a drive."

We all pile into the car and head out of the city. They are eleven, ten, eight and seven, and I've waited long enough. Their anticipation is breathtaking. We go on family trips and weekend excursions often, but it's almost never a surprise like today. And I'm not telling them anything. We arrive at the stables fifteen minutes later. The girls are screaming with excitement.

"Thanks for taking care of this, Benny," I say to the stable's manager as I slip him $100.

"I only wish Jack was alive to see this," he says.

"Yeah, me too."

I turn to my four little fillies and say, "Go on, pick a horse."

The four of them run to saddled horses; me and Benny help them up. I listen as he gives the girls a lesson in riding, much like the one I received from Jack so many years before.

"Take 'em out for a walk. They may even gallop a little,"

Benny says.

I watch as the girls, high up on their horses walk and gallop around the fenced-in yard. They are smiling ear to ear. My heart melts. All four beg me to sign them up for riding lessons. I willingly oblige.

❊❊❊

Saturday morning and the phone is ringing. I put the newspaper down and glance at the clock. It's a few minutes past seven. I look at Mary as she's getting up from the table to answer the phone. I have a feeling of dread pass through me.

"Hello," Mary says.

I listen intently as she has a conversation with the person on the other end.

"Oh yes, hi," she says. "Yes. Yes. Oh, I see. Okay, hold on, I'll get him."

She puts the phone down and looks at me. I can tell that something isn't right.

"Who is it, Mary?"

"It's your friend, Tony."

"Tony Mazzotti? Naughty?" I ask.

"Yes, Paul. I think something has happened."

Ten minutes later, I've got Naughty in my arms. He's crying uncontrollably. I look down at the body, face-down in a dirty alleyway behind a night club on The Block. I can't tell what caused his death. He could have been beaten to death, or the gunshot wound could have cause it, but either way our friend—our brother—Phil Carollo, Thrill, is dead. He had been drifting away from me and Naughty these past couple
296

of years, getting himself deeper into the Mob. And probably getting himself involved in activities he shouldn't have been in. I heard rumors, but whenever I confronted him, he always denied or played them off as not true. The last rumor involved drugs. For all I know, the Mob could have killed him. I'll never know the truth.

I should be crying too, but I'm not. I've seen death. I've seen friends killed. The hard heart I developed persists. I'm here to comfort Naughty. He's become more emotional over time, especially after his kids were born. He married several years ago and has three little ones. Thrill never married, another reason he drifted away. Me and Naughty only work a couple of nights a week. We've got regular jobs. Thrill worked five or six nights a week for the Mob.

"Look at him, Funeral," Naughty says between sobs. "Who did this to him?"

"I don't know, Naughty. We'll probably never know," I say. "He's been getting involved in stuff. You know he has, we've both warned him."

"But he didn't deserve this."

That is true. He certainly didn't deserve to end up dead in a dirty alleyway.

There must be 500 people at the funeral. I'm a pallbearer, as are Naughty, Jimmy, and Beans. This is the first time I've seen, and talked to, Beans in months. He's bawling like a baby, as are many others. I still haven't shed a tear.

"Why aren't you crying for your friend, Paul?" Mary asks. "You've known him all your life. You're best friends."

"I don't know why, Mary," I say. "After the war, maybe I just can't have normal emotions. Who knows?"

I think about Lieutenant Gibb and Finn and the dead German

kids, and of course the thousands upon thousands of dead bodies I saw at Gunskirchen. I wonder if I'll ever be able to show emotion about a loved one dying.

Of course, I have my nightmare that night, after the funeral.

❀ ❀ ❀

"Paul, the tavern down the street is for sale," my mother tells me over the phone. "Did you know?"

"No, I didn't know and I don't care," I say. I've got my hands full with the title company. Owning a bar is the last thing I want. I spend enough time in bars and clubs on The Block already.

"I think you should buy it," she insists.

"Why would I want to buy a bar?"

"I think you should buy it, Paul."

"I don't want to buy it."

"Paul, buy the tavern. You can hire your brother Frank to run it."

"Are you crazy, Mom? I don't want a tavern or a bar or a restaurant. And I don't want Frankie running it if I ever decide to buy a bar."

"Your brother Frank needs a job. I think you should buy the tavern."

She's never going to let this go. Once she gets a thought into her head, my mother can be the most persistent person I know. I need to placate her.

"I'll think about it." I must be crazy just thinking about buying a tavern.

But when I get home from the office, despite that voice in my head, I tell Mary about the tavern down the street from my mother's house. "Mary, my mother wants me to buy the tavern down the street from her house so Frankie can run it."

"How much does he want for it?" Mary asks.

Not exactly what I thought she would say.

"He wants $12,000. I stopped by the place before coming home. Nicer than I thought it would be. Even has a kitchen. Old Mr. Rossi owns the bar and the building."

"Can we afford that?"

Again, not what I thought she would say. And yes, we can afford it. The more I think about it, a bar might not be a bad idea—to hide the money I'm making working on The Block for the Mob.

"We can. But why would we want to own a tavern, Mary?" I ask. "I'm busy enough with work already."

"If Frankie's running the place, you won't have to do much."

"Do you really think I can trust Frankie to run a bar? You don't know him like I do. He doesn't know anything, Mary," I say. "No, I'm up to my ears with work running the company. I've got no extra time. The last thing I want is have to run a bar when Frankie disappears."

"You won't. Your brother will run the bar and he won't disappear."

I can't believe I'm agreeing to do this. A thousand things can go wrong.

"Here you go, Mr. Rossi, $12,000 cash for the bar," I say. "What about the building? You want to sell the building, too?"

Mr. Rossi is smiling ear to ear while he thrust the keys into my hand. I'm signing the paperwork for not only the bar, but for the building, too. I'm now the proud owner of a bar with a kitchen. The twelve grand gets me everything in the place— stools, tables, chairs, booze—everything. I'm still trying to figure out who is getting the better deal. The guy is old and just wants out of the business, plus, I've known him for years; he lives upstairs in an apartment above the bar. Since I bought the building, he'll be paying me rent with the money I just gave him. Maybe I'm making out better?

"Paulie, trust me, I won't let you down," Frankie says. "I'm your brother."

"Do you even know the first thing about running a bar, Frankie?"

Frankie Signori, my younger brother, is probably the least dependable person I know. He's been out of work for months, living with Mom. He never could hold down a job, always looking for a get-rich scheme.

"How hard can it be? Buy some booze and sell drinks to the customers," he says. "And I've got lots of ideas to make the place better."

If it was only that easy. I've been hanging around bars and clubs most of my life, so I know a thing or two. If he messes this up, I'll kill him.

"Look, Frankie, you mess this up, I'll give you a beating like you've never had," I tell him. "What drinks can you mix?"

"I know a few. Besides, I have this bartender's book."

He shows me a book about mixing drinks. I shake my head. How could I have been so stupid? The last thing I want in my life is to own a bar.

"Look, Frankie, I don't want to have to babysit you. Understand?"

"Yeah, Paulie, I understand."

"I hope so, Frankie, for your sake, I hope so."

❄❄❄

"Paul, it doesn't look like the tavern is open."

My mother is on the phone bothering me about the bar already. But I'm thinking to myself, How can the bar not be open? I've owned it for four months and, much to my surprise, Frankie is doing a pretty good job. I'm down to checking on the place—Paul's Tavern I named it—once a week. The books are balanced and he's making his monthly payment. I made him a deal where he'll own the tavern after a year if he keeps up with the payments—$1,000 a month—until I'm paid back.

"Where's Frankie?" I ask.

"I haven't seen him for two days," my mother answers.

"What do you mean you haven't seen him? He's not staying at the house?"

"Well, sometimes he sleeps at the bar."

I unlock the front door of Paul's Tavern. It's dark, no one is here. That no-good-brother-of-mine, I say to myself. Where are you? I check the cash register behind the bar. It's empty. All the cash is gone. I walk into the office and open the safe. Empty—all the money is gone.

"Frankie!" I yell. "I'm gonna kill you!"

❄❄❄

"Paul, your brother wants you to send him money for a plane ticket. He's sorry about the bar and wants to come home."

"He can find his own way back to Baltimore from California," I say. "And when he gets here, remind him about the beating I promised to give him if he messed up the bar."

I've been lucky these past several weeks because Mr. Rossi, the previous owner and occupant of the apartment above the bar, agreed to run the place until I find someone else to take over. I had to agree to let him live rent-free, but he's not going to be around forever. He wants to move out of the neighborhood. I've also had to spend much more time at Paul's Tavern than I would like. Reluctantly, I send my brother money to buy a train ticket home, but I'm not sure I ever want to see him again. I guess deep down I knew this would happen.

Mother once again comes to the rescue—or she thinks she does. "Paul, my brother George is looking for work. He'd be perfect for the tavern."

"Why isn't he bartending on The Block?" I ask. George has been a bartender at one of the clubs for years.

"He was, but not anymore. The timing is perfect," she says.

I never knew my mother was such a busybody. Ever since my old man died, she's been in everyone's business. I know George, and I never liked him. I haven't worked any of the clubs he bartended at, but I know people who know him. Nothing all that bad is said about him, but nothing good is said, either. I decide he's better than me having to run the place, so I hire him. I even give him the same deal I gave Frankie—$1,000 a month for a year and the bar is yours.

George disappears four weeks later.

I find out the Mob, the guys I work for, are after him. He didn't simply quit his job on The Block, he ran from it. He thought he could hide out at my tavern and the Mobsters wouldn't find him, or maybe he thought I would protect him. He's one of the only family members that knows I work for the Mob. I could have protected him if I knew what he had done, but he didn't tell me. Some people must learn the hard way—you absolutely do not double-cross the Mob. Ever. Thrill probably found out the hard way, too. And it cost him his life.

George was dumb enough to start his own numbers racket behind their backs, running numbers out of a bar the Mob owns. When they found out, they wanted their cut. George didn't have the money so he disappeared. You can't disappear in Baltimore. You can't hide from, or run from, these guys. They always find you. After he disappeared from my tavern, he turned up a couple of weeks later. Eventually, he paid off his debt, but he never worked on The Block again.

Meanwhile, I'm stuck running Paul's Tavern—again.

❀❀❀

"Do you still want out, Paulie?"

"Out, Jimmy? What do you mean?"

"Out of the Mob, because now's your chance."

"Yeah, of course I still want out."

Things have been crazy on The Block for weeks. The Mob all over Baltimore is getting busted. The biggest gambler around, a guy named Lord Salisbury, is under federal indictment. Lord is his nickname—it doesn't take much of an imagination to figure out why. I've met him many times at the Oasis as I work at his club. The story is, he's bringing everyone down with him now that he's been sentenced to fifteen years in prison. Salisbury owns the Oasis Club, and from its basement, he ran the city's largest gambling ring. He's been running the book —setting the odds, taking bets, controlling the gambling—in Baltimore for years. The cops finally caught up with him.

Lord Salisbury has been one of the city's most famous people for as long as I can remember, more famous than the politicians who supposedly ran the city. Maybe he got too powerful and the powers that be needed to bring him down. He was also one of the most connected men in the city—part Jewish Mobster, part club owner, part numbers runner, part sports-book, full-time gambler.

"Five of the guys are gonna get sent away to prison, including your old friend Beans, and another seven are getting deported back to Sicilia," Jimmy says. "The New York Mob, the Gambinos, are coming down to take over and they don't know you. You're too low on the totem pole, which is good for you, and I'm not gonna tell them who you are. So, now's your chance."

It's 1970 and I've got five daughters. My oldest is seventeen years old, and the youngest is five. It's also been seventeen years since I first asked to get out of the Mob after Phyllis was born, and was told I was in it for life. I don't know if I want to cry or laugh. I can finally walk away.

By the end of my career as a Mob enforcer, I'm only working a couple of nights a week. Me and Naughty are back to being watchers more than anything else. I had been offered many times to move up to "management," but I always said no. I was content to be low on the totem pole as Jimmy put it, not wanting to boss others around. Sure, I trained my share of head-bashers, and readily gave advice, but I never wanted what Beans or Jimmy did. There are lots of young guys, big muscle guys, that walk the floors and watch for the red light. We are like the old guard, taking care of business by way of reputation more than anything else. I was also lucky—the Mob never asked me to go on a hit—they never made me kill anyone. I know the men who do get the orders, and I'm glad not to be one of them.

I can't decide if I'll miss coming to The Block. Probably not.

This being my last night, I may never come down here again. My friend Naughty was given the same opportunity to walk away, and he jumped at it as fast as I did. I've got a life away from here. I've got a family and a legitimate business to run. I've also got a bar I don't want and no one to run it but me. The only good thing about owning the bar—it was great for hiding the cash I made from the Mob. Now, I won't need that excuse. To this day, Mary has no idea about my involvement with the Mob.

I must have been crazy to have joined in the first place. Thank God, it turned out not to be for life.

Julius "Lord" Salisbury disappears in August 1970, walking away from his Baltimore house, and his family, to never be heard from again. Maybe he fled to Israel, like some say, or maybe he was taken out by the Mob the old-fashioned way. No one knows, and those who do, are not talking.

# Chapter 20

# CHANGES

I find myself spending more time at Paul's Tavern and less time at my title company. It should be the other way around, but the company runs itself and I've got employees I trust. My day starts at seven in the morning when I open the office for business. By now, Mary knows as much about the title business as I do; she comes to the office in the early afternoon, and I leave for the bar. Today I've got a couple of visitors.

"Can I help you guys?" I ask.

"We want to talk to the owner," one of them says.

"You're talking to him," I say as I check them out—two large black men, dressed like flamboyant street hoods.

"Okay then, Mr. Owner, we're here to give you protection. How's $500 a week sound?"

"I don't need protection."

"Why, sure you's do. You's a white man in a black neighborhood," the taller of the two says. He then reaches down and picks up a bar stool by the legs. "What if, for instance, a man comes into your bar and picks up this here bar stool. Then he throws it against your nice mirror back there. Breaks the mirror, all them bottles of booze, breaks everything."

On the wall behind the bar is a long mirror. I have glass shelves attached to the mirror that hold the booze. There could be as many as a hundred bottles. I turn away from the two men and look behind me at the mirror and the many bottles. Looking back at the hoodlums I size them up. One is tall and well-built, wearing a long brown leather coat and a hat with a feather. He's the guy doing the talking and holding my bar stool. The other guy is shorter and built like a bull with an afro and sunglasses on. I make eye contact with my doorman, Rosie, a black man. He's been with me at the bar for about six months, watching the door, bouncing for me. I've also got a guy sitting at the bar—it's early afternoon and we're not open yet, but I've known the drunk at the bar for years so I let him in. My cook and a couple of waitresses will arrive in an hour or so. I officially open at three and start serving food at four. We make the best pizza, meatballs, and marinara sauce in the neighborhood.

"Hold on a minute, I need to check on the guy at the bar. I'll be right back."

I slide down the bar, stopping in front of the customer. But he's not the reason I moved. This is where I keep my pipe. I still have the iron pipe, my enforcer's pipe with the thin rubber coating and leather handle, after I stopped working on The Block. I wrap the leather strap around my wrist and slide the pipe up my sleeve. I've dealt with punks like these two my entire life. I pour a beer and leave the mug on the bar next to my drunk friend.

"Here you go, Billy," I say as I start to move back toward the hoods.

I stop in front of the tall man doing the talking and let a minute of silence pass before speaking. "So, what were you saying again?"

He bends back down and goes through the motion of picking up the bar stool. He lifts it over his head and then says, "I was sayin', what if a guy…"

He can't complete his sentence. I slide my pipe down my arm and it appears in my hand. I spin the pipe around for some momentum and whack the guy in the side of his neck. For a split second, I see nothing but black. He drops to the ground like a ton of bricks, the stool bouncing off his head. I don't give whacking this guy a second thought.

"Paulie, behind you!" Rosie yells as the other guy is coming around the bar.

I pivot on my back foot, turning to face my attacker. I raise
310

my arm above my head, pipe in hand, and smash it down on his head. He likewise drops to the ground in a heap.

"I think I killed 'em, Rosie," I say.

"We should dump the bodies," Rosie replies.

I've always liked Rosie. I pause and think for a few seconds before I decide to go to the phone. I dial up the neighborhood police precinct.

"This is Paulie from Paul's Tavern," I say to the desk sergeant.

"Oh, hey, Paulie. How's it going?" Sergeant Carney says.

"Going good, Sarge. Who's on the beat today?"

"Let's see," he says. "Joey and Bobby are on today."

"Good. How can I get ahold of 'em?"

"I'll radio 'em and have 'em call you. You need anything, Paulie?"

"No, no, just need a favor."

Five minutes later, the phone is ringing.

"Paul's Tavern," I answer.

"Paulie, it's Joey. Sarge says you needed a call."

"Yeah, Joey, it's like this," I say. "Two punks came in the joint trying to shake me down. So, I popped 'em in the head with my pipe. I think I killed 'em."

"Hmm," the cop named Joey says. "Tell you what—go ahead and drag them out onto the sidewalk. Prop 'em up against a tree."

I grab one of them by the wrists, Rosie grabs the other, and we drag them out of the bar and onto the sidewalk. We leave them sitting up against a tree, both still out cold. Hell, they might even be dead. A couple of minutes later, I hear the siren of an ambulance. Then, two cops walk into the bar.

"Hey, Paulie," Joey the cop says.

"Paulie, do you think Mary can make me some more of those crabcakes she makes? Best I ever had," the other cop named Bobby says.

"Yeah, sure she can," I say, "But what about the two dead guys on the sidewalk?"

"Good thing they wasn't in the bar, Paulie," Joey says.

"That would have been a bunch of paperwork for us and a lot of trouble for you if they were," Bobby says while laughing. "We've got no idea what happened to 'em or how they ended up on the sidewalk."

❉ ❉ ❉

"Rosie," I say later that night, "You think you can run the bar?"

I've had it with this place. I've been stuck here since my Uncle George disappeared on me a few years back. The neighborhood has gone through a dramatic change over the years. Most of the white people moved long ago, my mother being one of the last hold-outs. Rosie has been with me long enough. He knows what's going on.

"Sure, I can," he says. "What you got in mind?"

"The bar's yours if you want it. Pay me $1,000 a month for twelve months and I'll sign it over to you in a year." The bar makes enough in a month to cover the thousand dollars and leave some remaining for Rosie to live on. "I'll even cut the rent," I add since I own the building, too.

"You got yourself a deal, Mr. Paulie," Rosie says with a big smile on his face. We shake on it. "I won't let you down."

312

I sure hope so. I've heard that before and have been let down. I don't know Rosie that well, but I feel as though I can trust him. He shows up for work, is never late, and is always willing to do whatever is needed—like watching my back when street hoods show up. And then help drag them out of the bar. I don't think he's married, and come to think of it, I'm not sure where he lives.

"You married, Rosie?"

"No, Paulie," he says with a chuckle. "Do I look like the marrying type to you?"

"No," I say, "I guess not. You live around here?"

"Couple of miles up the road," he says.

I get the impression he doesn't want me to know too much about him. "I'll still come by every day for a couple of months to make sure everything is going good, and on Sunday, I'll teach you how to balance the books," I say as I change the subject.

"That sounds great, Paulie," Rosie says. "I can't thank you enough."

"I like you, Rosie," I say. "I think you'll do great."

"Mr. Paulie, one question—do I get to keep all the money we make over $1,000?"

"That's how it works. If you pay the bills, and pay me, you can keep the rest."

Have I finally gotten rid of the bar?

❀❀❀

"Paul, this is Richard from B and B."

Richard owns B and B Liquors, where I buy my booze for the bar.

"Hey Richard, what can I do for you?"

"Paul, do you know that the account is three months past due?"

"What?" I say. "I checked the invoices on Sunday. They're all stamped paid."

"I'll check with my guys to see if there's a mix-up," Richard says.

"And I'll head to the bar and pick up the invoices. Be at your place in about an hour," I say.

The invoices, like I thought, are all stamped paid with initials written in the paid box. My mind is spinning, but I've got a pretty good idea what's going on.

"Here you go Richard," I say as I hand him the invoices.

He gives the paperwork to his delivery men. Both shake their heads no. The writing on the invoices isn't theirs.

"How much do I owe—$1,100?" I ask.

"Yeah, Paul, that's right."

"Can I get it to you in a week?"

"For you, no problem."

I'm waiting for Rosie to show up at the bar. It's been five months of what seemed like smooth sailing, and now this.

"Rosie, I need you to look at something for me," I say.

"Sure, boss."

"These invoices say paid. Trouble is, Richard at B and B says they haven't been paid. These are three months past due."

Rosie's dark face turns a shade of maroon. How did he think

he could get away with pocketing the money and not paying the bills? I don't need him to confess. I can see that he's guilty.

"If I don't have eleven one-hundred-dollar bills in my hand in one week, you'll be floating face-down in Jones Falls."

Jones Falls is the local river. Rosie knows me well enough to know that I am not joking.

❀ ❀ ❀

I'm back at my bar with nobody to run it but me when the most outrageous looking black man I've ever seen walks in. A peacock doesn't do him justice. But he doesn't look hostile— he's all smiles. It's been three days since Rosie paid me in full, and I paid Richard.

"And how are you doing on this fine day?" he says to me.

"I'm good," I say. "What can I do for you?"

"I'm here to see Rosie."

"Rosie doesn't work here anymore."

"That can't be, he owns the place!" he shouts.

"No, I own the place," I say. "Have for the last eight years."

"No, sir! That boy sold me a partnership in this here bar. I paid him $1,100 three days ago!"

"He owed me the same amount. Paid it in full three days ago," I say.

"Why that cheating-good-for-nothing!" he says as he's reaching into his coat.

I'm looking for a way out of this mess as I'm watching him pull out a gun. The barrel of which never ends; it's the longest I've ever seen, a .44 magnum. He holds it in front of him, pointing toward me. I'm sweating bullets.

"If you ever see that rat, you tell him I'm looking for him and I'll kill him on sight."

"I told him the same thing after he paid me," I say as I wipe away the bead of sweat.

I guess it was only wishful thinking that I could trust Rosie.


❁❁❁


I decide to run an ad. I'll sell the bar to the first person to answer it and make the same offer that I did for Rosie. This time it's $12,000 paid in full, but I think I'll ask for a couple thousand up front and be done with it in ten months.

The first person to answer the ad is a black guy about my age. I tell him the price; he tries to haggle with me. It's got to be $2,000 up front and $1,000 a month for ten months. After several minutes of back and forth negotiating, he agrees to my offer. An hour later, he's back with the $2,000 cash. I've got a simple contract ready for him to sign. After he signs, I spend the rest of the afternoon educating the man on how easy it is to run a bar. Keep the liquor salesman happy, the kegs of beer cold, and the shelves stocked with booze and you can't help but make money.

"I own the building, so I'll be by to collect rent and the monthly payment the first of every month. Since you already paid two grand, this month's rent is covered," I say.

Four months later, my mother is calling me. "Paul, there are cops everywhere," she says. "They're in front of the bar."

She has been my eyes on the bar for the last few months. Mom is one of the last hold-outs on Collington Avenue, still living in the house I came home from the war to. I only show up to collect my rent and $1,000 payment the first of every month, like I told him, and have stopped checking on the bar. The guy hasn't missed a payment in four months.

"Where are the cops, Mom?"

"On the street in front of the bar."

"What are they doing? Are they in the bar?"

"They're everywhere, Paul. You need to get down here."

I arrive twenty minutes later—and sure enough, there are cops everywhere, and I don't recognize any of them.

"What's going on?" I ask the first officer I see.

"Busted the bar for selling narcotics."

"He's selling drugs out of the bar?"

"The owner of the bar is. He's a big-time dealer. Was using the place to distribute."

No wonder it was so easy for him to come up with a couple thousand dollars in cash.

"Technically, I own the bar. The guy's making payments to me. I also own the building. Mind if I check things out?"

"Go right ahead."

I make my way through the bar. Much is busted up—a broken table, a few stools and chairs, some bottles—but the walls, bar-top and mirror are fine. I go out the back door and up the stairs to the apartment above the bar. The new owner has been renting the apartment, also. The door is open and police are carrying stuff out.

"What are you doing up here?" a passing cop says.

"I own the building," I answer. "What's going on?"

"Oh. Well, sorry about all this."

The police obviously know that I have nothing to do with the selling of drugs. I peak my head around the door frame and check the apartment.

"What the heck!" I yell. "Who's gonna pay for all this?"

The walls are torn open; drywall and wallpaper is all over the floors. The entire front room has been destroyed.

"Since we found drugs hidden in the walls, it's not our responsibility. Sorry."

I'm stuck with a repair bill. And the bar, again. Good thing I got $2,000 up front.

\* \* \*

I run the same ad as before, and the bar is sold two more times. But the jinx continues and both purchases fall apart after only a few months. Finally, the third prospective buyer looks to be the real deal. He's well-dressed, not flamboyant and flashy, and doesn't talk with the local street slang. He sounds educated.

"It's $2,000 up front and $1,000 a month for twelve months," I say. I've increased the cost to cover the repair bills. Believe me, it's still a great deal.

"Sold," he answers. "Here's the $2,000."

I watch as he counts out the hundred dollar bills and places them on the bar-top.

"You ever run a bar?" I ask.

"Nope," he says. "I own a clothing store downtown. But I've always wanted to own a bar."

"Let me show you around, go over the books, show you the ropes."

"That would be much appreciated," he says.

"I own the building, by the way, so the bar pays me rent. You have a problem with that?"

"Nope."

"You want to buy the building?" I ask a few seconds later.

"I might. Let's give it a few months," he says. "I look forward to doing business with you Mr. Signori," he adds.

"Likewise, Mr. Lucas," I agree as we shake hands.

Everything is going great until neither the rent check nor the monthly payment show up on time five months later. I haven't had to go to the bar in four months.

"Is Mr. Lucas here?" I ask the bartender.

"No, but he said if you show up, to give you this address. He's there."

The address is downtown, not too far from The Block, but in a part of the city that is overwhelmingly black. I've got my youngest daughter Lori with me. She just turned ten.

"Feel like going for a ride, sweetie?"

"Sure, Daddy," Lori says.

"We'll get ice cream after I run an errand."

The address is a clothing store; it must be the store he told me he owns. It's stocked with high-end clothing and is packed on a Saturday afternoon. We're the only white people in there. I'm not bothered by this in the least. My bar has catered to a black clientele for years. Mr. Lucas spots me and waves us over. He's all smiles.

"Sorry to make you come down here, Mr. Signori."

"It's not a problem, Mr. Lucas. What's going on? Any trouble with the bar?"

"Nope, the bar couldn't be going better. I've got your rent money and monthly payment, but I wanted to talk to you before I sent it," he says. "If you follow me to the bank, I'll pay you the remaining balance on the purchase of the bar."

My first thought is that this is too good to be true. Then I think he must be up to something. I'm silent long enough to make him uncomfortable.

"And I'd like to make an offer on the building," he adds.

An hour later, I'm signing over the deed on both the building and the bar. Besides my wedding and the birth of my children, and I suppose getting out of the Mob, this may be the happiest day of my life. It's the 200th year of our independence, 1976, and I feel free. No longer tied to the Mob—haven't been for years—and the bar is sold. Four of my daughters have graduated from high school, three are in college. All but one of the girls lives with Mary and me. My little one, Lori, is ten. And to top it off, my little title business is more successful than I could have dreamed it to be. My life is good.

❋ ❋ ❋

*I'm crawling on my hands and knees away, but the bodies are everywhere, all around me. They're moaning, their expressionless eyes are staring at me. They're clawing at me with fingers of bone. I try to push them away, but they keep coming, surrounding me. I'm piling the bodies on top of each other. The stack is getting taller and taller. I'm floating in the air. The dead bodies are floating with me. Clawing at me. Scratching me. I'm on the ground, running, but I'm not moving. The bodies are all around me. They're covering me. I can't breathe. I'm screaming.*

This is the third time in the last two weeks that I've had my nightmare about the Nazi concentration camp. Lately, I have also been dreaming about my old lieutenant, Lieutenant Gibb. And Sergeant Finn. And First Sergeant Wall. They all appear to me alive, but Gibb has a bullet hole under his eye and the back of his head is gone, and Finn's face is all bloody from the splinters that killed him. Wall hops on one leg. I ask them why they're here, in my dream, but we just walk together. Then we're standing over the bodies of the dead German kids dressed in soldier uniforms that we killed. I see their faces exactly as I had seen them in 1945. I see the vision of the five shadows, but there are only four of us standing over the dead bodies. I haven't thought about those kids in years. I haven't thought about Gibb and Finn in years.

Why? Why have they come back to haunt me? Is the nightmare reminding me that my life will never be perfect? That I've done too many things in my past? That I have many things to ask forgiveness for? I believe in God, I'm just not a church going or praying man. Mary is—she goes every Sunday and is after me to start going.

❀ ❀ ❀

"You would have liked today's sermon."

"I would have? What was it about?" I doubt that I would have liked the sermon is what I'd like to say.

"Forgiveness, Paul. How the Lord forgives. And it's never too late in life to turn your life over to the Lord," Mary answers.

"Sounds interesting."

"After service next Sunday, we're going to a revival. You should come. Some of your old friends from the neighborhood will be there."

Old friends from the neighborhood? Who has Mary been seeing?

"Old friends?"

"That's right, Paul. We're all in Bible study together," Mary says. "Mark and Julie, Dave and Maria, and you remember Tom and Carol, right?"

"I remember all of them. I didn't know you were still in touch."

I made it through the war without praying, and I never prayed during all those years on The Block. I never needed to pray and I never needed the Lord. I don't even pray when I'm at the horse track betting on the ponies. Or pray that my number hits. My number used to hit a lot back in the day, every time Beans or Jimmy handed me a wad of cash for bashing men's heads. What would God want with a guy who made money bashing heads for the Mob?

"And your old friend Tony and his wife are part of our group," Mary adds.

My friend Naughty?

"Tony Mazzotti? Naughty? Is part of your group?" I ask.

"He is. He's been asking about you," Mary says. "And I don't think he goes by Naughty anymore."

I haven't seen him in months. Maybe it's been a year. If he's got himself involved in this, maybe it's not that bad. But I've always taken care of myself. I'll think about going to this revival of hers, for Mary, and I guess for Tony, too.

❈ ❈ ❈

"This isn't for me, Mary," I say after only five minutes. "I'll be waiting for you at the restaurant."

I couldn't get out of there fast enough. People chanting and praying out loud. The pastor, with his arms in the air—preaching, I guess. I couldn't follow him. I told Mary I'd give it a try. I tried, but it's just not for me. I don't feel anything. Besides, who'd want to save me? Save me from what?

The following Sunday, I'm talked into going again. This time, I last all of ten minutes. But at least I'm thinking about what the pastor said when Mary and Tony and their friends show up at the restaurant after the revival.

"What did you think about tonight revival, Paul?" Tony asks. I'm having a hard time not calling him Naughty.

"I'm not thinking about it at all," I say, not willing to admit I was. "I'm sitting here drinking a beer and waiting to order food."

"Come on, Paul," one of the leaders of the group named Carol says. "Nothing that was happening at the revival touched you?"

"I only stayed ten minutes, Carol. I must have missed the good stuff."

"It's good from beginning to end," Tony adds.

"If you say so," I say.

"We do, Paul," Carol says. "Accepting the Lord will change your life, if you give it half a chance."

❈❈❈

"When did it happen for you, Naughty? Shoot, I mean Tony. Old habits die hard."

"Right after Thrill was killed," he says.

"That was a tough time," I add. "I still miss him."

"I took his death real hard, Paul. Real hard," Tony says. "I took stock of my life after he was killed and didn't like what I saw. I was married, but I didn't act like I was. I had three kids but was a terrible father. I drank way too much. And this whole thing with the Mob. I couldn't wait to get out. I needed a change, Paul. I needed something. I found God. My life changed. Not overnight, but gradually, you know. Now, I couldn't be happier or more fulfilled."

I listened to what my friend had to say. It got me thinking about my own life. Am I a good husband? A good father? A good man?

"Why didn't you tell me?"

"I guess I thought you wouldn't understand. But I am glad you're starting to take the right steps now," Tony answers.

# Chapter 21

# SAVE A WRETCH LIKE ME

I'm at my third church service and have agreed to try another revival tonight. I've walked out of the last two. Even so, some of lessons I've heard from the pastor are starting to make sense. I can't say that I understand everything, but I listen. The more I listen, the closer I pay attention, the more I like what I hear. I never knew the Bible, not growing up with it. I only learned what the nuns at St. Leo's wanted us to learn, which wasn't much, and I stopped going to school in the fifth grade. I last to the halfway point this time, but I can't stay to the end.

"You're a good man, Paul," Mary says. "Your heart's always been in the right place."

"I guess so, Mary," I say. "At least I think it has."

There is so much she doesn't know about me, but I have very little regrets. I'm not a bad person—I may have done some bad things—but I'm not bad, and I love my family. Isn't that enough?

"You're a loving husband and father. Of course, your heart is good," she says.

I vowed early on that my family would be raised with love, no matter what. Unlike the way I was raised—by a father who never said he loved me. I tell my girls every day that I love them. Mary too, she hears the words, and knows that I mean them.

"I've tried to be a good father and husband," I say.

"You are," Mary says before planting a kiss on my cheek.

But I can't stop wondering why the Lord would want someone like me. Better yet, why accept me? I worked for the Mob for thirty-four years, not counting my time in the Army. I owned a bar. I drink. I smoke. I gamble. And I fight. I've busted more heads than I care to remember.

"You need to give our Savior another try," Mary adds.

"What would he want with a guy like me?" I tell her for the hundredth time.

"That's not how it works, Paul. Accept Jesus Christ as your Savior and give your life up to him and nothing from your past matters."

It can't be that easy, is it? There must be more to this saving thing.

"I'll give it another try next week for you, Mary" I say after I give her a kiss. "Did I tell you that I love you today?" I add.

❊ ❊ ❊

"Paul, are you ready to be saved? Are you ready to accept your Lord and Savior, Jesus Christ?" Mary's friend Carol says to me, again.

"I don't know what I need to be saved from," I say.

I'm not expecting this. I've seen people go forward after church service and accept the Lord, and I've seen it at the revivals, but I haven't been one of them. I have not gone forward and I don't plan to. I'm not sure that I have accepted the Lord. Have I? But I have been thinking about Jesus and what he has become to me. In my heart, I do believe, but there is still so much I need to learn. Can I be saved?

I look around the living room in Carol's house, at the people I've been going to service with. I look at Mary. She smiles at me and closes her eyes. She nods her head. Carol is standing over me as I look up at her from my seat.

"Give it time, Paul Signori, and you will be."

Another month passes before I go to a church service again and the revival that follows. After, at Carol's house for Bible study, she asks me if I am ready to accept Jesus.

This time I blurt out, "I am. I am ready to accept Jesus Christ as my Savior."

I'm not sure why I say the words, but they just come out. The room suddenly goes quiet. I can't hear a sound. I see a small black dot, tiny, but growing. The blackness is approaching me but is still in the distance. I have no concept of time; the dot could be moving at the speed of light or slowly creeping toward me. Closer it comes. All I can see is the black. I'm now completely covered by the blackness. My eyes are open, but I'm blind. I want to panic, but somehow, I feel a calmness. I don't know how long I'm immersed in the black.

Slowly, the blackness around me is receding. I'm in a state of deafness and blindness, but my senses are returning. I start to hear people around me clapping, barely at first, but the noise grows. My vision, once engulfed in darkness, has light breaking through. The black is becoming a dot again. Large at first, covering most, but now I see the edges. As the blackness is vanishing, I have dozens of visions flash by.

Beating the little kid to a bloody pulp when I was ten. My first paid street fight when I had to be pulled off the guy. When I saved Sarah and kept punching the man's face. The deaths of Sergeant Wall and Lieutenant Gibb. The fifth shadow and the German kids we killed. Visions of a knife to my father's throat. The street hoods I hit with my pipe, and many more dark events. And finally, Gunskirchen Concentration Camp. Thousands of bodies disappear—vanish from my sight.

People are starting to come into focus.

"Paul, are you all right?" Mary asks.

She is the first person I see and hear.

"Mary, you're not going to believe what just happened to me."

I tell the group what I have experienced. They are smiling and nodding in agreement.

"What you have just experienced is your past leaving you. The Lord has cleansed you, Paul," Carol says. "You have been saved. How do you feel now?"

"I feel good. I feel calm."

I am truly at peace.

"Mary, this is the greatest feeling I've ever had," I say to her later that night.

I sleep better than at any time in my life. The perfect sleeping, nightmare free, continues for days. Then weeks. Then a month passes. My cleansing has cured my war-time nightmares. I am rejuvenated.

I can almost remember my dream from last night. It's on the edge of my consciousness. What I remember is the figure of a person, or maybe an object. But there was something in the dream, something I can't explain. I do not have the dream again—at least not yet.

❄❄❄

"Paul, I'd like you to give your testimonial at the next service," My pastor, Pastor Baldwin says.

After I accepted the Lord and was saved, I've been a regular in my new Pastor's office these past weeks. He is a patient, caring man, and a good teacher of Bible lessons. I'm an eager learner, but I didn't expect this.

"I'm not ready to get up in front of everyone, Pastor Baldwin," I say. "Besides, who'd want to hear my story?"

"I've got a feeling it's an interesting one."

Reluctantly, I agree. But I'm not sure how much of my story I'm willing to tell. I'm not sure I want Mary to hear what I've got to say. Will my testimonial be more of a confession to Mary rather than a testimonial?

"If the Lord can accept me, and forgive me, then there is hope for everyone," I say as I gaze into Mary's eyes in the front row of seats in the packed church. "I'm not sure where to begin."

I pause for a few long, uncomfortable seconds. Then I continue, "When I was eight years old, I was recruited into the Mob. I was a bag boy. I ran the numbers for the local Mobsters. By the time I was fourteen, I was a street fighter for money and a watcher in the clubs down on The Block. By sixteen, I was a Mob enforcer, we called ourselves head-bashers. I've spent more time in bars, strip clubs and night clubs than I'd like to admit. Spent most of my life in them. I worked for the Mob for over thirty years. And I never told anyone. Anyone who was important, anyways. Certainly not my family."

I feel a level of shame making this confession. I'm having a hard time continuing to make eye contact with Mary. She is sitting quietly, but I know she is shocked. All those nights I was playing cards or bowling were a lie. All that money I earned, without sharing how I earned it. But just as Pastor Baldwin said, my testimonial will be the final cleansing, the getting-it-off-your-chest confession that will make accepting Jesus Christ complete.

I go on to tell about the war and the friends I saw killed. I briefly mention the concentration camp; that experience may be more than most people can handle. I tell the congregation about the bar I owned. I tell them about my relationship with my father and what he did to his family. I even tell the story of selling Mr. Joe his scrap iron back to him. On and on I went, the words flowed out of me. I finished my testimonial with the moment I was saved and the blackness leaving me. Afterwards, there is a line of people who want to shake my hand or give me a hug. My testimonial touches many people—probably inspires a few who may have been on the fence.

Mary's not happy with me. On the ride home, she's quiet. I'm smart enough to let her have some time to herself. She starts to come around in a day or two, and eventually, she forgives me.

❋ ❋ ❋

I'm sitting up in bed shaking and sweating. It's the dream with the vague figure of a man or a creature. I reach out and touch Mary's arm, stirring her awake.

"What is it, Paul?" she asks sleepily.

"A dream, Mary. I'm not sure what it is I see, but I'm real shook-up by it."

"I can see that you are," Mary says, "But you don't know what you saw?"

"Something powerful," I say. "Maybe something evil."

Every night since my testimonial, the nightmare is becoming clearer. I can now see the figure clearly. I think it's the devil himself, but I'm afraid to acknowledge what it is for fear of what may happen to me.

The dream comes into focus tonight.

*The devil is grabbing me, pulling me under. Hands with fingers of bones, scratching me, tearing at my skin, pulling on me. Harder and harder the bony hands pull, trying to pull me under. Under the ground. I'm struggling against his power, but I'm too weak. He is winning, I'm going under.*

I sit up in bed screaming.

"Paul!" Mary shouts. "What is it, Paul? The war nightmares again?"

"No Mary, worse—much worse," I say, sobbing. "The devil is pulling on me, pulling me underground. Just like the devil from the dreams I had when I was a kid."

I have the nightmare every night for a week. Each night, the horrible face of the devil gets clearer. Every night I'm closer to being covered.

"Pastor Baldwin, please help me," I say to my Pastor.

"How, Paul? How can I help?"

I tell him about my nightmare.

"The devil is battling for your soul, Paul. And he doesn't like to lose. All those years you lived without the Lord, you may not have known it or realized it, but the devil was influencing you. It was very subtle, but he was there. He wants you back."

I think about the blackness and my visions.

"Why in my dreams?"

"Why not in your dreams?" Pastor Baldwin says. "You've accepted Jesus Christ; you've seen his power. Start using that power against the devil."

"How?"

"Fight him in your dreams with scripture. Use the words of our Lord against the Prince of Darkness."

"But how? Can you teach me?"

"Recite scripture, Paul. It's your most powerful weapon," Pastor Baldwin says. "James 4:7—*Submit yourself to God. Resist the devil, and he will flee from you.* Or try Ephesians 6:11—*Put on the full armor of God, so that you can take your stands against the devil's schemes.*"

I spend the night reading scripture, preparing myself for

tonight's nightmare. I know he will come in my dream. I hope I am ready. The dream comes and I desperately try to remember the scriptures I read, but I can't. My mind stays blank and I'm overcome with fear. I'm losing this battle every night. I don't know how much longer I can hold on.

"You can't give up, Paul. Study the scriptures, memorize them, but also believe in the Word, believe in what you read. You will remember, and you will win this battle—too much is at stake," Pastor Baldwin says after I tell him I'm losing to the devil in my dream.

I read and study and memorize. I do my best to understand, but when the dream comes, I'm no match for the devil. He has a hold on me and won't let go. During the third night after studying scripture, I think I'm gaining strength.

"The devil takes pleasure in winning over the weak. When he comes up against a man of strong faith, he doesn't stand a chance," Pastor Baldwin says after I tell him the dreams with the devil are starting to fade. "And you are a man of strong faith."

By the sixth night of the battle, I've turned the tide. The devil is in full retreat. By the end of the week the dream is gone. Perfect, fulfilling sleep has returned.

This had been the most frightening experience of my life. I believe I was in a battle against the devil for my very soul, and I almost lost. Had I lost in my dream, I don't know what would have happened to me during my "awake" life. Would I still have been saved? Would my life still be turned over to the Lord? Or would I somehow return to the man I was? Whatever that was. A man without the Lord, a man without peace. Although only a dream, I believe the battle was real, and the consequences on my life were equally as real.

My heart started to soften after I met Mary, and a little more with the births of my children, but now it is complete. I have no hardness left in my heart. I am finally able to cry for my friend, Thrill. I feel as though my life is complete. Just like Tony, I'm the happiest and most fulfilled I have ever been. I am finally at peace. And it's because I accepted Jesus Christ as my Savior.

I spend the rest of my life as a follower of Christ.

Epilogue

# THE INTERVIEW:
# OCEAN CITY WORSHIP CENTER

Pastor Bryan: This is something I've wanted to do for a long time. It's my great honor to introduce this man, Phil Sigismondi. He's ninety-two years old, a World War II vet, married for sixty-two years.

Phil Sigismondi: Sixty-eight.

Bryan: Married for sixty-eight years. He and his wife Lorraine have five daughters. He's a church elder, a mentor, a prayer warrior. He's a great man.

*Applause*

Bryan: Phil, tell us about your childhood. What it was like being a kid way back when?

Phil: I don't remember having a childhood. I was always taking care of things, my family, working. My father was a drunkard. He was always beating on my mother and taking all the money away from her. Going out drinking. He never said he loved me. Or any of us kids, or my mother. I never heard the word love at home. When I got older, I depended on myself. Helping the family out. Since my father took all the money, my mother would ask me to get her some. I would tell her "I'll go to the bank." The bank was the junk yard down the street. I'd pull my wagon around back and load it up with scrap iron and bring it around front and sell it back to the junk yard owner.

*Laughter*

Bryan: How old were you?

Phil: Nine or ten.

Bryan: What else did you do for money?

Phil: I'd go around to all the stores, collect cardboard and paper. The junk yard guy, Mr. Joe, he'd buy paper, too. I'd wet the paper and wrap it around bricks to make it heavier.

Bryan: You told me another story.

Phil: Yeah. The vase. One time, I found a vase in the back of the junk yard. I cleaned it up and brought it to Mr. Joe. He offered me twenty bucks. I told him I needed twenty-five. He said it reminded him of a vase he had out back. I said, "I don't know about any vase out back, just this one." He asked, "Where did you get it?" I said it was my grandmother's. He asked, "Why do you want to sell it?" I said, "What do I want it for?" He paid me twenty-five bucks and I gave it to my mother. About four or five hours later, Mr. Joe shows up at the house. I can't use the words he used, but he told my mother I sold him his own vase. Wanted her to send me to him when I got home. My mom had spent ten dollars, but he told her to keep the fifteen because he knew she needed it.

*Laughter*

I can't use the words he said to me, either, but he made me pay him back the money. He said I couldn't wet the paper anymore and I couldn't put bricks in the middle, but he'd still buy my scrap iron. I'd go to the bank two, three times a month.

Bryan: Did you go to school?

Phil: My father pulled me out in the fifth grade.

Bryan: What did he have you do?

Phil: I went to work with him. Brick work, cement, carpentry.

Bryan: You told me the story about who taught you to read.

Phil: Mrs. Russell. She lived on the third floor, above us. She was always looking out the window, watching us play cards. She called me upstairs one day, said I didn't know how to play cards. She'd teach me. Then she made me read. Whenever I stopped at a word, she told me what it meant. She taught me how to spell, too. I still misspell some of those words.

*Laughter*

Bryan: What did she do for a living?

Phil: She was the Madam of the house. Prostitutes. Down on The Block.

Bryan: But she had a soft spot for you.

Phil: She did.

Bryan: When did you start working for the Mob?

Phil: Seven or eight years old. I was a bag boy. I ran the numbers for the Mob. I'd pick up numbers from stores, grocery stores, bars, clubs—you name it. I'd bring back money and give it to the Mob.

Bryan: Then you had more responsibilities?

Phil: Yeah, that's right. We started watching out for the girls. But that was mostly after the war.

Bryan: Okay, we'll get back to that. Tell me more about your relationship with your father.

Phil: I never had one. I never heard the word love.

*Phil is struggling to talk*

Phil: I didn't hear love until I heard it from my wife. And the more I heard it, the more I liked it.

*Laughter*

Bryan: Tell what happened when you saw your father hitting your mother.

Phil: After the service, when I got home from the war, I walked in on my father beating on my mother. I grabbed him and threw him against the wall. Then through a screen door. I hit him again. When he was on the floor, I picked up a knife and held it to his throat. I said, "If you ever hit her again, I'll kill you." Then I nicked him in the throat with the knife, cutting him.

Bryan: You wrestled with that, right?

Phil: I did, for most of my life.

Bryan: Over how many years had you worked through forgiveness? How did the Lord help you?

Phil: I didn't forgive him until he was on his deathbed. But you can't judge people without knowing all the facts. After he died, my mom told me he wasn't always like that. He loved me and Nicky. He would roll around with us on the floor, playing. He fell off a truck and broke his collarbone. Spent weeks in the hospital. They gave him morphine, but when he got home, we couldn't afford morphine, so he started drinking. That's when it hit me—if I would have known that at the time, I could have helped him. My opinion of him would have been different.

Bryan: One of the things you may not know about Phil is that he always asks, "Have I told you that I love you today?" He says that to everyone. Why is that?

Phil: Because I know a lot of people who probably never hear it. It's nice to tell people that. It makes people feel good. I tell them I love them and the Lord loves them. It lifts people up.

*Bryan asks Phil about a story he told him that took place in a grocery store about telling a stranger he loved her. Phil tells the story.*

Bryan: You have five daughters. Tell us how you changed, how you became a good dad without an example to follow.

Phil: With help from Lorraine. She's really the one, she did more than me. But I always wanted to give the girls more than I had. And I always wanted them to know how much I loved them. I told them every day. Now, when they call, they always say, "Have I told you that I love you?" Even the grandkids now say it. I did that. And once you hear you're loved, it sounds good.

Bryan: Tell us about the money you made working for the

Mob and how you're the luckiest man alive.

Phil: The Mob always paid in cash. I'd hide it in the house, or in a coat pocket. Lorraine would find the money and I'd tell her that I hit the number. I'd throw the cash in the air, tell her to take as much as she wanted.

Bryan: And you'd hit the number three or four times a year?

Phil: Yeah, that's right. Luckiest man alive.

*Laughter*

Phil: Then her sister wanted to know my system!

*More laughter*

Bryan: So, when you got older, before the war, you're a teenager. What did you do for the Mob?

Phil: I worked down on The Block, protecting the girls. Making sure they got paid and no one hurt them.

Bryan: Tell us about the light coming on.

Phil: I wasn't sure you wanted me to bring that up.

*Laughter*

Bryan: Why not? You were a teenager?

Phil: Well, this was mostly after the war.

Bryan: Okay, we'll get back to that. So, you wanted to go into the military?

Phil: That's right. The Navy. But they said no. I couldn't see good. I said, "I see just fine." Then I saw a poster about joining the Army, and how if you joined, you could pick what you did. So, I joined and picked the Horse Cavalry. But that only lasted a year. Then I started driving an M8.

Bryan: That's when you met Ronald Reagan?

Phil: Reagan and Jack London. They were making a movie.

Not a Hollywood movie—a movie for the Army called *Boots and Saddles*. I was in charge of the mess hall and Reagan came in. Everyone stood at attention. He got his food and came over to our table and asked if he could join us. He didn't like to eat alone. Then Jack London came in. They talked with us about making movies.

Bryan: What did you do when you went to war?

Phil: We were an observation unit. We went out and found the enemy and called in artillery. Then we stayed and watched where they hit. The Indian radio operator would radio back.

Bryan: Indian? Why?

Phil: The Germans couldn't understand what he was saying. They didn't know his language. He talked to other Indians.

Bryan: What did you do?

Phil: I was an M8 driver. Sometimes, we got ambushed. My lieutenant got hit with a bullet under his nose. Came out the back of his head. I held him up and the Indian radioman held the back of his head. We got out of there and got him back to the hospital, but it was too late. He was already dead.

Bryan: Tell us about World War II, how did you handle it?

Phil: Took it like everything else. We did what we had to do and depended on each other. But it sticks with you. Seeing a body lying there beside you. You start to get used to it.

Bryan: How old were you when you got back home?

Phil: Twenty-two.

Bryan: You were still just a kid. When you got back, you went back to work for the Mafia?

Phil: Yes, I did.

Bryan: And worked for the Motor Vehicle Administration? Where you met Lorraine?

Phil: I started at Motor Vehicles, and this guy Smitty, was always pointing Lorraine out. I said, "Who is she? She's jail bait."

*Laughter*

Phil: Every place we went, we ran into each other. Big band, dancing—she was always there. She'd be at a table with her boyfriend. Me, Joe, and Nicky would be at the bar.

*Laughter*

Phil: I'd talk to her a little. Then the fights would start. We were always fighting. I'd get hurt or something, and have to ask her and her boyfriend to take me home. She was always angry at me.

Bryan: How did you know you wanted to spend the rest of your life with her?

Phil: She was different than all the other girls I knew. She was always polite, talked nice, smart. And pretty. She was a nice girl.

Bryan: What did her parents think of you?

Phil: At first, her father didn't pay any attention to me. I'd come to the door to pick her up, and he'd say, "What do you want?" I'd say, "I'm here to pick up Lorraine." One time, I come in the house and he's got the horse racing sheet in front him. I say, "Oh, you like the horses. Oh, good, I've got a tip.

346

Brandy to win at San Francisco." He says, "Doesn't have a chance." I told him to put money on the horse. He didn't know the race had already been run and the Mob guys all got the tip. He made the bet. He liked me after that.

*Laughter*

Bryan: Where did you tell Lorraine you went when you worked for the Mob on The Block?

Phil: I told her I was playing cards. That got me in trouble sometimes. Once, I told her I was with her father, but her father showed up at the house. When I got home, she asked me who I was with. I said, "Your father." She said, "No, you weren't, my father was here tonight." I got in trouble, I told her I was playing cards with the guys.

Bryan: Tell us about The Block.

Phil: The girls would pick up a guy and take him upstairs. She'd ask me and Joe to watch out for her. If the red light came on, there was trouble. Usually, the guy didn't want to pay. He'd say he didn't have any money. We'd make him leave his watch or ring, and we would give it back when he came back with the money.

Bryan: What about taking shoes?

Phil: We only did that with the married guys. A married guy didn't want to have to go home with no shoes. He'd get in more trouble from his wife than from us.

*Laughter*

Bryan: How long did you work on The Block?

Phil: After Phyllis came along *(his first daughter)*, I said, "I must be crazy to be doing this." I went to the lieutenant—that's what we called him, Pete—and I asked to get out. He said, "No way, you know too much, you can't get out." Then, he came to me one day and said, "Now's your chance." I said, "For what?" He said, "To get out. Fifteen Mafia guys got busted, eight sent back to Italy and seven going to jail. New York Mafia is coming down and they don't know you, so, if you want out, now's the time."

Bryan: Tell us about Pastor Baldwin wanting you to do a

testimonial.

Phil: He asked many times and I always said no. I was afraid. I didn't want Lorraine to know what I'd been up to.

*Laughter*

Bryan: But you finally did a testimonial?

Phil: I did. And Lorraine got mad.

Bryan: How was the ride home?

Phil: Very quiet.

*Laughter*

Bryan: Tell us about coming to the Lord.

Phil: Lorraine was going to charismatic meetings. She said some of my friends were going, Joe and Paul. I said, "What, are they sick, too?" She says, "No, they gave their hearts to the Lord." She asks if I want to go downtown to a meeting, and after, out to dinner with everyone. I went. I'm sitting there when all of a sudden, they all get up. I ask, "What are you doing?" Lorraine says, "Praising the Lord." Then they all start speaking funny. Lorraine says they're speaking in tongues. I say, "I'm out of here." That was a little spooky. I waited for them at the restaurant. Later on, I went to another meeting, they're all praying. Lorraine and the lady in charge start to pray over me. She asks if I want to receive the Lord. I hesitate. Lorraine has this peaceful look on her face. I say, "Yes, sure, why not?" They're both praying over me. I see—

*Phil hesitates, struggling*

Phil: I still see it today. A darkness came over me, blackness, light was being pushed out. Lorraine said it was the Lord cleansing me. After that, look out, there was no stopping me. It was Lorraine, and the Lord who did it.

Bryan: After that, you were speaking in tongues?

Phil: Oh yes!

*Laughter*

Bryan: What would you tell someone who's on the fence?

Phil: If the Lord is after you, watch out. There's no getting away. If you put the Lord first, you can't go wrong. I'm not perfect, not perfect yet. Well almost.

*Laughter*

Phil: Let the Holy Spirit guide you. He'll lead you, but you have to concentrate on him.

Bryan: Marriage. You've been married for sixty-eight years. Any advice?

Phil: Don't take it lightly. Remember when you first asked her to marry you. Hold hands. Don't forget those things. And always tell her you love her. Every day.

# ABOUT THE AUTHOR

*Bag Boys* is Chris Conway's third book, following the release of *The Devil's Voice*, a crime thriller, in 2015 and *The Glove Slinger*, an historical fiction novel set against the backdrop of World War II, in 2016.

Chris' writing interests began over a decade ago when he was researching a non-fiction book on World War II. His fascination with World War II spurred him into writing *The Glove Slinger*. His next book project is to tackle a novel on the Vietnam War and its aftermath. Another book project Chris plans is to write the sequel to *The Devil's Voice*.

Chris is a graduate of Cal State Long Beach and is a successful businessman. He lives on the Eastern Shore of Maryland with his family.

87458916R00212

Made in the USA
Columbia, SC
13 January 2018